RAINBOW COUNTY and OTHER STORIES
WINNER
LITERARY FICTION
NATIONAL SMALL PRESS BOOK
OF THE YEAR AWARD, EROS

"His most prized theft was cut from a portfolio of reproductions of...photos of the legendary strongman...in an
appealing variety of masculine, but modest...poses."
—"Rainbow County"

Actual photo image by Guglielmo Marconi c.1865-1870

RAINBOW COUNTY
and
Other Stories

Jack Fritscher

PALM DRIVE PUBLISHING
SAN FRANCISCO CALIFORNIA

All *inquiries* concerning performance, adaptation, or publication rights should be addressed to Publisher, Palm Drive Publishing, PO Box 191021, San Francisco CA 94119. *Correspondence* may be sent to the same address. Send *reviews, quotation clips, feature articles, and academic papers* in hard copy, tear sheets, or electronic format for bibliographical inclusion on literary website and in actual archive.

For author history and literary research:
www. JackFritscher.com

Cover photograph, "Gay Cowboy, Reno," shot by and ©1979 Jack Fritscher covering the gay rodeo with Randy Shilts for Associated Press wire service, August 5, 1979. A second Fritscher photograph from this series, published nationwide in newspapers August 6, 1979, was the first mass media image to introduce gay cowboys to American popular culture. *San Francisco Chronicle*, First Section, page 3, column 1.

Cover design realized by Christine Dec Graphics, Sebastopol, California
Cover ©1999 Jack Fritscher
"Afterword: Gay American Literature" ©1997 Claude Thomas
Palm Drive Publishing Literary Series 2000
Published by Palm Drive Publishing, P. O. Box 191021, San Francisco CA 94119

Rainbow County™ is a protected trademark.

Library of Congress Catalog Card Number: 98-86625
Fritscher, Jack 1939-
    Rainbow County and Other Stories / Jack Fritscher
    p. cm.
    ISBN 1-890834-28-9
    1. American Literature—20th Century. 2. Homosexuality—Fiction. 3. Gay Studies—Fiction. 4. Erotica—Gay. 5. Sadomasochism—Fiction.
Previously published ISBN 1-881684-12-1, LT Publications

Printed in the United States of America
10 9 8 7 6 5 4 3 2

www.PalmDrivePublishing.com

For Mark Hemry,
editor, producer, lover

Contents

**In the Twilight's Last Gleaming,
He Had Left Civilization behind...**

THE SHADOW SOLDIERS

War criminal!" Lieutenant J. G. Steve Drosky, USAF, could hardly believe the verdict pronounced by the slope military judge, down for the mock trial, from Hanoi. Drosky sweated in the blazing Asian sunlight. He stood, tied, in the central compound of some godforsaken village in North Vietnam. He wore the same green nylon flightsuit he had worn the day his A4 Skyhawk had been shot down.

In the last two weeks of the war, he had been streaking up the Gulf of Tonkin, under bright skies, toward the torpedo boat base at Hon Gay, north of Haiphong.

His big American-Polack body smelled ripe in the jungle heat. Sweat, darkening the nylon under his pits, ran down his skin. His cheeks, chin, and throat itched with the—how long was it?—ten-day bristle.

His hands, crossed at the wrist, had been tied tight by a young Viet Cong who had spit his contempt in Drosky's face. Drosky spit back. He had a bruise to show for it. The purple bloomed through his dark blond stubble of beard. In the tropical heat, the sun was darkening his fair skin and lightening his eyebrows and moustache.

He was hungry. He was thirsty. He needed a cigaret.

His big uncut dick itched under the foreskin he hadn't

been able to reach to strip back in over a week. The VC, fearing his bull-sized build, kept his wrists tied behind his back, alternately in ropes and in irons. He knew the crack of his hairy ass was crusted. The fucking slopes were intent on humiliating the best and the brightest of the American fliers every way they could.

Through each interrogation, Drosky had given only name, rank, and serial number. He was learning fast that he, and probably the other two Americans, also tied for trial and sentencing in the shadowless high-noon sun, were the only three people in the whole compound who gave a fucking shit about the Geneva Convention. Drosky had never before seen the other two Americans until he had been dragged out of his solitary-confinement cage for this fifteen-minute trial.

Drosky figured one of the two other Americans for a flier. He was strapped up spreadeagle ten yards to the right of Drosky. He stared straight ahead, as if once he had seen something so terrible he would never look at anything again. The judge's words "life sentence" hardly seemed to register on the flier's face. Drosky calculated from the weathered look of the lean pilot's body that he had been bound to the bamboo tripod for some days and nights. His flight suit had been sliced off and he was exposed: head and torso and legs. The VC had stripped him down to his green boxer skivvies and boots. His dog tags glistened against his hairy chest. Even crusted with the sweat and dust of this filthy captivity, he looked to Drosky like the kind of good-looking skyjockey who, stateside, gets volunteered for recruiting posters.

To his left, Drosky checked out the other captured American. He had been trucked into the compound about an hour after Drosky's tied wrists had been hoisted up painfully behind his back to a tall metal pole the village children had once used to tether their game ball. Drosky figured he wasn't going to be any braver in this one than he needed to be. He wasn't any John-Fucking-Wayne; but he was an Air Force officer, a career pilot, 28-years-old, married, with one kid, a son. His shit was together. But the sight of the VC troop truck pulling into the compound with the second American had sickened him.

A half-dozen young VC soldiers, commanded by a squat burly captain with a shaved bullethead, milled around the handsome young Marine. The USMC grunt was hanging suspended by his shoulders from the metal canvas-cover struts arched over the bed of the truck. Unable to touch his feet to the floor to steady himself, he swung back and forth like a side of young American veal. He was too young to be beef.

Drosky figured the kid for no more than nineteen. Twenty, tops. He was a fresh capture. The sidewall clip of his buzz cut was less than a week old. He was stripped shirtless, down to his green fatigues and boots. A bamboo pole cutting into the small of his back held the crooks of his arms immobile against the pull frontwards of his forearms which were manacled by the wrists tight across his hard belly.

Drosky figured him for the kid who captains his high-school football team in the fall and joins up the next spring, right after graduation. On the third finger of the young Marine's left hand, Drosky spotted the flash of what looked like a new gold band.

That was a mistake.

All in-country military personnel had been ordered to avoid wearing wedding rings into combat. The VC liked to use the information that a prisoner was married against him. Drosky himself, after his shootdown, stripped off his flight glove, removed his wedding ring, held it a long moment, and then tossed the gold band far from him into a rice paddy.

That act more than anything made him realize he had left civilization far behind.

Drosky found it hard to tell anything much about the kid's face. His eyes looked tough enough, though he seemed to refuse to look at Drosky, even when the VC took hold of the bamboo pole and lifted him, high and long and slow, so his whole body-weight hung excruciatingly from his manacled arms in the slow march toward Drosky. The Marine was embarrassed. The bondage itself had become torture. As the VC carried him in agony close past Drosky's face, they stopped, and forcibly turned the handsome Marine's face for Drosky's inspection.

The dirty VC hands held the suspended American's head painfully still. Drosky studied the kid's mud-crusted chin and lips and nose. The young Marine avoided Drosky's stare. A fresh cut clotted through the kid's left eyebrow. The VC displayed him hanging in front of Drosky's own tied body. The squat captain with the bullethead moved in. Carrying a swagger stick, he approached the young Marine's mouth. With one quick blow he broke off the kid's two front teeth.

"You like?" the captain said to Drosky.

Drosky felt sick to his guts. It was a shit-load more than blood crusted on the bound Marine's face. It was jungle filth, the kind of human mud that snakes slither through to kill things that only come out at night.

The slope captain threatened the bound Marine with a couple of pulled-punch swings at his tight-closed lips and clenched, broken teeth. He poked his swagger stick at the dirty face and parted the caked lips. Drosky watched the swollen full cheeks of the cherry boy's face. Another threatening tap. The kid was scared.

The Corps had taught him obedience as the best solution to every situation.

The boy pulled his lips back. Bullethead tapped at his bleeding teeth. Another tap. Hoisted in midair suspension, he hung helpless. He parted his jaws. Obediently. Bullethead nudged the tip of his swagger teasingly into the boy's mouth. Churning deeper. Poking deeper. Fucking deeper into the terrified Grunt's mouth. Past his gagging. Past his vomit.

The young Marine's body stiffened and swung defenselessly. His eyes opened wide in terror at the force-feeding he saw coming: again. Bullethead ordered up a bucket of fetid water, and with the kid's mouth pried open with the swagger stick, motioned for the ladling of crickets and small tree frogs to begin. They poured the slime down the kid's throat.

Drosky himself began to gag at the same moment that Bullethead triggered, with his hard-churning swagger-stick, the gag reflex in the young Marine painfully swinging by his arms in the humid sunlight. Bullethead stepped back, and the young VC soldiers laughed, as the young Marine tossed up the dark jungle slime of the force-feedings he had endured hours before when they had pinched his nose closed and fed a hose past his lips, through his teeth, over his tongue, and down his throat to his belly, slipping a small live snake down the tube, watching the kid's belly expand and contract with the dying snake.

Finally the Marine raised his eyes to look the three-feet directly into Drosky's eyes. He was crying, and he said, with his voice deep and husky from the rubber tube and the filth of war, "I'm sorry, sir."

Bullethead slammed him across the cheek with his swagger, and the guards carried him to another iron post twenty feet upwind of Drosky. They hung the bamboo pole securing his arms from the ropes. But this time, stripping his combat boots from his feet, they let his toes touch the muddy ground.

Blood ran from his nose.

The other flier, the Major, seemed to have chosen to notice nothing. Drosky figured maybe he was smart. Maybe that was the way to survive. But Drosky could not help hearing the flies and seeing the pile of vomit that the VC had gorged up out of the Marine's guts. None of them, Drosky knew, was ever going to get out of this alive. Charlie was fierce about the Americans. Drosky knew enough captor psychology. The odds were against the three of them. Severely abused prisoners rarely live to tell their stories.

The young Marine, at the pronouncement of his "war crimes," stopped his sobbing. He spit two words from his bloody mouth. "Fuck you!" He spit his brown spit at the VC squatting in the hot sun. They laughed and spit back, and then, bored, moved out of range, leaving the three Americans hanging, each in his own private agony, to the scorching sun, the suffocating humidity, and the low drone of hungry flies.

Drosky realized that even a short life, sentenced by these sadistic animals, might be longer than he could handle. But he figured they were maybe more sound than fury. In his guts, he was a fighter. He felt his tongue thickening with thirst in his mouth. He thought of old football scores. The feeling had long gone out of his hands. He thought of intricate flight plans. For two days, the three men, fed only rice and boiled fish heads, were left strung up exposed to rain and sun in the compound. Drosky ran multiplication tables forwards and backwards. He picked out names for his captors: like shaved-down Captain Bullethead.

Drosky had enough fight in him to want to punch out and fucking kill the VC making a game of humiliating the American soldiers. Untied, Drosky figured he was big enough to take them all on. Fucking Charlie! But he was not untied. He could not stop the VC coming out, forcing him to his knees, pulling their short fat dicks out, pissing on his face and chest, hosing him with the high-pressure force of their short, thick, rice-rocket dicks. His own Polack sweat was like a moist shield on his blond skin. He hated the drunken piss of the young VC soldiers. Most were no more than vicious teenagers. One of the fuckers, built like Mr. Mekong Delta, came out from his hooch almost hourly. He was some hybrid seed the French Colonials had abandoned when they fled Indochine. He was half-French. Almost handsome. Drosky figured him for the camp stud. Threatening Drosky with a pistol, Mekong forced him to his knees, causing his arms, still tied behind him, to pull painfully up past his shoulders. The shirtless Eurasian, powerful as a young tank, liked to force Drosky to watch him strut his stuff. When he whipped his dick out, he displayed his pizzle like some prize water buffalo at a cattle show. He was hung: big, uncut, and mean. He threatened Drosky's face with the heft of his hang.

Drosky knew a pervert when he saw one.

Swallowing Mekong's piss was humiliation enough. His wagging dick, hardening, was no way, José, acceptable to Drosky, who knew the facts of the way life sometimes was: he'd circle-jerked a couple times in high school, and let one of his drinking buddies one drunken night back at the Air Force Academy climb on top him, and bump bellies, till the cadet came and passed out on top of Drosky, who only half-endured the episode. While he'd been doing his buddy a favor, he'd been thinking thoughts about the girl who became, and still was, his wife.

Drosky knew, if he ever got out of this alive, some of this he'd never be able to tell her. He knew, if he lived through all this, he'd never be able to tell anyone.

Drosky vowed to keep forever to himself how the muscular, young, half-French VC with the middle-weight powerlifter's build, stroked up his big dick. He was proud to sexually humiliate the American. He liked to show off his enormous size. "We are not all small," he said, spitting into Drosky's eyes. With his big wang bobbing from his uniform, he took cash from the circle of drunken slopes who'd bet on anything. They argued and wagered how far down Drosky's throat Mr. Mekong Delta's heavy artillery could slide, before the pussy American, they called him, choked and begged for mercy.

Mr. Mekong Delta liked to suffocate bound fliers on his enormous meat.

The muscular half-breed flexed his arms and made a fist. Drosky read his threat. If he bit the frog-gook, he'd lose his teeth. For openers. In the trade-off of death-before-dishonor bullshit, and raw survival, Drosky opened his mouth. Reluctantly. The rape situation left him little choice. He allowed his lips to be parted by the knob-head of the dick. It was hard, long, and big. Mekong slammed his right fist hard into his left palm, six inches above Drosky's face. Drosky took a deep breath, and dropped his lower jaw, just the way he'd instructed his wife, but ever so much more tenderly, before she was even his fiancée.

The circumference of the monster cock raised Drosky's upper lip high enough to brush his thick moustache into his nose. He was revolted by the slick slide of the huge cockhead depressing his tongue and probing back toward his defenseless throat. The muscular in-and-out thrust and tease began. Mekong was on show. The drinking and bets increased. Mekong punched his fist and palm together again.

Queer to them, Drosky knew, was only when a man was on the receiving end. The man dishing it out was not only untainted, but was about as manly and patriotic as a soldier could be. To the VC, the sexual abuse of an invading American was an honorable way to insult the aggressive macho warriors who, so much bigger than Asians, dropped in full battle armor out of the sky into the forbidden jungle, light-years from the lives they'd known.

Mekong's big fat dick forced its way with vengeance into Drosky's virgin mouth. With the bets running high as blood lust, the heavy-built VC took Drosky's blond head in his brown hands, and, pulling his dick out to the wet edge of Drosky's lips, spread his thick legs, and stanced his hard butt, for the final deep ram past Drosky's teeth, across his tongue, and finally...finally...through the raped and bleeding back of his mouth, deep down his gagging throat.

Drosky felt the man's huge military rod slam deep back in his head, and then descend, penetrating, down his gullet. He had never felt more violated in his life. Mekong held Drosky's face impaled on his cock. Drosky went through gagging into choking and felt himself heading down a deep dark airless corridor. His penultimate thought was refusal to die like this. Instinctively, with hardly any purchase around the big dick, routed through his mouth, and rooted in his throat, Drosky fucking goddam tried to bite the pervert's dick off.

All hell broke loose!

Mekong screamed at Drosky's toothsome lunge. Near Drosky's left ear, a pistol fired loud into the ground. Mekong yanked his bitten dick out fast. Drosky tasted the film of blood where his teeth had scrapped the cock. He wished he'd more than only skinned the gook dick. He knew what was coming as Mekong's heavily muscled arms drove the hard-handed fists into his face. Mekong beat and kicked Drosky half-unconscious. He slumped over into the mud, falling off to his side. He could not reach the ground, not even for a moment's rest. His arms, still tied at the wrists behind his back, stretched beyond pain up his back, higher than his head. Half-kneeling, half-hanging, he passed out.

When Drosky awoke, he knew he was in worse trouble. The full length of his body had been completely coiled in tight hemp rope. Like wire around a spool. The

VC squatted on their haunches around him, seeming to map out strategies for some mission Drosky could not make out. Occasionally one of them yelled at him and kicked him. This was it. He was sure they'd hang him by his heels, skin him alive, chop off his nuts, and finally his head.

A truck pulled up and stopped, brakes squeaking, motor running, next to him, blue exhaust choking him. Several VC came at Drosky.

"Open mouth!" Captain Bullethead shouted.

"Back so soon?" Drosky said. His mouth was parched.

"Open mouth!"

"You guys are real oral." Drosky was no silent fool.

"Open mouth!" Bullethead brooked no resistance.

Drosky refused. He locked his cracked lips together.

Bullethead took one of Drosky's blond-stubbled cheeks in each of his martial hands and squeezed hard until Drosky's eyes winced and his mouth was forced open in pain. Bullethead signalled to an ugly young soldier. He smiled. Drosky fixed on the ugly soldier's missing front teeth. The soldier crumpled old newspaper into balls and shoved them one by one into Drosky's mouth. Drosky wished he had kicked out the ugly motherfucker's teeth himself. Bullethead kept the agonizing pressure-pinch on his cheeks. A second soldier took Bullethead's swagger and shoved the dry newspaper balls farther over Drosky's tongue and deep into his throat.

Drosky started to gag and panic. He could no longer breathe through his mouth. The hard dirty fists forced the dry newspaper rolls in until his mouth and cheeks were stuffed. He could not salivate. He was scared. Death in combat had always been heroically, patriotically acceptable. But not this.

Drosky stared hard at that ugly, grinning, broken-toothed motherfucker's mouth. He memorized the face. He would remember it if he had to take vengeance in hell. His anger saved him. He was mad enough. He'd beat these fuckers. Somehow. Someday. Somewhere. He concentrated. By will alone, he breathed around the dry wads of newsprint clogging his throat. Through his nose. Slowly. Carefully. Evenly.

Then the grinning toothless asshole blindfolded him. The VC lifted Drosky's body, tightly coiled in endless rope, into the truck. He was helpless. For the first time in his wholesome, athletic, All-American life, he was scared shitless.

They drove him slowly in a 72-hour convoy toward Hanoi. They stopped in villages along the route to display him, the bound and gagged American war criminal. At one stop, he was sure, when they took the blindfold off that he was about to be beheaded. At another village, a crowd of more than five hundred soldiers milled around, seeming intent on stoning him to death. At another encampment, he was stood bound and gagged and wired to a post in front of a firing squad. The boys were, all of them, recruits no more than twelve or thirteen. For an hour, they were put through repeated execution drills: the command, the count, the captured American M-16 rifles, their cold young eyes squinting to the rifle sites, the raised sword, the shouted command to *Fire*, the empty clicks of a dozen unloaded rifles barreling in and sited on Drosky's face and chest and groin.

During another convoy stop, the VC rolled and wrapped Drosky's big body in filthy blankets that completely covered his head and face. They left him alone, unguarded, and bound in the enclosed bed of the truck. Sweat poured off his big body. Again he felt he was suffocating, dying, smothering under a wrap of dirty rags at the side of a nameless road far from home.

He vowed to escape. He struggled, unable to move any of his body coiled in the tight rope. He rolled his head side to side, as much as he could, trying like a man driven mad to get free of the smothering wool. No one paid any attention to his struggling. He was one American. One man. They were thousands. They were getting to him. His bodily functions were out of control. Everything was getting way out of control.

Within minutes, Bullethead unwrapped Drosky's head, removed the blindfold, and pulled the newspaper from his mouth.

"You are war criminal," Bullethead said. His voice was as even as his steady dark eyes. He knew how to exploit fear. "We are going to hang you."

"Horseshit," Drosky whispered. His tongue was thick in his mouth. "Horseshit!"

"For attacking and insulting the Vietnamese people, you must be punished."

Drosky remembered the young Marine and the silent Major back in the war-trial compound. Nobody in this day and age treated prisoners of war this way. There was the Geneva Convention. North Vietnam was a signatory.

"Geneva Convention," Bullethead said, "is for prisoners of war. You are...war criminal."

Bullethead signalled for a half-dozen soldiers to hoist Drosky out of the truck. They untied the rope winding around his body, but they kept his hands tied behind his back. The stench of his own flesh no longered bothered Drosky. He was beginning to like the aggressive smell of his own big American body. He figured it was about the only weapon he had left.

The VC called him a filthy pig.

Drosky cut his cheese as loud as he had ever farted during gas-lighting ceremonies in high school, when he and his jock buddies had drunk a lot of beer, pissed a lot of piss, eaten a lot of chili dogs and lit with matches the gas-farts they blew out their asses as they mooned each other in contests for the loudest and most explosive stinkers.

A filthy pig? He'd show them a filthy American pig. He farted again.

The VC backed away from him.

Bullethead ordered him strung up by the neck, with only his toes touching the ground. The bright sun burned into his face. He squinted, reconning the area. Tied near a truck, similar to the one in which the VC had transported Drosky, was the young Marine. Drosky was surprised, and not too happy to see the kid again. He was a survivor at heart, but Drosky could tell, the way that Bullethead approached the kid, that he planned to waste him. Better he'd been shot dead than stand in as their amusement for their bored night's encampment. Drosky was glad he himself was older and tougher than the young Marine. His Academy training warned him the VC were perverts when it came to Americans.

The kid's too juicy, Drosky thought, much too juicy to be out here, a thousand years from nowhere.

The blistering sun was setting over the far trees, sinking into the horizon like the last light protecting them from the heart of darkness.

The twilight encouraged the hungry VC.

They stripped the young Marine naked, more naked than the kid had ever been, only six months before, showering after a Friday night high-school football game. More naked than he had been the night of the day that goddam gold wedding ring had been slipped on his finger. More naked than his first group shower as a USMC boot.

Drosky figured the kid was, like him and his own son, from some small town where they never thought of circumcising their boys. He had an unusually large lip of foreskin hooding the blind head of his healthy cornfed cock.

Bullethead directed his special vengeance against the young blond Marine. The VC spread the kid belly-down over a metal oil drum. His full rounded white buttocks glowed in the twilight's last gleaming. Vagrant clouds of

cooking-fire smoke blew over his body and toward
Drosky.

Drosky tried to look away, but Bullethead assured
him what he feared. This was for Drosky's benefit. An
experienced flier could be used; but young inexperienced
Marines were pleasantly expendable. Some VC hunted
Americans for sport. For the pleasure of the slow kill.

Drosky wished for the whoop-whoop of a chopper. For
a direct artillery hit to blow them all away. Anything.
But the Nam night was quiet. Only the occasional far-
off boom of an explosion muffled by distance broke the
low murmur of the jungle night.

The young Marine lay tied immobile over the 55-gal-
lon drum with TEXAS OIL stenciled on its top. Two lines
of VC formed on either side of his spread legs, nodding
to each other and taking wagers. The Marine's bare butt
was higher than his head and feet. The VC soldier at the
head of each line held a rubber fan belt in his hand.

On a signal from Bullethead, the alternating beating of the Marine's white butt began. The VC on the left
swung his arm repeatedly over his head like a lasso, and
then, with a war cry that broke the quiet of the firelit
encampment, ran full-speed at the Marine's defenseless
body, arm swinging to full arc, slicing down across the
unmarred white meat of the American ass. The kid
reared his head as the slice of rubber slashed red-hot
into his flesh.

Then the soldier at the head of the left column took
his running lick with his frayed rubber fan belt, striking
a red welt crisscross the slash from the right. Passing
the fan belts back to the head of the lines, the grisly
relay race of whipping tore first the skin, then the bloody
flesh, and finally into the deep muscle of the Marine's
buttocks.

Bound and helpless, the Marine found and became
his own his best silent courage, became his shouts,

became cries, became screams, became shrieking, be-came moans, until, Drosky knew, his voice shredded and was gone.

Bullethead ordered five or six of the soldiers to stroke their own short-arm dicks to penetrate the groaning Marine's bloody ass. Drosky hated the sonsabitches mounting the bloody butt with no more passion than their quick humiliating vengeance. Disciplined to fero-cious obedience, they shot on command, shouting their patriotic hate for the stinking American. Their dicks dripped with the Marine's blood and sweat. They laughed, and spit on him, and congratulated each other like night marauders after successful penetration of en-emy lines.

Drosky disengaged. He composed a list. Anything to somehow balance this horror half a world away from everything he ever knew. He'd buy his wife a ring. He'd buy his son his first ball glove. He'd buy himself a car stereo. Some cassettes...a goddam hunting rifle. To kill the goddam sonsabitches. His fear had been one thing. This horror...this atrocity...was another. Drosky had heard how American soldiers massacred the villagers in Mylai, and worse; but all the fucking politics and all the fucking villages-wasted-to-save-them had nothing to do with this boy's personal final agony.

"You like show?" Bullethead spoke in close to Drosky's face, puffy from the noose of rope tightening slowly around his neck.

Drosky spit at him.

Bullethead smashed his face with an uppercut.

The VC toyed with the tortured Marine. Intent on playing him out. They untied him from the oil drum. He punched out at them with what was left of his husky strength. Drosky was glad to see some fight left in him. The VC wrestled him to the ground, and staked him out spreadeagle on his back. Bullethead ordered the Marine's wedding ring pulled off his finger. He pointed with his swagger stick at the dirty blond penis. The VC laughed at the size of the finger-ring compared to the thick American dick. In one rough-handed minute, they spit-worked the Marine's big cockhead through the ring, and forced the gold band down tight around its root.

The pressure of the hands pulling, forcing, stubbing his dick through the metal caused the whipped and spreadeagled Marine's cock to stand at full attention. Drosky watched the helpless kid look in horror at the betrayal of his own dick, hardening against his will, flopped back on his dirty belly, then rising, turning, filling—its thick veins made thicker by the strangling pressure of the ring.

A young dick on a naked man, bound, and exposed, full of heavy unmilked sperm, aches to blow its pressurized nut off. The Marine's body, caked with sweat and dust and slime, was too resilient. He was taking too long to die.

Drosky knew what was coming. He watched the involuntary hardening of the Marine's cock. He watched the filthy shaft of the abused dick writhing, filling, rising. He watched, unbelieving.

The big USMC dick pointed straight up from the spreadeagled body. The shaft, rooted in crud-caked blond crotch hair, was dark with dirt; but the pressure of the wedding ring finally forced open the big lip of uncut foreskin.

Drosky could hardly believe the size of the big wet pink head rising rosy-clean and bulbous, crowning the boy's huge shaft, with the heavy collar of foreskin rolling back under the intense pressure.

The head glistened above the filthy tortured body. A drop of clear juice pearled up in the Marine's piss slit. It rose, bubbled bright, then flowed slow and wet down the shaft of filthy cock.

The VC gathered in close, cutting off Drosky's view. Something in him made him think how fucking proud he was that these envious slopes could see a beaten, tortured, bound American male body with enough balls to affront them with dick harder and bigger than they had ever seen before.

The young blond Marine's erection was his ultimate "Fuck you, asshole!"

Bullethead ordered his soldiers to stand back. He wanted Drosky's view clear and unobstructed. With a pointing of his swagger stick, Bullethead signalled for a renegade Montagnard scout to carry out the finish of the night's entertainment.

The Montagnard, from a primitive village time had forgot, squatted next to the Marine's body. Drosky could not afford any longer to feel sorry for the kid. Any feeling now was too expensive. He tried to think of nothing as he watched with increasing disconnection from the scene.

The naked Montagnard rubbed something, grease and something, across the broad hairy chest of the Marine, stroking the curling mat of blond fur almost sensuously, working the oil into the blond brush, across the chest, down the hairy belly, and deep into the crotch around the huge erect dick. The young kid's body glistened in the firelight.

The sky was moonless.

The Montagnard, squatting on his haunches next to the Marine, slipped his hand into his breechclout, and pulled out an American-made lighter. In one hand, he held his rifle. With the other, he thumb-rolled the lighter to a flickering flame.

For a moment, the bright intensity of fire in the dark Montagnard hand froze the encampment in place. The small flame threw huge shadows against the dark trees.

The Montagnard moved the flame in close between the Marine's oil-slick pecs.

Drosky saw the smooth nipples reflect the flame.

In one swift move, the Montagnard touched the flame to the young Marine's chest.

Ignition!

The Marine's chest flamed up in twin mounds. A fast, burning flash of grease and hair crossed his chest, then raced fuse-like down the length of his furry belly to his grease-packed groin. The flames exploded around his heavy-haired balls, and seared up the flesh of the huge erect cock.

The Marine's body arched taut against the spread-eagle stakes. His wrist-bound hands turned to fists. His ankle-bound feet pointed toes down. The flash of flames burned for no more than seconds, but Drosky counted them an eternity.

The tortured Marine had no voice left to scream.

Drosky shouted for him.

Bullethead moved in close to Drosky. "Bo rown," he said, "Bo rown." "Bow down."

Drosky understood. He was on his toes, hanging by his neck. Bullethead wanted the American to bow down. He was tempting Drosky to hang himself.

Drosky stared instead out into the heart of darkness. Then closed his eyes.

Bullethead raised his hand and with toughened fingers forcibly pulled Drosky's eyelids open and turned Drosky's face toward the Marine.

The Montagnard unsheathed his knife. With one hand he pulled large pinches of muscular flesh from the Marine's seared chest and sides and belly. With each pinch, he carefully sliced the blade through the skin.

Drosky prayed the kid would die in shock; but the strength and health of his young body held off agonizingly even that brutal comfort. He writhed in the tight bonds as the Montagnard carved superficial flesh wound after flesh wound. The knife dripped red in the firelight.

The VC were losing interest in the renegade Montagnard ritual. It was night. They were tiring of their deathsport. The winners wanted to collect from the losers the wagers they had won.

Bullethead nodded at the Montagnard.

The dark face grinned. With his knife, he skillfully skinned the Marine's uncut penis from head to base. The raw shaft of the cock foamed red. The Marine, his hoarse voice reaching for one final scream, opened his face: mouth and eyes and flaring nostrils.

The Montagnard reached down for the one big handful of full blond balls. He slipped his blade deftly in under the sac. With one clean upward stroke, he castrated the Marine whose eyes, to Drosky, saw nothing more. Not even the revolver that Bullethead forced deep down and back into the Marine's open, screaming mouth.

There was only one bullet in the gun. Drosky agonized each unmerciful moment as Bullethead grinned and clicked, clicked, clicked the chambers, prolonging more for Drosky than for the Marine, to whom nothing any longer mattered, until, finally, after the fourth slow click, the hammer found the one loaded chamber, exploded, and blew the handsome Marine's face away forever.

Something drained out of Drosky. Something subtracted itself from his soul. He heard sounds, like other voices speaking. They were saying: "Steven Drosky. Lieutenant J. G. Service Number: 8291930." But it was not other voices. It was his voice in the darkness, mumbling in the sleeping camp.

Drosky knew deep down in the hollow growing in him that he was a prisoner, that no one would ever touch him tenderly again. The life left behind him had been a good one. Now no one even knew he was alive.

He was no longer flesh and blood.

He was a shadow soldier.

No one who cared for him or mattered to him even knew for certain any longer that he existed.

* * * *

For eight solid months, deep in the solitary confinement of a fetid tiger cage somewhere near Hanoi, Drosky fought to keep his sanity, and as much physical strength as he could scrape off the tin-plate diet. He ate putrid meat paste cut sometimes with pieces of pork fat, watery pumpkin soup, and small loaves of dirty bread pocked with weevils and rat feces.

Guards walked over the grates above him. They ignored him. He exercised. He meditated. No one spoke to him. He did not exist. He scratched designs on the wall. No one listened when he spoke. He pulled lice from his filthy prison clothes. He knew other Americans were nearby. He had heard, on two occasions, a man's far-off whistling of "The High and the Mighty."

Drosky was sitting on his wooden cot, meditating, when the first American he had seen in nearly a year was pushed into the small cell. He looked like a dirty wet rag.

The two men stared at each other.

It was the longest moment that Drosky had ever lived. Longer than all the solitary confinement. Longer because recognizable human touch was only an arm's reach away.

The two prisoners moved slowly toward each other unable to speak.

Drosky knew only that with one second more without some touch in the middle of all this lonely hell, with the warmth of another human so close, after so long, he would crack and snap forever.

The other prisoner was some shadow of his former husky self; but his eyes, staring unbelievably at Drosky, burned bright as coals. He had thought this new cell would be as empty as all the other cages in which he had been kept.

Drosky reached out to shake the man's hand. Their firm grips seemed some long-unused gesture, from a world a million miles away. The man reached for Drosky's arm. The two prisoners, complete strangers, pulled themselves close into one another's bodies. They hugged and held and cried and patted with an understanding born of their long solitary imprisonment.

They touched in ways unspoken. In ways that only men who have endured long torment can comfort one another. They lay together in a way to soothe deep wounds that the wives they knew they'd never see again could never have been able to understand and reach.

They were complete strangers, but they were soldiers, prisoners, men suddenly together, perhaps for only one brief night. They were men starving for human affection, tenderly exchanging all the grinding, weeping, hugging, laughing consolation they could give one another.

"The war." The man whispered in the last chill before dawn. "The war," he whispered softly into Drosky's ear, "is over." He touched Drosky's startled face, and soothed him back down, holding him on the cot.

"Home!" Drosky's voice was hoarse.

"No." The man spoke quickly. He could not let the defenses he knew Drosky had built up, crumble. He would need them all. He told Drosky how nearly eight hundred POWs had been repatriated some months before. "We lost," the man said. "We evacuated Nam with honor. They told me that when I was jailed up in Hanoi, and they laughed. Some honor. We surrendered. I think we surrendered. They sent most of us back. They said they sent all of us back."

"O my dear sweet Jesus Shit," Drosky said, "we're bargaining chips."

"They're going to fuck with us until they're tired of fucking with us."

In the hot July, depressed, Drosky and his cellmate lost all appetite. They were shackled to the bunks in iron ankle stocks and beaten more frequently. The uneaten food was collected by the Vietnamese to feed the pigs raised on the prison grounds. Drosky was no way ready to help the enemy.

He dumped their uneaten rice into the slop-bucket they shared.

The guards usually steered clear of the loosely lidded slop cans; but new guards had replaced the old. They needed to make their impression. They were harder, less lax in discipline. They had been schooled to bring the Americans to their knees. The regime had finally revealed their plans to use the shadow prisoners they had denied, and would continue to deny, had ever existed.

The new guards hauled Drosky from his cell for the first time in months for interrogation. They accused him of yet another crime against the Vietnamese people: he had thrown away his uneaten ration of food into the cell slop can.

For an hour they beat him, and then with his cellmate, surrounded by guards carrying a dozen slop buckets, Drosky was marched to the shallow mudwallow where the cans were daily emptied.

A new guard, so young he was vicious in the enjoyment he savored in the beatings he gave, handed Drosky a bamboo screen. His meaning was clear. Drosky and his cellmate were to use the sifter in the mudwallow to reclaim the rice Drosky had thrown away. The young guard drove them into the wallow with a rubber truncheon.

Calf-deep in the slime and mud and filth, the two prisoners were forced to kneel. The guard, in heavy rubber boots, waded in behind them. With both hands on a bamboo stick, he forced Drosky's cellmate's head toward the bobbing surface of the pit.

For long seconds, Drosky feared they were going to make them eat the stuff. Negative, Drosky thought, I'll die first.

But the guard pulled back. He knew other plans existed for keeping these Americans as prizes of war. Their skill with weaponry and English was to be used sometime; no one knew when; and they were more valuable alive than dead. And alive, there were vast periods of long nights of vengeance, of long chances to discipline and humiliate and break them to be tractable to the needs of the new postwar regime.

The guards kept them on their knees sifting the rice from the muck for hours. Both men were exhausted from the screening. Drosky had to hold his cellmate's head up from the slimy surface.

The young guard laughed, and said something, which Drosky interpreted, about how the two Americans at night lay together. The guard spit at them, and ordered the soldiers to remove them from the mess pool.

They were hosed down. Drosky's cellmate was locked into bone-biting torture cuffs behind his back, and his feet were secured in metal stocks at the foot of his cot. Drosky, who was not secured in the cell, had to help him with his pajama trousers when he had to use the bucket. Drosky had to wash and clean him.

Bound hand and foot for weeks, the man asked Drosky to be tender to him, to touch him, to lie upon him for warmth. Drosky was no longer surprised at his own feelings. He no longer cared what anyone would think. No one who counted would ever know how relieving was his contact with the bound flier whose only relief was in

Drosky. Finally, Drosky no longer even started the night sleeping on his own cot. He found a way to curl in next to his bound companion.

The new guards woke the two men late one night, and beat them both.

Drosky was clubbed senseless in the corner of the cell, watching his friend, still bound to the cot, being beaten with rubber truncheons and bamboo sticks. Drosky remembered seeing the thrashing man's nose flatten, turn sideways, break, and gush blood. "I love you, man!" That was the last Drosky saw of his cellmate.

When he regained consciousness, he was alone again in solitary confinement. In the slow grind of months, Drosky picked up enough with his pidgin vocabulary to learn of other Americans shot down years before over the Ho Chi Minh Trail. They were being transferred slowly, in great secrecy, from Laos and Cambodia, to Hanoi.

The new regime was expert in reeducating the fliers. Some caved in under extreme torture. Some cooperated out of sheer boredom after years of solitary confinement. The Communists needed the Americans they had shadowboxed away. The US fliers were needed to train a new wave of young VC troops how to repair and fly the planes and choppers abandoned years before in the hasty retreats from Vietnam, Laos, and Cambodia.

They teased Drosky with newspaper clippings. He grew sick at the mention of the term MIA. He wasn't missing in action. He was a prisoner of a war he was still fighting, of a war that was long over, as far as the world was concerned. But not for Drosky. As long as he was held captive, he vowed to resist as long as he had strength and life.

No one, he knew in his heart of hearts, was really, truly trying to negotiate for the MIAs about whom Hanoi claimed to know nothing. He could hear the other American prisoners, voices muffled, in faraway cells. He learned to tap a code on metal pipes that brought coded messages back. For some, there were small brutalizations, in the cages, on the spot. Others were taken off to full-scale torture sessions. Men were disappearing from their solitary cages. Drosky knew that some of the disappeared were already teaching in classrooms. Those who refused had been murdered.

Drosky needed to survive. In every way he could he flipped the bird. He hated the enemy. He hated them when they finally decided it was his time for higher education. He hated them as they broke into his cell, surrounded him, and dangled the coils of torture ropes before his face.

He was determined.

They were determined.

They would make him of use to them, or they would kill him.

Finally it had come time to shit or get off the pot.

Drosky felt a thrill of fear.

In the boredom of interminable solitary confinement, he had almost begun to welcome the rough touches of the guards.

They pulled Drosky's arms behind him, tying his wrists together. He was blindfolded, and his shorts were ripped off, exposing his buttocks, balls, and dick. The guards punched his gut and kicked at his ass and shoulders. One kneed his nuts and sent Drosky sprawling to the floor, scraping his face. He rolled on his side. Winded, he felt hands binding his ankles tightly together with coarse rope. They rolled him onto his belly. The guards took the long torture ropes, cut to precise lengths, and tied tight half-hitches up Drosky's left arm from wrist to shoulder. As each loop was strung, a guard stood on Drosky's arm, and pulled the rope tight into his lean muscular flesh. Again, the rope was wrapped a few more inches up Drosky's arm and tied into a new half-hitch. Every several hitches the guards stopped and slapped Drosky's forearm and biceps like some salami to be coil-wrapped as tight as possible.

Then the guards half-hitched Drosky's other arm.

The bondage was torture and pain itself.

Three guards pulled Drosky's separately bound arms together behind his back, and tied his bound arms together, passing ropes even tighter around on top of the first bindings, wrapping them excruciatingly together: wrists, forearms, elbows, all touching, and then, with their booted feet standing on his arms, they cinched tight against each other his upper arms, all the way from his elbows up to his broad shoulders, until his shoulders were nearly touching.

Drosky felt both shoulders begin to pull out of the sockets. He was in guttural pain. Its center was in his chest which strained out from the tension of the ropes pulling his shoulders back above his bound arms. His arms had already lost all feeling. They were swelling, deadly gray, and cold.

Then he felt their hands tying his legs in tight half-hitches from his ankles up to his knees.

Drosky thought this torture-bondage was the worst he had ever suffered.

Until he felt them raise up his torso.

Until he felt them raise his tightly trussed arms by the wrists, up, backwards, up his back, and above his head.

Until he felt the guard's knee forcing his back forward.

Until he felt the knee's pressure on his back, forcing his face down past his dick and balls, until his nose was between his knees, and his blindfolded eyes were squashed against his legs.

Until he felt the hands pulling his dislocating arms

by his wrists back up over his bowed-down head, tying his wrists pointing straight up from his shoulders to a rope that stretched taut forward and down to his bound ankles.

Until in the room with the piss-soaked floor, there was only his screaming, his mouth muffled against his own naked thighs.

Drosky concentrated against their vengeance...*to give no information or take part in any action which might be harmful to my comrades*...their knees and hands bent him expertly...*to continue to resist by all means possible*...knowing in their long experience with torture...*to make no oral or written statement disloyal to my country*...that they were too vengeful to let him escape by dying...*to give only name, rank, service number and date of birth*...knowing he could only stand so much immobile, suffocating, wrenching, spasming pain...*that I am an American fighting man*...one word in the shadow of this killing pain...*responsible for my actions*...that in all this torture, one word from him, one word...one word only, one word he could never say...*dedicated to the principles which made my country free*...one word that could stop them...*to trust in God*...one word no one a world away would ever, could ever hear him say...*and in the United States of America*...one screaming, broken, thigh-muffled, gagging, pleading *yes!*

Pilatus

The soldier
is no longer
the property of the state
when he dies
he reverts
to his family,
to the mourning women
moving among the cabbages
at the grocer's
dropping Kleenexes,
to the father
come up from whatever fields
to read the withering telegram.
No longer state's property:
their own, at last.

The women move together
fluid
from cabbages
to long trays of meat
(that man in butcher white
washing up)
no freer they
for him,
killed.

That butcher in spatter
commonplaces usually
about fair trade,
but today,
washing,
improvises how the young man
(again theirs)
uh, kept them free.

**Somewhere across the Tracks
from Tennessee Williams'
Desire for the Black Masseur...**

GOODBYE, SAIGON

Some SOB's you never forget. I can still remember what the big-hung bastard looked like and exactly what happened. The sounds, tastes, and smells come prousting back sometimes when I least expect. Sometimes, while jerking off, I can even feel the way it was, because this experience is true and really happened.

Fall 1969. Hippies. Yippies. Vietnam. Student protests. Green recruits leaving. Seasoned vets returning amid green body bags. Redneck State Troopers. County jails in the south. All familiar to an 18-year old college freshman born, bred, and raised in Columbia, South Carolina: home of the University of South Carolina and of Fort Jackson, a major processor of returning Viet vets.

Picture me picturing myself: one of those young Southern blond boys, ripe as a peach, lean and hard and hung, eight inches long, thick, virtually virgin, tired of jerking off, tired of fast glances at upper classmen standing in the shower or at the row of urinals, wanting forbidden sex. Hardon thinking about men's dicks and balls. Tentative with tent pants. Got to try it. Finally: got to find dick! Reading coded classifieds in an underground copy of the *LA Free Press*. Jerking off. Sniffing around a similar ad in the college paper for "swinging roommate." Hardon. Answering ad. Making arrangements to meet.

Nervous. Turned on. Stiff dick running down the leg of
well-worn Levi's. Throwing on OD Army shirt with pro-
test buttons. Running hands through cool hair. Sweat.
Stiff cock. Ready. Yeah. I was ready.

Scheduled to meet at 10 PM, but arrive half hour
early. Man, about forty, answers door and invites me in.
Two young soldiers in creased khaki lounge on couch.
They glare at my hippie appearance. Both chug Southern Comfort from pint bottles. Legs kicked up. Crotches
aimed like rifle-sites at me from between well-polished
boots. Older man winks at me and says he's going out
for more booze. Takes one soldier with him. They split.

I pull out a joint, sit cross-legged hippie-style on floor,
my eyes at level of one remaining soldier's crotch. He's
no more than twenty-one. Start talk. Pass joint. Soldier
hands me nearly empty pint. Drink. Smoke. Watch crotch.
Hardon. Soldier grabs his crotch and plays with it
through stiff khaki.

"You want this, don't you, boy? You want this cock,
huh?" Soldier stands up and walks toward me. His dick
hard against his uniform. He reaches down and grabs
me by the OD Army shirt and pulls me up and pushes
me into the wall. "Fuckin' hippie puke!"

Crack! His free hand crashes against the side of my
face. Blood. Pain. I taste salt. More blood comes from
nose. Surprising: no pain. Not much any way. Another
slug. I fall to the floor. One hand up for some protection.
Maybe this is the way it is. I watch his face. Fuck. Just
stoned and ripped enough to be sort of outside myself
watching this drunken fucker stomp me. Blood taste. Surprise. My shirt gets shredded off. I feel his strength as
he knocks me back on the floor. This ain't half bad! He is
brute handsome. I start to say something. No time. His
polished boot pushes heavily on my balls. Harder and
harder.

"Fuckin' hippie puke's gonna get it and get it good."

Boot crashes against my crotch. Hard. Real pain now. Blood taste. Fear. I roll over moaning. No chance to move. He's on me. His weight pins me to the hard wood floor. He rips my teeshirt off. Hesitates. Then starts banging my head against a small pillow on the floor. The pillow slips. My head hits the hard wood floor. Head throbs. Vision blurs. Sounds stop.

Wake up. Feel okay. Can't move. Hands tied behind my back. Propped up against wall with my ripped teeshirt in my mouth. Can't talk. Can barely breathe. Soldier walks toward me. His shirt unbuttoned exposing impressive chest, tattoos, dog tags, bandages red with fresh blood from straining. He gropes his big box as he drains his whiskey pint. Tosses bottle across room.

Soldier stares at me. Unclips his belt. Reaches inside his fly to pull out his cock. Big stiff cock. He stands for a moment looking at me, watching me react to the sight of him, stroking his cock with one hand. His other hand brushes against his bandages and his chest.

"See these, fucker?" He points out older scars as well as the fresh blood on his bandages. He is no more than twenty-one or twenty-two. "I got these...so assholes like you...can run around and be college...assholes and hippies. Now it's your turn, asshole. You're gonna see what pain feels like and how to hurt." He reaches down. Grabs me by my long hair. Pulls me up. Face to face. Wow. He glares at me with thick white teeth clenched. The scars are angry red weals on his hard young body.

"Look at 'em, asshole!"

He pushes my face into his side. This is heavy. Almost fucking religious. His enormous cock stands at rigid attention. I smell his sweat and the Southern Comfort on his raunchy breath. He's alien like nothing I've ever seen. I want to take his prick down my throat. I want to swallow his seed. He holds my cheek against his tight belly close to his scars.

"Look at 'em good. You see 'em? Take a good look. Fuckin' hippie puke."

Big scars up and down his well-developed side. I see them. Old wounds. New wounds. Shrapnel frags. The red bandages. The bandages coming undone in the sweat and roughhousing. Fresh battle scars. Stitches. Fuck! It's only twenty-four hours from Saigon to here.

"Fuckin' hippie puke." He keeps saying it like a mantra that keeps him alive. "Fuckin' hippie puke."

He pulls my head up to his face. He is handsome. I don't want him to stop. He rips the teeshirt out of my mouth. Grabs me by the throat.

"You gonna take care of me, ain't you, asshole!"

More fear. Mouth dry. Iron taste of blood-caked lips. My blood. His blood. Can say nothing. Just afraid. Just real fear. As long as his huge cock stays hard, I figure I'm more the subject of his lust than his violence.

"Lick these fuckin' scars, asshole."

He pushes my face back down to his wounded side. I taste his sweat and blood around the rough scar tissue.

"That's right, fucker, lick 'em good."

His cock still hard. His other hand pumping it. Huge mushroom head topping thick shaft. He forces my face harder into his side. He hesitates. Stumbles. Too much booze. Falls against the wall holding his side. I've worked my hands loose from behind my back. Scared. I watch him glare at me through his pain.

He recovers. He walks toward me. His eyes narrow with the hard-boiled intent of a mean face-fucker. His cock thrust forward. Full attention. Grabs my neck. Forces me down on my knees. His big hands tightening around my throat.

"Suck me, asshole! Suck me good."

He shoves his cock into my mouth. I choke and pull back. He hits me with his fist. Kicks me with his fucking heavy combat boots. Intense pain. Fear. He stops as

I fall on the floor, bleeding, breathing hard. He stoops to one knee, checks out my eyes, unfastens my belt, pulls my Levi's down around my knees. He half drags me across the room.

"Roll over." He commands the order.

Face down, both hands protecting my balls, I shake. Several long minutes pass. I watch him, sore as hell. He holds his side. Pulls off his khakis. He sees me watching him. He spits a hawker in my direction. I stick out my tongue but I miss the phlegm. He laughs. He throws his boots at me as hard as he can. One hits the back of my head. The other, my side and ribs.

He walks over, stripped but for the dog tags and the white bandages hanging loose off his side, bobbling his huge dick, cantilevered over his hairy balls up past his navel. No noise except for heavy breathing and the jingle of his dog tags.

"You're gonna take care of me, fucker. You're gonna have to take care of me."

He swings his dick. His bone. Like a club. A gun.

"You assholes owe me!"

He grabs the cheeks of my ass. Spreads them. Spits on my virgin hole. He holds me down and starts to take my asshole. The power of his big weight, his hard muscle, his sweat, his cool dog tags against my back. My asshole resists. He shoves harder. Intense pain. His cock getting harder and harder inching its way up into my unwilling asshole. He starts pumping.

I struggle under him to get away. Can barely move under his weight and strength and anger.

He starts hitting me with his fist as he bangs his cock up my asshole. He stops long enough to hold the bandages falling from his side. His hot wet blood runs with sweat down his belly to my butt, blood-fucking me, juicing my ass, easing the pain, driving in deep all the way. He's breathing heavy. Hitting me with his fists.

Cursing. "Fuckin' hippie puke." Then shoots his load and falls motionless on top of me. My asshole pushes his rigid dog-soldier cock out. He raises a few inches up off me. The blood causes our two skins to stick together. Fused so tight, it's almost the sound of ripping flesh as he pulls his belly from my back, stands up, and stumbles a few feet to pass out on the couch.

I try to stand up. My head, side, asshole throb. Finally up, I wipe the load of his cum into the blood running down my back, butt, legs. His blood. My blood. Our blood. Not sure. I dress fast and beat it, hoping he won't wake up. He lays passed out, holding his side, his young face relaxed down in sleep, the violence numbed, drifting in a certain, separate peace, burned like a flashbulb snapshot into my brain of a wounded naked soldier crashed out on a couch in a living room that exists now only in memory.

Mine. And maybe his.

Back at school, I ended up in the infirmary with two bruised ribs, a slight concussion, three loose teeth, and a story about getting beat up by some pro-war rednecks. A likely story in South Carolina in the late Sixties. I never mentioned my bruised asshole. After a couple days, I no longer had to hold onto the walls in the john.

Of course, I'm no longer a hippie. Who is anything they used to be? But I'd sure like to get in touch with that 1969 Viet vet from Fort Jackson. I wasn't very willing then, but that experience and those memories have kept me pulling my meat nights when nothing else but memory will get me off.

Maybe I'm a sick fucker, but sometimes what seems the worst of times is the best of times after all. Maybe we exorcized each other's demons. Maybe I was that "welcome home" parade he expected but never got.

Rough Trade

Chico knows the Game I like.
I've bought him more than once
out of the allnite deli a block off Sheridan Square.
He knows I dig his attitude, his long blade,
his thick Newyorican cock,
his martial arts, his kungfoolishness I call it,
so he hits me so good, putting his bladepoint
in that tight olive-complected triangle under my chin.
"C'mon, baby," he coaxes.
His point tilts my head far back.
Our Village alley is dark. My mouth opens. Breath...
leaves my lips...uh...in some silent shout for help,
and Chico is all my help, nodding his head,
coaching me further. "C'mon," he teases.
"C'mon, man, wider, baby."
His cock grows harder
with his blade against my soft throat.
His cold steel draws a trickle of my hot Afro-Irish blood.
He thickens, glistens, bargains his big cock deeper
down my throat, pumping his dark dick into my face,
building his unsafe pre-lube to a 15 buck cum,
slipping in his point, tempered steel, an inch
below his cock buried in my throat,
acting out redsnuff orgasm,
lipdeep in his greaser crotch.
His smile when I cum.
He knows guys are looking
for what he won't actually give.
He goes with a 10 buck tip.
Chico. Jeez. Man.

**Stuck Fuck in the Middle
of Nowhere...**

*FROM NADA TO
MAÑANA*

Nicaragua. Shit! Managua, a nightmare. Hanging upside down by my boots lashed to the fan in the center of the room, I spin in slow circles, bombed. My blood, my sweat run down from my feet to my face. Inside my camouflage boxer shorts, my thick dick, bigger than my daddy's, hangs down past my navel. Prime uncut American meat. Choice Kansas cornfed. I feel my foreskin peep open around the blood-thickening head of my cock, descending hard. It's Jack Daniel's making me turn around and around, tripping me out, on who I am, who I was, where I was, and where I'm headed. My hand reaching on my dick feels better than good and brings me floating down from the circling fan to the bed.

I'm getting this sick feeling. The kind you feel when you know you're living on the edge. The kind that only feels right when your jaw aches from one punch too many in the good-time bar of the Hotel Managua. The only pain that feels better is the ache in your own knuckles from breaking some other poor fucker's jaw. Weird shit, man. A barroom brawl gives me a hardon. But that's another story.

I wrap my bruised fist around my dick, strip the foreskin back, and slowly piston it like a steam train starting up back in the hills with swarthy young Sandinistas riding shotgun on the cattle guard. Grinding noise and puffing smoke. Soot from the 'stacks blowing back into the cattle car packed with boxes of rifles, half from the USSR and half from the good old USA. Nicaragua's like Abbott and Costello: Who's on first? You think I care? I pledge allegiance to cash, although I confess a weakness for American dollars. I may be a merc, but, born in the USA, a traitor I'm not.

My dick in my hand feels as smooth and sweet as the tough young soldier, who, no more than a snot-nosed eighteen, laid back two nights ago in an empty box car on a slow-rolling train, and smiled his *Si-Señor* smile when I stood over him, kicking his combat boots apart, spreading his legs, kneeling down between his thighs, reaching under the bandoleros of cartridges x-ing his torso, unbuttoning his shirt, rubbing my calloused hands over his hard chest, diving in on his nipples, pinioning his muscular arms back with his shirt, licking his sweaty armpits, tongueing down his tight belly to the cinched equator of his belt. His juicy young Latin body was all promise of big dick.

"Americanos," he said, "you all want the same thing."

"The same thing you want."

"Asshole!" He said it and smirked.

"Dick." I corrected him.

"Asshole wanting dick." He spelled out what he meant.

"Red-white-and-blue cocksucker," I said.

He shrugged his shoulders and moved both his young hands to the pistol in his belt. Sex and death and the whole damned thing. But his palms passed over his pistol and he smoothed his hands down over his camo crotch. "How much you say," he said. He laughed when he saw I thought he meant to sell his dick for trade. "No," he said. "How much you bet me my dick is bigger than yours?

My dick shoots more than yours. Eh? *Mano a mano.*
Twenty-five bucks maybe? Fifty? A hundred?"

"No way, José," I said. "Fifty." I sized him up. He was
a handsome fucker. No more than a kid. I figured, like
the rest of them, he'd been soldiering for six years, since
he turned twelve, and he had grown fast from boy to
man before the murmuring dark of his first night in camp
was broken by his first penetrated grunt of pain turning
to unexpected pleasure before sun-up. Every country, I
know, because I've seen plenty, trains their young recruits the same, the same being the older soldiers doing
what I was trying to do to this young Latin stud to kill a
long train ride from *Nada* to *Mañana,* and us still more
than a 150 klicks from Managua, Nicaragua, "such a
heavenly place," as the Tin Pan Alley lyrics go: "You ask
a señorita for a sweet embrace." Shee-it! Fuck the
señorita. Or better, don't fuck her. Fuck her brother.

"Put up." He grinned. He stuck fifty bucks American
on his Russian pack. His white teeth flashed between
his perfect brown lips crowned with his black moustache.
He was an arrogant young bastard who followed the
handsome Daniel Ortega, the way our revolutionary foot-
soldiers followed Washington. He smiled when I stuck
fifty bucks next to his crisp cash. The rattling boxcar
vibrated around us as it pulled through the hot, humid,
jungle night.

"You want to measure it," he asked, "soft or hard?"

"First soft. Then hard." I rubbed my fingers over my
own covered cock. He rubbed himself the same. His
tongue moved slowly, tip first, from between his lips,
exactly the way the tip of a hardening cock slides out
between the tight lips of foreskin. He slick-wet his berry-
ripe lips. My heart leapt to my throat the same in sex
as in combat. My cock tucked and rolled. I moved from
between his legs and knelt on the outside of his left
thigh.

Bold, he popped the buttons on his fly, raised his butt, and stripped his hips and thighs down naked. His huge uncut cock lay atop the furrow between his hairy legs. A good Twelve Incher. Maybe more. Maybe a lot more. The jungle night was tossed by deep shadows under the tropical moon. He grinned at me. "You can beat my meat?" he asked. His voice swaggered. Back in the States, he probably had cousins, illegals, hustling 42nd Street. If they were hung like him, they'd be rich in no time flat. His soft olive-skinned cock stretched long as a snaking hose. My fingers tipped along the incredible length of his dick that was as soft as velvet. The tight curlicues of his dark pubic hair forested its base and his big studnuts.

"Are there anymore at home like you?" I asked.

He grunted. "This is South America, *señor*. There are always more at home like me. That is the point." He gently but firmly pushed my hand away. "Are there anymore," he asked, "at home like you?" He spit past the open target of my face into the darkness. In the light of the full moon spilling into the open door of the slow-moving railcar, his smile was part contempt, part joke, and all young lust. "Now," he said, "you show me your big North American prick." For the first time he called me his nickname for me, "*Señor El Norte*, show me your big white dick."

"You talk big."

"I am big." He tightened his naked groin muscles and flexed every veined inch of his exposed cock.

Whether I was hung bigger or smaller, I had won the bet by getting him stripped part-naked. Very sexy. Fifty bucks had peeled his dick from his uniform. I stripped my rod free, flopping it out, kneeling next to his left thigh. His eyes widened. He grabbed my cock at its root and stared at it as if he had never seen big blond *Estados Unidos* dick up close. He liked it. I liked it. Jeez! Stuck fuck in the middle of nowhere, rattling like two beebees in a boxcar, probably going nowhere fast, we were a fair match, dick to dick. Different, but we had a couple of beauties. We both knew it. We both recognized it. His lip of dark olive foreskin was, maybe, an inch longer than mine; but soft inch for soft inch, our bet was a meatman's draw; but hard, he'd win, I could tell, by a mile. I took his dick in my hand while he held on to mine.

"Even steven," I said.

"Okay," he said.

"There's only one way to win this fucking fifty bucks," I said. If there's anything I find worth studying, it's a man with a big soft cock. But if there's anything I want, it's making a man's big soft cock stand up stiff and hard. "This time, kid, I'll bet you another fifty, that you're bigger hard than I am."

"That's no bet, *El Norte*."

"But it's a sure thing to get me what I want."

He laughed, spit in his hand, and stroked my stiffening rod, until my dick stood rockhard pointing straight in his face. My hand worked his meat, mauling him up to full attention.

Anybody standing along the tracks that night could have seen in the door of the train rumbling by in the hot Nicaraguan moonlight the single-frame shot of two soldiers hand-pulling each other's meat, stripped to the uniforms dropped around their knees, slapping and rubbing chests and bellies, tongues wrapping, sucking spit, blowing air down throats, rebreathing, sucking the air back out, twisting nipples, making hard-assed love in an almost empty cattle car on a half-deserted troop supply train.

War is a hard time in a harsh place and nothing soft passed between us in our rough wrestle toward cuming. We panted and grappled like soldiers. Our dicks bobbed and weaved. I pulled him to his feet and jammed our bellies together, grinding meat into meat, sportfucking, challenging for the kill, hands pulling the other's dick, gun barrels jousting, ramming cockheads and long shafts between sweaty thighs, fucking slick dick between hot legs, balls bouncing, big dicks slamming, ready to burst, rocking with the roll of the train.

He put his hands on my buzzcut head. He had big arms. He tried to force me down to my knees to suck his cock. I grappled with him, wanting to ram my dick down his young throat; but he was too strong. I let him be too strong. He resisted me. I let him resist me. The next roll of the train slammed us against the wood wall. I stumbled on my pants tangled around my combat boots, stumbled because I wanted to stumble, because every time, fucking with young soldiers, I lose the upper hand, I feel I've won.

I'm the kind of hunter who eats what he stalks.

He forced me to my knees. The full glory of his huge cock manifest itself over my face. My mouth opened and he drove himself in, head and shaft and crotch hair, balls banging my chin. I took him the way I'd wanted him, all the way in, sucking him in deep, swallowing him in deeper, holding his huge cock, his teenage daddy-cock, that, who knew had made, and would make, how many babies, sucking his salty seed-taste deep inside me, till I could hear, above the rumble of the train, the roar in his throat that charged his slam-driving fuck of my face with his big cock.

Each lunge brought him closer to cuming. My left hand held his *toro* balls tight against my chin. My right hand slapped my own cock to the edge. Spit ran from my lips, dripped on my chest, wet my cock. He grabbed my ears in his hands and holding my head dog-steady almost pulled his twelve hard inches from my mouth. I sucked hard on his grenade-head not to let him escape; but escape was not what he wanted.

He wanted surrender.

He started a slow drive into my mouth, inch by inch, sliding the full length of his massive rebel meat down my throat, still holding my ears, then driving the final inch down my throat, cutting my breathing, me trying to gasp around the eight-inch circumference of his dick, feeling his explosion coming, like far-off cannon fire, advancing, igniting, cuming, blowing off, exploding deep in my throat, concussions of his seed spewing hot shrapnel molten-deep in my throat, gushing out around his cock, flooding my cheeks, his cum shooting out of my nose, blowing out of my snotlocker, my own cock cuming under the passion of his relentless face-fucking. I wanted what I got and I got what I wanted.

When he pulled his weapon from the deep holster of my throat, I slumped forward on my knees and wrapped my arms around his strong young thighs.

"You win," I said. "I know when I'm beat."

"Your president too," he said, "should know that about us."

All the world's a smart-ass.

The fucking palm trees in the moonlight passed by the open boxcar door and I thought the trees were moving and we were standing still.

So here I am, cha-cha-cha, crashed in this crummy hotel room, with a throat still sore from two days ago, and a memory I'll never forget of Carlos, or Paco, or Esteban, or whatever his name was, unless his name was Jack Daniel's which is a name, sweet Jesus, I never forget, because I am *Señor El Norte*. I know, because a young Sandinista with brown eyes, a saltlick taste, and a twelve-inch dick told me so. But he's gone. Maybe dead by now. That's too romantic. He's not dead. Tonight he's cribbing in somewhere, probably with some pretty chiquita banana, maybe not drinking as hard as me, but then he's too young to have much to forget. He's not thirty-four, crapped out in a room with an honest-to-

Christ flashing neon sign outside the window, listening to the monsoon rainstorm batter the glass. *El Norte* has got to get his ass out of Nicaragua! A man can be out too long, especially when he's between assignments. He forgets who he is and which side he's on. I been paid cash money by at least three different flags to tackle the same covert mission. I use that money well, which is how I started drinking sometime the night before last at the only male whorehouse in greater Managua, a famous place—if you ask the right people—no sex maniac ought to miss. I been a regular for maybe a year. Luis de Aguilar, the owner, invited me to a game and a gamble that keeps me coming back. He knows I'm hung big and he knows I like size, so he prides himself on scouting the biggest cocks he can to beat my meat. Luis de Aguilar knows I'll pay up to a hundred an inch for better-than-ordinary, nicely-attached young dick. One of my Size Nights at Luis de Aguilar's can cause inflation to ripple through the Nicaraguan economy. But, hey, I'm Goddam *El Norte*. I get paid big. I spend big. I suck big. Bigger is always better, and maybe because I'm blond, Latin meat looks all the sweeter: brown shafts, cocoa foreskins, olive-ripe dickheads. Cha-cha-cha.

That's how I know I better split. There's plenty of mercenary work, but, fuck it, I've been out so long all I want to do is play. Suddenly this summer, I'm turning into that fucking Sebastian Venable, and I remember how dark young Latin men did lunch with him. But that hardly stopped me that last night at Luis de Aguilar's, when Jack Daniel's and Sebastian and I went out into the heart of darkness for one last time, straight to the neon flash of *La Cantina de Luis.*

When a country's at war, anything goes. In the back rooms off his main bar, Luis de Aguilar had converted a storeroom into pari-mutuel betting, sort of like on horses, where those who bet on the winners divide the bets or

stakes, minus a percentage for the management. Luis
de Aguilar was no more a fool than the dozen or so CIA
operatives and other US and Russian military advisors
positioned around the small smoky room, watching the
action, where the bets weren't on horses but on the horse-
size cocks of the contestants. Take me to any hot little
room in any war-torn little country on a Saturday night
in a makeshift bar where men forget to be reminded
about women, and I'll introduce you to half the Penta-
gon.

Luis de Aguilar's gambling show was in Round 3
when I arrived. I liked it. I saw three young studs. Two
trig-looking Nicaraguans, and one blond Swede—a merc
with big, tattooed arms. Hold this picture! They were
standing buck naked, butts twitching, with their dicks,
wrapped hidden in soft brown chamois rolls, laid out like
bagged sausage on a crotch-high wood counter. The
Swede was jittery. He kept both hands busy dialing the
nipples on his big hairy pecs where the number "2" had
been painted with black gun grease. The shorter Nicaraguan, a black-bearded Bull, naked next to him, put his
fingers in his teeth and whistled for Luis de Aguilar. "The
gringo plays with his tits," he said. "He cheats."

"Fuck you, Numero Uno," the Swede said, swiping
his big paw at the number painted on the short man's
pecs and belly.

The crowd called out for more. The contest was for
size of cock; but sometimes size of mouth was a good
kickass kickoff. The crowd of bettors was able to see no
more than each contestant's body. The three players stood
naked except for the tight wrap of chamois-skin leather
around their cocks. The bettors, lunging with money,
cigars, and whiskey, handicapped their bets based on
general body size. They gauged particularly the size
of fingers and noses and feet, three sure signs of cocki-
ness. Nearly everyone bet on who had the largest dick,

but some hedged their stake, betting on who had the smallest, which, considering Luis de Aguilar's back-office auditions, wasn't that small, since a man auditioning less than eight inches would never be invited to strip down, chamois-wrap his dick, flop it out on the table, and stand naked, working the crowd, trying to get the bettors to go for him, because, win or lose, he got a sweet percentage of the total bet on him. What a contest! Three naked men trying to convince a crowd of national soldiers and international paramilitaries to bet big cash on the size of their big cocks.

I sucked off Jack Daniel's again. My own cock stirred at the temptation to enter Luis de Aguilar's inch-worm contest just one time before I split Nicaragua. What man doesn't fantasize he could win a cock showdown. As the bottle splashed down from my face, I recognized the third contestant, the second Nicaraguan, not the short Bull who had complained about the Swede's tits, but the taller, juicier one, the hairier one, the one I hadn't realized was so hairy—two nights before—on the supply train when all I wanted was to deep-case his big foot-long throat-sausage. The fucker had won my hundred bucks. What did I care? I'd swung long and hard on his massive meat that he, with great pleasure, *señor*, had crammed as far back down my throat as he possibly could. He hadn't killed me with it, but I suspected men lay dead, dying happy, smiles on their faces, with their throats torn open, where he had face-fucked before.

"Ola, Luis de Aguilar!" I shouted. "Two hundred on Number 3. What's his name?

"*El Capitan*," Luis de Aguilar shouted. He was a tout, fast with nicknames.

El Capitan, oh yeah, recognized me, he did, and grinned. He pointed at his wrapped cock resting on the table, then shook his fist, warning me not to reveal the long secret of his one-eyed pants snake. God! It thrilled

me to think of the nerve some young studs have, like
they're God's fucking gift to man, which they are, to strip
down and lay their dicks out on tables for strange men's
inspections and bets, because they're confident they're
sporting the biggest dick around. Who, at what age, first
tells them that?

The three young men stood 1-2-3, *Uno-Dos-Tres*,
shoulder to shoulder with the Swede sandwiched like
white meat in the middle. Soldiering had hardened their
tough young bodies, but in their faces, especially in the
face of the eighteen-year-old *El Cap*, a sweet trace of
boyhood's sunset glowed. Their muscular bodies sweated
under the bright spotlight of the gaming table. The
shorter Nicaraguan stood his ground like the Bull he
was. The Swede was the kind of perfect military blond
who always shows up whenever anyone throws a war, a
crusade, or a bar-room brawl. *El Cap*, lean as a Latin
boxer, was the mean fighting machine that keeps a hungry guerrilla army going past all endurance.

Blue smoke from fine Havana cigars, gifts from cousin
Fidel, wafted through the bright light. The crowd, most
in jungle camo uniform still sweaty and bloody, armed
to a man, loud with booze, eager with lust, cheered as
the last bets were placed. Outside, machine guns fired
off in the night. Hardly anyone bet the short swarthy
Bull had the biggest dick. Most went for the tattooed
blond merc, swayed by his attitude and the size of his
powerful Swedish body; but the smart money quietly bet
on *El Cap*. I'd sucked him in the dark and had no real
idea how much bigger than big he might really be hung.
I wanted to know. I wanted his long gun of a prick down
my throat again.

Luis de Aguilar fired his pistol into the ceiling. Plaster dust fell. A basso whore upstairs screamed drag-so-
prano. The crowd cheered. Not a man in the room would
have bet he himself would see tomorrow. The three

naked men, with their dicks bagged and laid out along three yellow school rulers nailed to the table, concentrated, thinking those thoughts a man thinks when he wants to, hands-off, make his cock hard. The Swede's chamois bag inched forward first. The short Bull grunted and his bagged dick edged past the Swede's. *El Cap*, running his own dirty movie on the inside screen of his closed eyes, ignored their contest like a runner pacing the leaders till they run themselves down.

The race was on. The Swede's dick was approaching 8 inches. At 8 inches on the yellow ruler, Luis de Aguilar's move was to unwrap the dick from the chamois bag, but the naked, hardening dick had to stay, untouched by hands, inching along the edge of the yellow ruler, until it hit 10, when the contestant could finally take his meat in one hand to palm-drive it up past 11 inches, to 12, 13, however far it would harden.

The house record was painted in red on the green table: 14½ inches of bone-hard cock, set by a Texas cowboy who drove his red Ford pickup into Managua one night so three-days-drunk he never knew he had crossed the border out of Texas into Mexico and had kept heading south on unmarked backroads, and ended up in Managua, Nicaragua. Cha-cha-cha! That's the great seduction about Central America: a man can drive there.

The bearded Bull was in a sweat; his big cock ached for a handjob, a blowjob; he had the meat but he needed the pull. The Swede hit 8 on the yellow ruler and Luis de Aguilar stripped his big fat blond cock free of the chamois. His dick was a beauty: thick blond porcelain veined with blue traceries, tipped with a big nipple of uncut foreskin. The crowd applauded. Even those who hadn't bet on the Swede had to cheer the sheer beauty of his manhood rolling, stretching, lengthening, toward 9 inches, then past 9, untouched, toward 10.

The Bull wasn't doing bad for himself. A dozen mestizo soldiers from his ragtag outfit spurred him on, yelling to him like they personally knew how big was his cock, shouting obscenities to him to make it bigger, reminding him what a big face-fucker he sported between his hairy thunder-thighs. The squat Bull bared all three of his gold-rimmed white teeth in his black-bearded face and strained. His chamois-roll slid past 8 inches. Luis de Aguilar stripped his bullcock bare, careful to accidentally touch it, careful to accidentally stroke it, entrepreneuring the man's hardon, figuring to make the contest more interesting for the house at *La Cantina de Luis*. The Bull roared as Luis de Aguilar, who was also known as Lois de Aguilar, stroked his cock.

The crowd cheered. A beer bottle flew overhead and smashed against the wall. The Bull's dick thickened and inched past 9, straining on the yellow ruler for the 10 he knew he was hung with, the 10 inches and maybe more, depending on how excited he was, like this moment with the crowd cheering his size, aching to beat the gringo blond, worrying about the too-quiet kid next to him with his dick wrapped in chamois and lying alongside the yellow ruler like a secret arms shipment about to be exposed on the table.

The Bull's dick hit 10 inches. Luis de Aguilar blew his whistle. Bull grabbed his dick, stroking it carefully, watching the Swede's dick inch toward 10 and hit the magic number. Again Luis de Aguilar blew his whistle. The Swede took his own dick in hand. Shoulder to shoulder, the two soldiers beat their meat, slamming their rods down side by side, blond against olive, along the yellow rulers. The Bull was pulling 11 and the Swede was right behind.

"*El Capitan!*" I shouted. "Number 3!"

El Cap grinned at me and spit, the way he liked to spit, past the two soldiers masturbating next to him. He flexed his powerful butt and blasted his wrapped cock straight past 8 to 9 inches on his yellow ruler. Luis de Aguilar blew his whistle. The crowd roared. Men started clapping. "Take it off! Take it off!" Luis de Aguilar unrolled the chamois from *El Cap's* cock. A cheer rose up. Untouched, *El Cap's* dick writhed and rolled, stretching hard past the 10, 11, and 12-inch marks. He was stud with a bullet. The wet eye of his advancing cockhead, peeping through its big dark foreskin, was set on 13. The Bull and the Swede paused in amazement. "Oh shit!" the Swede said.

"Oh God!" The Bull should never have looked at the size of *El Cap's* cock. His own lust for sucking big dick undid him. He shuddered, spasmed, tried not to, but couldn't help cuming, turning, shooting his hot load slop across *El Cap's* thick pipeline still heading untouched past 13 on the yellow. The Bull fell back. His own 10-inch boner, 8 inches around the base, stuck straight out from his bull-body, dripping sperm like the animal cock it was. He raised his thick arms in salute. The crowd cheered. Sweat I wanted to drink ran from the inside of his big biceps down into the twin thickets of his dripping hairy armpits. The Bull may not have been the biggest stud, but he was big and he was stud. A General, an advisor from the Potomac, waved at him two one-hundred dollar bills which easily matched his winnings from Luis de Aguilar's Inches Derby, and made him the General's conquest for the night.

The Swede, buck-naked against the snazzy color of his tattooed arms, stood alone next to *El Cap*, who had yet to touch his inchward cock. The Swede spit in his hand and stroked his own rod, working his blond beauty for every last micropinch he could add to his hardon. He stripped his foreskin back, pressed his thighs into the table, tweaked his hard nipples, slapped his dick down the length of the yellow ruler, and watched the head hit square on 13. The crowd cheered. The Swede grinned yeah-yeah, but he knew it was all he had in him. If there is a hell, it must be having the goodluck/badluck of a 13-inch cock that's still not big enough.

The Swede had no alternative. I'd have done the same thing. He nodded to Luis de Aguilar who blew his whistle. He spit in his hand, looked straight into *El Cap's* eyes, got his go-ahead, and did the honors. He touched, actually touched, *El Cap's* untouched cock topping 13 on the ruler. He lifted the cock up, his face amazed at the cock's gorged volume-weight, teasing the cock's tip with his fingers, stroking the cock's silo-length, feeling the cock's throbbing growth, then finally, *El Cap's* cock size so overwhelming, falling to his knees in front of *El Cap*, opening his mouth, his brilliant blond moustache catching the light, his own big meat bouncing with lust, wanting the young rebel soldier's cock rammed down his throat, begging for his head to be drilled.

The crowd went wild.

El Cap turned to me. I held up three hundred dollars which was only a fifth of what I was going to win from my bet on his cock. He winked. Three hundred was okay. He held up one finger to signal me his intent. Then he dropped his big balls into the blond's waiting mouth. His olive dick showed to huge advantage measured up across the grid of the square-jawed blond face that looked like the map of Sweden. Men whistled. The blond crossed his eyes adoring at close range the monster cock.

Finally, *El Cap* pulled his hairy nuts dripping saliva from the Swede's bulging cheeks. The blond's own meat was ready to blow in his hand. *El Cap's* dick loomed over him. His mouth opened, and to the slow stomping of feet that grew louder and faster, *El Cap* drove his drill-rig cock inch by inch past the blond's moustache and lips and tongue and deep down his throat where he rooted in and held his position, with at least four more inches to go, hearing the crowd shouting *Ole!*, watching the Swede's eyes, crossed again, in his blond face impaled on the huge dick, waiting for the Swede to give the nod for the final thrust, and taking, when the nod of surrender did not come willingly from the blond, the final choking slide down his throat, so final, so good, so victorious, the vanquished Swede shot his load between *El Cap's* naked calves, and the house came tumbling down.

El Cap pulled his dick slow out of the gasping blond merc's throat. Luis de Aguilar ran to him with a tape measure sure he had a new house record; but *El Cap* gently pushed him away, and said, "Not now." He meant not ever. He had no intention of being a man measured by his cock.

Yeah. Sure. Cha-cha-cha. Later that night, and for several weeks thereafter, hanging around Managua, with several side jobs crossing to Honduras, dodging Contras, I was privy to every fucking inch of the private parts of my own *El Capitan*, and my lips, now that they've been stitched back together, are sealed.

All I'm saying is that, measure for measure, against *El Cap*, that famous-hung drunk cowboy who drove his 14 ½ inches in from Texas one night to Luis de Aguilar's Inch Derby probably ain't much to write home about, which is something me and Jack Daniel's have got to do one of these first *mañanas* before *El Norte* finally hauls his ass out of where he don't belong.

The Young Turks Dream of Derek Jarman

The beautiful young men,
forced-laboring in Sardinia,
sweating in the steel mills,
hung, hanged by the wrists,
strung up for whipping.
Young men, naked,
sweating, greasy, hairy, filthy slaves,
tortured by the gruff Polack foreman,
the whipmaster, hanging
the handsome, bound, young men
up-side-down,
suspended stripped,
nude, naked for industrial torture.
The leather whip cuts across
young muscled back.
Somebody's sons.
Somebody's brothers.
One, a great beauty, a convict convicted
of crimes against nature,
suspended by his spread ankles.
Ah. The handsome moustached slave,
more perverse than the whipmaster,
grows hard,
beaten by the muscular foreman.

They know not they are watched,
from a distance, and close up,
by men who enjoy
their brutally sensuous punishment.
Young men born to suffer,
working at hard labor,
imprisoned in the Sardinian penitentiary,
serving sentences indeterminate,
pulled from chained solitary confinement
to labor by the sweat of greasy muscle.
Hard,
they are, one by one,
stretched spreadeagle,
suspended up-side-down
by their boots,
spread against steel grills,
bound, tied, forcibly whipped
in the total male sensuality
of young men serving time,
serving a cruel master,
punished,
in a dream,
in a steel dungeon.

After Pasolini's *Salo*,
After Miller's *The Road Warrior*,
After Tarantino's *Reservoir Dogs*,
After Oliver Stone's *Natural Born Killers*,
Comes a...

RoughNight@Sodom.Cum

Tonight, twenty minutes into the Future, in a high mountain desert, beyond the Federal Gestalt Line, manimal screams echo deep from the ritual painstream chambers of the Giant Robo Prince Sodom. Above his forested estate, the nuke-red moon hangs full over his vaulted stone mansion. Lunatic shine lights the hyper-secret acreage of high-tech torture courts, discipline barracks, killing fields, and burial yards.

The vast compound, laser-laced border to border, invisible even to sophisticated Federal Gestalt satellite scrutiny, is completely surrounded by a fifteen-foot solid rock wall, capped by a ten-foot high-voltage cyclone fence. The top of the metal barrier is accordioned with coils of gray Federal prison wire barbed every six inches with 35-mm razor blades, cut like SS lightning bolts, calculated to shred the well-muscled flesh of any big-pec'd, big-nippled, big-built prisoner fleeing the agonizing slow-death sadomachismo tortures of the heroically handsome Annihilator Sodom, Prince of Pecs, and his killer cadre of masculine-identified nipple-driven bodybuilder terminators.

Prince Sodom's secret of success?

The Ever-Repeating Spin Cycle of Robo Bloodlust. In the present "Great Irony" that follows the end of the classic "Long Before," the more Prince Sodom separates his tastes from the Federal Gestalt, the more sought after he becomes, until his tastes have become cult. In *The Book of Prince Sodom* it is written: "In the soul-less Federal Gestalt, miss-led males, many of whom are actually failed heterosexoids, and some females, who are more *vir*-aphobic than sapphonic, act out sadomaso in analytical workshop groups ironically devoid of sexual passion. They are eccentric exhibitionists performing in traveling freak shows for perplexed voyeurs. Prince Sodom's classic platonic ideal restores the genuine male-male *radix* of erotic passion and authentic sex appeal based on face, physique, muscles, cock, perversatility, virility, grooming, and psychic presence suitable to the ongoing decades of a man's life. If the torturer or the tortured lacks sex appeal and beauty and grace, which are always inexplicably relative to one another, there is no erotic point to either's mechanical skill which becomes, not erotic, but rather the penitence of religion, or the process of therapy, or the performance in the center ring of the circus—all of which are betrayals of true erotic torture."

Out in the Federal Gestalt, males, growing up, secretly memorize chapter and verse from *The Book of Prince Sodom*. Many are called, but few are chosen. Those with true vocations turn themselves into willing pilgrims who approach the Cult of Final Belonging reserved for the Friends of the Friendless Friends. Twice a year, athletic supplicants, from youth to maturity, kneel nude at the gate. They stare at the huge marble statue of a naked, erect, and very muscular *Pleurant*, whose colossus head and face are hooded for Eternal Vigil. Untouched, they touch themselves: their muscles, their nipples, their dicks, their butts. Prince Sodom walks among them. He is brilliant. He poses. Each man he looks at mirrors his poses. Sodom's double-bicep pose guides the aspirant's double-bicep pose. Sodom's nipple-and-pec display tutors the cultist's nipple-and-pec display. Thus led, the lucky, the selected, become the elected. Beefy guards escort them away, between the legs and under the erect cock of the marble *Pleurant* through whose asshole they enter, never to return, disappearing eagerly into the mansion of Robo Prince Sodom.

The Giant Prince Sodom's battalions of massively pec'd, tit-squirting musclemen know he can, and will, turn even the best of the best into death-sport slaves if ever they trespass his severe commands. Among the most perfect bodybuilder guards is an even higher aspiration: to be selected by the Prince of Pecs himself, for the pleasure of pure lust, to suffer glad allegiance through agonizing physical torture of absolute mutual bloodlust that makes a man one with his Prince.

This night's screams jolt Sodom's massive Robo Cock to stand at hard attention. On his huge pectorals, his fiery red nipples, three inches long on lifted coronas, their skin treaded tough as hard-rubber radials, drip with titcum. Sodom's hyper-masculine frame is built, in precise techufacture, into a Pastfuture Warrior to reformulate in the present "Great Irony" the most perfect male bodies lost with the collapse of the classic "Long Before."

Across his hairy chest, Sodom cinches a defining leather-and-chain harness snug around his beefy pecs. His high black boots are spurred, soled, and hobnailed with blood-soaked boot spikes. His big, unshaven, predatory chin juts out from under his brutally handsome face. An exquisite Conneryian sneer, forged of exotic pain and titdeath, plays across his virile lip under his thick moustache. His eyebrows arc over his insatiable amber eyes, intense eyes that burn to see big beefy bodies writhing in excruciating pain only males can experience. The thick hair of his head is shaved down to a rasp he uses as a cruelty against tender flesh. His armpits are a sweat mat of hair bathed only by human tongue. The Giant Prince Sodom, built bigger than any bodybuilder, any powerlifter, any professional wrestler, is no video contest-game player from the satellite-dish leagues of the Federal Gestalt.

He is a Giant Robo Rogue.

In the "Long Before," when the very young Prince Sodom was on the cusp of manhood, he had burned the rule books and murdered the referees. He had raped his mother and raped his father and then killed them both. He had asked the Federal court for mercy, because he was an orphan. Then he had killed the Federal judge and escaped over the top of the Federal Gestalt Line where his legend grew, because he had done openly what all other people want in their hearts to do.

He is an untouchable outlaw. His unruled lust is death-defying, death-dealing, and real beyond any comfort of denial.

This night, on view before Prince Sodom, a massively pec'd young bodybuilder, hangs crucified, spikes driven through both his hands, his widespread fingers individually screwed down, through the joints, by torque of turn into the wood. His cock and balls, wrapped tight at the base in a noose of barbed-wire, stretch under heavy weights. The head of his big cock bleeds from the night's fresh circumcision, cut with a serrated hunting knife. His severed foreskin has been sewn with surgical stitches, to add flapping length, around the tip of his protruding tongue. He can no longer speak.

His big pecs, sliced with razor blades, run rivulets of blood down to his tits, which for the week since his capture, have been exercised and vacuumed to a juice-squirting two-inch pump, surprising the moaning bodybuilder who, before his abduction, had known only muscle pump, itself as sweet as orgasm. His fresh young blood drips from his engorged tits and runs down the canals of his washboard abdominal six-pack. His feet, bound together with bare electrical wire, slide in his own blood across the floor, out from under him.

Prince Sodom, sprawled naked in full majesty on his throne of leather and hides and furs and skulls, is pleased.

Prince Sodom nods.

A Black Bodybuilder, playing with his own extruded tits on his twin mounds of pecs, his uncut twelve-inch blacksnake hard as a Niger River pole, flips a switch, electrifying the wire cinched tight around the crucified bodybuilder's ankles. The handsome victim's pecs crab together. His veins explode across his body to full vascularity over his contracting muscles. The electricity forces his feet into midspace, hanging his 235 pounds from his crucified hands. He screams. "Mercy, Master! Mercy!" The foreskin tip sewed to his tongue flaps wildly. Agony balloons out of his mouth: "AAAAAAH!"

Prince Sodom hardens at the sounds of sacrifice. Precum lubes his giant Robo dick. Men have died impaled on the length and thickness of his high-tech hardness. His tits grow, visibly, at the pain, at the torture, at the slow murder in progress. Sodom's tits crown each of his big pecs like spikes on a Prussian soldier's round helmet. He nods to the Black.

The electrocution halts briefly waiting the fifth shocking round.

Sodom calls up a brawny Russian Powerlifter wearing the half-mask of an executioner. His upper body is bullthick and pec'd to the max. His arms are the bulging weapons of a strangler. Under the Russian Powerlifter's armpit, tucked in his sweaty thick pit-hair, rides the handle of a hammer. The Russian Powerlifter stands foursquare in front of the crucified bodybuilder who looks at him with pleading eyes. With his free hand—the palm with finger and thumb the size of a huge meathook, the Russian Powerlifter, once a Federal Gestalt cop, makes a bone-stone fist and slams the moaning bodybuilder in the face. The handsome nose explodes in blood and snot and collapses flat as a pug boxer's.

Prince Sodom expects the unexpected of his men. He applauds the Russian Powerlifter's improvisation. The massive man bows and signals for a 2x4 oak plank to be held in place by two beefy red-haired college-football jocks, eagerly recruited, who are in training as next-generation torture-killers. Both athletes are harnessed with black-leather football shoulder pads. Big-gauge rings, tuned to receive electrical obedience charges directly from Prince Sodom, jut golden through the red aureoles of their growing tits.

They are called the Redd Twins. Like Romulus and Remus, they have the oral need to suckle the hard nipples of wolfmen and bearmen and bullmen and pigmen who are first of all musclemen and best of all titmen. Their golden pecs are almost identically matted with curling red hair. Their scientifically enlarged big hard cocks are padlocked into tight metal tube-sheaths that corset their thick shafts up to their dripping cockheads swollen bulbous, purple, and lethal.

Months before, the Redd Twins had arrived, unbidden at the estate, underground refugees from the Federal Gestalt Territory. They had come to join the Outlaws of Prince Sod, the Annihilator, convinced they wanted the rigorous coaching of Prince Sodom's training camp. They are single-minded, speed-focused on growth hormones, pumped from forced training at bench-press pec-and-chest workouts where they are electrically motivated in their last killer reps by the sizzling depth zaps delivered in direct charges to their huge inset tit rings.

The Redd Twins hold the oak 2x4 steady.

The Russian Powerlifter takes the crucified muscleman's tits in his hairy fingers. "Scream for Prince Sod," he says.

The tongue with the sewn-on foreskin hangs from the screaming mouth like an uncut dick, unable to speak. "Scream! Hot fuckin' body! Yeah! Yeah!" The Russian Powerlifter finger-pinches the fat raw nipples flat and then slowly pulls them long and hard with his sharpened finger nails.

The Black Bodybuilder begins to tweak his own drooling nipples and stroke his own uncut meat. His mouth opens wide showing strong white teeth around an emergent pink tongue hungry for flesh.

The tit-tortured bodybuilder looks down at his bloody pecs and his mangled nipples. He screams snot and tears. His voice sinks to a low, constant moan that is picked up by a microphone sutured to the base of his throat and wirelessly converted to a revving, deep, electroid hum in the copper cockring around Prince Sodom's big balls. From his victim's whimper, amplified up from moan to scream, Sodom tunes in to the pain. He amplifies the sobs and absorbs the screams around the rootplug of his cock and balls. He turns his *vibrato* reception dial up and down with his thick fuck-finger to approximate the endorphin rush he tweaks in himself vicariously from his victims. Sodom wants to be inside every experience in his vast compound.

"Strut for me," Sodom says to the Russian Powerlifter. "Show me *your* pecs. Prepare to show me more of *his* pain. Strut! Side Chest Shot! Strut! Make him beg, scream, cry, till his voice is gone and we cut his throat with my blade. Pump your pecs! Strut! Front Chest Shot! Walk that bodybuilder walk. Chest out! Rub your biceps across your nipples. Strut! Till we cut off his handsome head with my laser-saw. Strut! Strut! Strut!

Power-down into a Most Muscular Pose! Strut for me.
Again! Peak your pecs down into the Ultimate Crab Shot!
Lick your pecs! Wipe your big biceps across your pecs!
Suck your nipples. Again! Front Chest Shot! Forward!
Forward! Strut for me! Strut!"

The Russian Powerlifter struts—his huge uncut dick
preceding him hard—and pads his big bearlike poses
and moves across the stone compound floor. Other naked slaves, stretched spreadeagle between pillars of
stone, calm their fear of his approach with their desire
of his attention. They have seen his brute teeth bite
nipples off sculpted chests, chew them into ground bloody
tit burger, and spit them down the throats of other
chained bodybuilders, force-feeding them. They have seen
him hook-whip the flesh from the pecs and tits of men
built like young gods, until, half-unconscious with the
pain, their pecs stomped with boot-spikes, slashed repeatedly across the chest, nipples electrified, they are
buried alive as they lay dying, stabbed, castrated, bound
with heavy corded ropes tying their muscular arms tight
against their pumped torsos, their transfixed faces, their
heads encased in clear plastique bags taped tight around
the neck, buried alive beneath the bubbling curds of the
paramilitary sewage pits.

The Russian Powerlifter struts to a hot brazier, pulling out red-hot pliers, holding them aloft, triumphant,
his thick armpits open, wide, rampant, bushed with black
hair long enough to curl onto his massive pecs tangling
with the forest of hair surrounding his long, vulcanized,
red-rubberlike nipples. He struts the strut. He is Prince
Sodom's Favorite. He is, in fact, grateful knowing that
the next victim in the palace of serial murder might be
himself. He takes hardon enjoyment in however his Pec
Master Prince Sod might favor him, victor or victim.

Prince Sodom leers at the crucified bodybuilder. He
slow-strokes his cock with both hands. Two beefy tit

slaves, former heavy-weight Pro-Wrestlers, each naked but for tall boots and black-rubber goggles, reach over his shoulders and massage his huge pecs and elongated tits. Their touch enlarges his nipples and his appetites.

"Burn his tits." Prince Sod says. "Start at the tip. Pinch those hot pliers down millimeter by millimeter. Fry him! Fry his tits!" He stomps his hobnailed boots on his throne. "Torture him! Make him scream for my jizm. Cum for pain."

Prince Sodom, shining brilliant, strokes his huge cock, pulls its fleshy mouth open, nods to the Powerbuilder Medax who slides a thick metal sound through the mouth of Sodom's cock and down the engorged shaft all the way into the balls. The extruding end of the probe is a second *vibrato* receiver that translates the vocal suffering and pain of the victim to the inside of Sodom's urethra so deep that the probe passes through the interior circumference of the exterior cockring receiver circling around the rootplug of Prince Sodom's predatory cock.

Thus classically prepared, Prince Sodom says ironically, "Play 'Misty' for me."

It is an order.

Pecs thrust forward, the Russian Powerlifter approaches the moaning, crucified bodybuilder with two red-hot pairs of pliers. He spits into the smashed face, dives in mouth-first sucking blood from the broken teeth, tearing off the foreskin sewn onto the tongue, chewing it, eating it, dipping and biting each nipple fiercely, making the tits wet with blood and spit.

"Scream for Prince Sod," he says, and grips the two pairs of branding-iron pliers down hard on the crucified muscleman's steam-hissing tits.

"No, Master, no! YYYIAAAA!"

Prince Sodom nods to the masturbating Black who hits the electricity.

The crucified bodybuilder, only a month before so proud and pec'y in his last Federal Physique Contest, where Sodom watched him win the trophy for Best Chest, rears up from the electric shock, the pain in his nailed hands nothing now compared to the squeezing, burning pressure on his sizzling nipples.

Sodom's dick juices up his tight belly. "Scream! Take it! Scream in agony! Agony! Yeah!"

The Redd Twin bodybuilders, holding the 2x4, stand obediently in place in respect and worship of their beloved Prince. They know what is coming. Their broken pug noses sniff and snort the smell of the hot burning tits. The purple heads of their iron-bound shafts bulge in anticipation. So magnetized are they by Prince Sodom's sexual true north, they do not notice that one of the newer guards, a dark young Turk, has slumped, passed out, to the floor.

Prince Sodom notices. He nods. He is ecstatic to eject the faint-hearted who waste a place reserved for the lion-hearted. He sticks his tongue out in the classic way of the lost "Long Before" and flaps it up and down fast, making a lop-lop sound. For perverse pleasure, he punches the Powerbuilder Medax in the face, and himself pumps the probe in his cock up and down, in and out. The Powerbuilder Medax rises stunned and begins to speak. Prince Sod pulls out his Gestalt handgun and shoots the Medax between the eyes.

Across the room, where the young Turk guard has fainted, three seasoned guards, jumping to attention, seize their junior comrade, strip him naked, and tie the unconscious man spreadeagled to a huge archery target.

The crucified bodybuilder himself slumps out.

"Enough of him for the moment," Prince Sodom says. He nods to a bulk-pec'd, blond, bearded Viking who knows his job. The golden warrior stands with his big

forearms crossed on his chest: his left thumb and forefinger roll-massage his right nipple, and his right thumb
and forefinger roll-massage his left nipple. On command,
the blond Viking marches to the unconscious young Turk
tied to the target.

"Bring him around," Prince Sodom says to the Vi-
king. "You are my Viking Whipmaster. Whip his chest!
Whip those pecs! Aim for his nipples! Bring him around!
In pain. Pain! PAIN!"

The Viking Whipmaster cracks his tit-pec whip. His
thick arms are downed with blond fur. He snaps his whip
across the oily dark pecs of the unconscious guard whose
handsome pecs have always been his pride and glory.
Instantly, the tearing lash whips the young Turk awake.
He screams realizing his new position. "No, no! Please,
Master!" The tit whip tears shreds of flesh from his
mounded pecs. One nipple is hooked out by the roots. A
gusher of blood shoots from the tit hole.

"Scream," Prince Sodom says. "Scream for your pecs!
Scream in pain! Give me your pain! Scream for your tits,
scum!"

The Viking Whipmaster beats the Turk's chest, spik-
ing his erect nipples, lacerating the first layers of skin
off the pecs, exposing the massive white muscle beneath.

"Flex your pecs for the whip," Sodom says. "Ninety-
nine strokes!"

"No, Master."

Lash. Rip.

"AIIIY!"

Whip. Shred. Tear.

"Master! Master! The pain! The pain! AYAAAAHHH!"

"Ah, the pain," Sodom shouts. "Worship the pain.
Worship me in your pain. Worship all tits and pecs and
muscle in your pain. Study me, learn me, know me in
your pain."

The Giant Prince Sodom, shot up with mainlined

painstream power, enlarges heroically in body size and aura presence. He nods to a handsome Newyorican muscle slave with twelve fresh needles through each bloody three-inch tit, both nipples surrounded by a circle brand burnt on his street-hard pecs. His black hair is grease-gunned slick back. Exposing his perfect white teeth, his long tongue licks around his lips, brushing through his black moustache. At the corner of his eye is a blue tear-drop tattoo *pleurant*. To him only sex matters. He has dedicated his life to following his tits around.

"You! Greaseball! Get your tongue on my balls while I watch that hot stud Turk squirm for me. And you two," he says to the renegade Pro-Wrestling slaves pleasuring his nipples, "Yank my tits. Tag-team 'em! Twist and yank 'em the way mantits are meant to be yanked. Work 'em! Watch and learn from what you see!"

Prince Sodom turns his gaze back to his suffering victims. The crucified bodybuilder is slowly regaining consciousness with the Russian Powerlifter and the Redd Twins standing at ease next to him. The spreadeagled Turk guard is shouting to the blond Viking Whipmaster in a desperate voice, hoarse with transcendence, begging for more pain.

"Pain! Master! Please! I flex my pecs for your pleasure. My tits! My pecs! YAAAAH!"

The Viking Whipmaster is up to a count of ninety lashes. His big body heaving, his own pecs bulging with every lash, his huge dick rockhard inflicting the pec pain that is pleasure beyond pain.

The whipped Turk's own nine-inch cock stands hard in salute to his Prince.

"Whip his cock!" Sodom, the Annihilator, says.

"NO! Master!" the Turk screams.

The blond Viking tears into the unprotected cock and balls.

"Whip that fucking slave! Harder, you, motherfucker,

or I'll have your Viking tongue nailed to your Viking dick
and have you hoisted by the nail. Whip him! Scream,
slave! Worship your Master's big hot hardon!"

The Viking Whipmaster's deft hand shreds first the
balls, then the shaft of the Turk guard's raging hardon,
saving the huge head protruding from his ragged foreskin for the last. The Turk victim is looping out beyond
screaming words. The blond Viking Whipmaster has
lashed him into a dark howling manimal. The Turk, desperate to adore Prince Sodom, manages one last final
roaring call, "Kill me, Master! Kill me!"

"The man is weak. The man is no man. I will give
him his last and final pain." Prince Sodom gestures with
one hand. "Finish him. Bring in the chorus for his big
finale."

A husky Spear Squad of five pumped Firbolg giants,
naked, greased from shaved-head to thick toe, uncut,
big-dicked, massively muscled, takes its place on sturdy
thick feet. Re-created from ancient DNA caught in amber on the faraway isle of Granuaile, they are wild warriors whose Druid priests predated the Celts. The huge
plates of their pecs are fully tattooed blue in intricate
pre-Gaelic designs that spiral down around their enormous three-inch nipples pierced with rings set every six-
teenth-inch from the base to the engorged tips. Their
hardons arch up, sturdy as the thick-handled spears in
their big hands, aimed at the Turk guard tied in bloody
spreadeagle on the huge target board. The tips of their
Firbolg nipples drip with titcum. They are Death Com-
mandos.

"Kill me," the Turk guard screams. "I die for Prince
Sodom."

The blond Viking Whipmaster takes two steps back.

"AAAAAH," Sodom says. "Spear him! First one, then
the next. Spear him, but do not kill him till the last."

Sweat and animal grease shine on the tattooed pecs

of the muscular Firbolg Spear Squad. The first Firbolg, his javelin angled up the same as his huge primeval cock, puts his mighty arm, back, and pecs into his thrust, sending his spear, THUK!, through the inside of the Turk's left thigh, its spearhead emerging bloody on the outside of the leg.

"Pierce him," Prince Sodom says.

The second and third of the Firbolg squadron launch their spears: each pierces one of the Turk's broad shoulders, THUK! THUK!, entering precisely at the outside upper corner of each of his bloody pecs, pumped with pain, pinning his shoulders flat to the target.

"Die for my jizm!" Sodom says.

The fourth Firbolg aims his spear direct on target through the bloody cock and balls. THUK!

"Torture," Sodom chants. "*Torture! TORTURE!*"

The hall of beefy, chested, big-nippled rogue males takes up his rhythm. "TORTURE! TORTURE!"

Robo Prince Sodom, connecting his techufactured electroid force-field, strokes his mighty cock with both hands. A second Medax, arms and pecs more muscular than the first Medax, approaches with tight green rubber rings banded down snug around the finger-sized base of his three-inch nips. The Medax plunges and replunges the sound-probe down the open mouth of Sodom's leatherized urethra. Violet electricity crackles in force-fields of sparky lightning wherever Prince Sodom's hands touch his own body. The head of Prince Sodom's cock flashes purple with priapic power. "Murder him!"

The spreadeagled Turk, thanking Allah he has finally raised the genuine bloodlust of Prince Sodom, lifts his head with the last of his strength screaming, "YES!" as the final Firbolg spearpoint enters precise as a javelin through his open mouth, a wide-open screaming target, sending its point, THUK!, out through the back of his head. The mortally wounded Turk, his hard shredded

cock shooting white clots of death jizm, stares at Prince
Sodom with the dying eyes of a grateful martyr experi-
encing the divine transcendence of feeling his soul leaving his body.

"That Turk had something to him after all," Prince
Sodom says. He motions the Firbolg Spear Squad to approach his throne.

In basso-chanting beef parade, naked, tattooed, oiled,
the Firbolg muscle warriors march to him.

"Cum on my double-titcocks," he says. "I want the
jizm of murderers on my chest."

The Firbolg Squad, re-created from the ancient warrior days before the coming of the Tuatha de Danaan,
obeys the ritual command, stroking their huge uncut
dicks, milking their legendary tits which rise oozing and
hardening like pairs of dicks symmetrical across each
chest, each Death Commando shooting three loads, two
of clear-gleat titcum and one of milky-white cockcum on
their Prince's masturbating dick and flexing pecs and
squirting nipples. The goggled tag-team of Pro-Wrestlers
massages the hot titjuices into Sodom's chest, making
the muscular Prince's mounded pecs and thermal nipples
itch with an itch only bloodlust can scratch. His monster cock, uncut, juts hard over his bullstud balls. The
Medax pumps the sound-probe in constant churn into
Sodom's urethra. Spontaneously inventive, the Medax
folds his own chin down to his own big pecs and, first
left and then right, sucks on his own big nipples, thirsty
for his own titcum. Prince Sodom appreciates the
Medax's Olympic degree of difficulty.

To his heroic Firbolg Commando Spear Squad, Prince
Sodom says: "For your reward, march to the Tir-Nan-
Oge gymnasium, the legendary Hall of Torture where
the Tuatha de Danaan trainers await. You each will be
imaged, for my later private screening, pumping out ten-
sets-per-hour of low-rep, bulk-building, pec-crunching

bench presses, thirty pounds heavier than your last workout. If you be crushed, you be crushed. It is my pleasure that you each be chained hand and foot for nine hours, your ringed nipples to be electrified every five minutes in one-minute jolts twenty zaps higher than your last recorded tit session, until your drooling wet tits shoot load after load of titcum. Give me your pain."

"Just so, Prince Sodom." The Firbolg Spear Squad obediently straightens to attention and walks off, chests out, pecs proud, tit-hungry to their reward, their big, hairy, oiled bubblebutts grinding in that slow moseying stroll peculiar to thunder-thighed bodybuilders hung massive with prehistoric mastodon cocks that drip drool.

"The Squad performed well," Prince Sodom says. "Remove the Turk's carcass. Sodomize him. Impale his ass with a wooden pole. Push the point out his mouth. Bury him horizontal on a spit, just so, in the sewage pits."

Prince Sodom looks toward the crucified bodybuilder hanging half-conscious between the burly Russian Powerlifter and the Redd Twins, all three bodybuilders finger-rolling their nipples in the crossed forearm maneuver. He nods to a third Medax who injects the crucified bodybuilder's veins with the endorphin RXush of CXonsciousness that revives him in a flash.

"I want more and more is never enough."

He waves away the wrestling slaves attending his cumslick chest and monster cock. Bored with their low-level touch, he places his own Robo hands on his nipples and electroid-milks them till creamy white titcum beads up on the glistening tips of his three-inch tits. He pushes away the Medax who pulls out the metal sound. The adoring Medax shoves the metal sound still wet and hot from his Master's urethra down into his own dick. Prince Sodom nods to the Viking Whipmaster and points over the head of the masturbating Medax at the crucified bodybuilder. "Whip him. Whip the pecs and nipples of the crucified slave. I want his pain luxuriant!"

The hairy Viking Whipmaster, his tongue licking his blond beard beaded with sweat and blood, takes his stance. His first lash is hard. The crucified bodybuilder trembles. The second and third lashes are harder, but less than the twentieth.

"Hot fuckin' body!" the Viking Whipmaster shouts.

Lash! Lash! Rises to *Slash! Slash!* The pain of the whip brings the young crucified bodybuilder to an even higher consciousness.

"Yeah! Yeah!" The Viking Whipmaster is bass-throated. "Flex your pecs for the whip!"

His enthusiasm pleases Prince Sodom who thinks to reward him well. Even the naked crucified bodybuilder responds, remembering passages he, as a boy, memorized chapter and verse from *The Book of Prince Sodom.*

"Please, Master. Pain," the tortured bodybuilder says. He digs deep inside himself for the words that will connect him to Prince Sodom, Annihilator. "Pain!" Hanging crucified, he valiantly tries the impossible: to crab-pose his proud pectorals to their full massive pec glory. Rippling striations roll through his pecs under his fair skin.

"Beg for more pain. Beg for my pain." Sodom smiles his exquisite sneer. His eyebrow arches. His Robo Cock throbs. His three-inch radial-tread nipples harden up like two cocks on their proud aureole coronas. His big hand massages the wide spread of his hairy mountainous pecs. "Say *more.* Beg for *more pain.*"

"More, Master, *more, MORE!*" The spikes driven through the bodybuilder's hands drip red blood that runs down the inside of his big forearms and bigger, blue-veined biceps, coagulating in the thick bush of blond hair in his forested armpits. *"More! More! More!"*

"You will have your wish. You will worship the pain. Your wish, your pain, is my will." Sodom nods to the Viking Whipmaster. "One hundred more lashes."

The Newyorican tit-slave rushes forward with a chalice. He forces open the crucified bodybuilder's sweet lips and empties the reviving red liquid into the man's throat. Prince Sodom is the Ultimate Master.

He knows how to create—that something so much more than endurance—perverse willingness, in his masculine victims.

"Flex your pecs," the Viking Whipmaster orders.

The crucified bodybuilder stares in complete adoration of his awesome Prince Sodom sprawled on his throne. Fortified by the vision of his Man-God Sodom, the bodybuilder achieving new will, new acceptance, flexes every muscle in his stunning body. The hundred lashes, WACK! WACK! WACK-ING!, slicing his powerful pecs to ribbons, are nothing compared to the torture waiting at the hands of the Russian Powerlifter, his wooden hammer handle tucked tight in his sweaty armpit.

The Redd Twins, holding the oak 2x4 board, grin eagerly over their hardon nips. The Left Redd Twin smiles with perfect white teeth. The Right Redd Twin smiles a beguiling grin with two front teeth missing, lost in a series of byes in a punching match where he beat up eleven of twelve opponents.

"Enough!" Sodom commands. "As if ever there is enough of pain." He reaches for a .45mm pistol holstered on a Beefsteak Bodyguard standing naked but for the gunbelt at his side.

"Look up at me, your Prince Sodom," he says to the Newyorican slave sucking his balls. The young man's eyes adore his lord and master who touches the slave between the eyes with the cold point of the gun barrel. Sodom pulls the trigger. A clean new hole explodes in the man's forehead as the force of the shot kicks his body backwards. He hands the gun to the guard. "Take his new fuckhole," Sodom tells the guard whose dick has grown hard at the sight. "Fuck it. Fuck his head while I watch this other business before me." He smiles as the big guard slides his huge uncut cock into the handsome young dead man's forehead.

"Finish your work," Prince Sodom says to the Russian Powerlifter.

The mountainous man signals to the Redd Twins who, by the sheer strength of their massive arms, hold the solid oak board beneath the bloody, huge pecs of the crucified bodybuilder. The Redd Twins' dicks stand at hard attention. The Russian Powerlifter pulls his sweaty hammer handle from under his bushy armpits. The Viking Whipmaster pushes the bodybuilder's head and chest forward, holding him in place over the 2x4 board.

The Russian Powerlifter is skilled. He pulls a twelve-inch iron spike, razor sharp on all four sides, places it at the top of the crucified bodybuilder's big left pec and in a dozen precision blows, drives the spike, with his hammer, down through the length of muscle-pec built to perfection through years spent in Federal Gestalt gyms. The crucified bodybuilder screams. His crispy nipples ooze plasma. Prince Sodom's dick juices, drips. The Redd Twins' muscles bulge, as the spike, passing through the crucified bodybuilder's pec penetrates the board, its tip protruding, two inches below the hard wood.

"YIIIIAH!" the bodybuilder shouts. "The pain! Take my pain, my Prince!"

Sodom says to no one in particular. "His prick is harder than ever." Satisfied, he nods.

The Russian Powerlifter looks at the Redd Twins. He ducks first to suck the drip of titjuice off the nipples of the Left Redd Twin, and then to lick the squirting titcum from the ripe stretched nipples of the Right Redd Twin. The Redd Twins follow the Russian Powerlifter closely as he raises his thickly muscled arm and with the heavy hammer in his big hand drives a second spike, deftly nailing the crucified bodybuilder's right pec to the board.

"AAAAIIYH!"

"More pain!" Sodom's eyes are red with bloodlust. "Beg me for more pain."

"More."

"Louder!"

"MORE!"

"Repeat it over and over." Sodom's Robo hand works blood rhythms on his monstrous cock.

"MORE! MORE! MORE! AIIYHAHHH!"

"Nail his nipples to the board."

Obediently, the hairy Russian Powerlifter re-grips the fried nipple tips and stretches them four inches, nailing first the left and then the right to the board. The bodybuilder is crucified not only by his hands. Spikes crucify his pecs. Nails crucify his tits.

He screams uncontrollably. Titcum drools, then shoots from his tortured nipples as he throttles in sexual ecstasy.

Sodom is pleased with his new punishment. His dick tells him so. "Twist my tits," he orders the huge-chested Pro-Wrestlers reaching around his massive shoulders. "Twist my tits. Milk my tits. Make my tits cum!"

He motions to the Black Bodybuilder. "Jolt him. Hard! To full consciousness."

The electricity surges. The smell of burning flesh around the crucified bodybuilder's ankles mixes with the heady smell of blood pungent in the death chamber.

"YIIIY! YES! YES! UNNNH! MORE! MY DICK WANTS MORE!"

Prince Sodom nods. "He is hard. He is hung. HANG HIM!"

The Viking Whipmaster slips a rough hemp-rope noose tight around the crucified man's thick neck making his tongue protrude across his broken teeth, past his lips, under his broken nose on his face transfiguring to even greater beauty dying than living. A wild look brightens the bodybuilder's eyes. The Viking Whipmaster slips a second noose around the 2x4 board. The crucified man screams, doubting himself, but not doubting Prince Sodom. He realizes he is to be hanged by his tits and pecs, and by his neck, until he is dead, with his arms outspread, hands nailed to the wooden posts, ankles electrified, his cock uncontrollably erect, driven harder and bigger by the injected endorphins of the RXush of CXonsciousness.

"NO! NO!"

"I will torture you until your *NO* becomes *MORE*," Prince Sodom says. "And then you die!"

"NO MORE! NO MORE! MASTERRRRR! YESSS!"

The Black Bodybuilder jolts the roped-and-nailed man in three sets of ten heavy reps. The magnificent body rises, convulses, blood and white titcum squirting from his four-inch nipples, dripping over the white oak 2x4 board. A muscular Teen Slave, pumped since his eighteenth birthday with massive 'roids therapy, picks up the chalice once carried by the Newyorican punk gangster. The Teen Slave knows his role: his hose-man cock pisses a stream of foaming yellow urine steaming into the chalice that he fills to overflowing. Grabbing a funnel hose, the Teen Slave shoves a black rubber tube down the crucified man's throat, force-feeding the Liqueur of Endurance. The crucified bodybuilder, gagging on the tube in his throat, envies the Teen Slave's unmarked, young, huge-pumped bubble-pecs, tipped with titcum-squirting raisinette nipples. He recognizes the Teen Slave. He recognizes the fresh face moving in close to suck the blood and breath from his broken nose. It is his adoring younger brother, stroking off his dick, sexually active in the erotic art of fratricide.

"Now," Prince Sodom says. "Now we are ready."

The blond Viking Whipmaster connects the two nooses, one from the pair of nailed tits and one from the thick neck, attaching their sturdy knot to an industrial chain hoist swung in overhead.

"Now I will see pain," Prince Sodom says. "I will see fear. Hang him! Hang him by his tits! Perhaps I will see...the passion...and death...sometime...of some God. Hang him by his pecs! Hang him by his neck. Slowly. Raise him slowly. Milk his huge bodybuilder chest of all its pain. Make his tits spasm, cum, and squirt titjuice!"

The chain hoist rattles through its pulleys, ratcheting the tortured muscleman higher and higher until his pecs stand as pumped and proud as in any physique competition. The hanging rope around his neck makes his eyes bulge. His tongue, its tip torn where once sewn over with his own foreskin, protrudes from his mouth. "AAAAAAH! The pain! The Pain! THE PAIN!"

Sodom feasts on the sight of the tortured muscle-pec-man hanging, nailed, whipped, tit-tips double-drooling clear gleat, massive hardon of freshly unforeskinned cock seeping clear pre-cum. "Without a signature hardon," *The Book of Prince Sodom* says, "death is not erotic transcendence, not erotic union, not erotic immortality, not erotic at all."

"THE PAIN!" The hanging man looks down at his big pierced pecs and his huge tits exaggerated by torture. His hands are nailed. His fingers are screwed down. He can only watch his unstoppably thick cock, with a drive of its own, turned on by the pain, turned on by the agony, begin to shudder on its own, shaking him hanging helpless, revving up, spermbustible, racking him, shaking him, wagging his hanging body the way a huge tail wags a helpless dog. "AAAH! I'm going to cum!"

Sodom palm-drives his own dick with both hands. "MORE! When he shoots his load, HANG HIM!"

"YOURS, Prince Sod!" The hanging, crucified body-

builder raises his handsome face: blue eyes, blond moustache. "My chest, my pecs, my tits, my titcum, my cock,
my cockcum are YOURS!" His body spasms, his big dick
cums, and hot white sperm shoots up his tortured body,
clots of jizm on his chest, snowballing down his nailed
pecs, dripping off the bloody leaking tips of his nipples
into his little brother's hungry, suckling, waiting mouth.

The last fast ratchets of the chain hoist him up, high,
strangling him, tearing the nails by the inch up his pecs,
lifting him in perfect ascension to glory in Prince Sodom's
Pantheon of Pain.

Sodom's own dick rides the death rattles. "Die for
my jizm, slave. Die for my cum! UuuuUUUH! Die! In
pain! Die! Die for my jizm!" The Prince's cum splatters
on the slaves around him. They grovel and fight his 'roid-
jazzed little brother for his bloody seed.

"Uuuuhh," Prince Sodom says. "What a studly sight."
Slaves suck cum off his fingers. "Bring to my bed tonight
whoever is the biggest, beefiest, chestiest bodybuilder. I
think I will make love."

"What shall we do, my Master," the Viking Whipmaster asks, "with this one, your lover from last night?"
The Viking Whipmaster points up at the crucified bodybuilder hanging by his pecs and neck, choking, breathing, writhing in hysteric euphoria.

"Such a man is a sight to be savored," Prince Sodom
says. "Let us enjoy him hanging for awhile. Have the
little brother drive his fist up his brother's ass. We have
pumped up the younger one so he has thick hands, hardened forearms, and meaty biceps. I want to see the crucified brother arm-fucked bicep deep. Then you, my Viking, and you, my Russian, can fuck the younger
brother's ass and make him suck your nipples till you
cum. But don't kill him. Thrill him. Build the hunger in
him. As for the older brother, in two or three hours, and
before he dies, call my swordsman. Order him to laser-

slice the body artfully at the three-quarter mark, below the nipples, just below the chest, severing the spine in one neat stroke. Then move a marble column. That one with the statue over there. Do away with the man's torso and body. Stuff his balls in his mouth with his big dick protruding from his lips. Lower his crucified chest almost onto the column, and leave him there suspended by the neck, so we can admire his face and the amazing look frozen in his eyes."

"His arms are still crucified."

"Cut them off at the shoulder. Leave the ropes and nails and board through his tits and chest. He'll make a handsome bust for our banquet in his memorable honor tonight. Everyone will know how I loved him."

* * * *

This note in all its sincerity is presented verbatim, as spelled, and hand-delivered in 1975.

"Somthing To Think about;

I would like to have you see me in pain! Having you see me, and hereing me in Pain. To see the sweet balls Pop all over me, and to smell the Pain grow in me more, and more. Mouth should drink from your juice cock, and see you sit on my mouth as I ake in Pane. Having my tongue dig in to you as you show more parts of me to feel you. Your ass should muffel my crys, and having me suck on your ass hole and when my cock sit up and hard, Your hands and mine will Tuch my sole and dance on my braine and you will know that I am a brother of Pain and you are the giver of Pain. And in that I will show you my love of you and Please you if you let me.

—Tony Tavarossi"

Foot Loose

Come on, muthafuck, eyeball these size 12's up close.
A man stands on his own two bare feet:
booted, socked, sweat-bared, raw-boned.
Heavy nails, man. Sniff that toe jam.
Worship the smell you're gonna suck.
Oh, yeah.
Sweaty manfoot, calloused,
rubbing across your soft lips.
Pull your tongue that you thought was made
for sucking cock and ass
across the thick-skinned sole of my foot.
Oh, yeah.
That's personal, fucker. Very personal.
Oh, yeah.
I walk thru wet steam rooms at the gym
and piss barefoot at dripping urinals.
You tongue manstough between my toes.
Oh, yeah.
Chew my heel, fucker.
Worship manhood from the bottom up.
Kiss my toes. Fill your mouth.
Feel the smooth nails down your throat.
Rub the ball of my heavy foot across your cheek.
Oh, yeah.
Smell the asshole I footfucked an hour ago.
Oh, yeah.
Worship manfoot, muthafuck.
Cry on my foot like some loving Magdalene.
Dry the wet and sweat and asstaste
with your growth of beard.
Be my footstool, fucker.
Oh, yeah.
I want your eyes' wild look.

Oh, yeah.
Lick my toes.
Oh, yeah.
Lick my arch of triumph.
Oh, yeah.
A guy could kick the shit out of you.

William Blake's "Thel":
On My Back to the Future
through the Tunnel of Love...

WILD BLUE YONDER

Inch for inch, pound for pound, Big Boyd Grymkowski was the best buddy a flyjockey could want back in those bombs-away days when our lives depended on each other in the United States Air Corps. Boyd was the aviator, the pilot, the captain, the jock, the stud. He even had a girl back stateside. Sweet Lorraine.

I was his ball-turret gunner, squished like a human booger into the all-glass nose of his airplane. He called me that. His "Booger." Wrapping his big arm around my neck. Giving my crewcut head a, wow, ow, dutch rub with his big knuckles, asking me, "What's an air cock?" Shoving me down between his thighs, dropping his big stud dick into my willing mouth. High in the skies over Europe, we were higher than any high-wire act without a net those last days of WWII whistling "Booger Wooger Bugle Boy," because that was the nickname we strong-armed our flight crew into painting real bold behind the nose of our plane, them not knowing the real "Booger" joke or how it was between Big Boyd and me.

I remember one of our last times together, me and Boyd, heading out before dawn across the wet tarmac, outside in the last deepest dark before the French dawn, ahead of the other flyboys, who were still combing their wet hair, acting in the mirrors like they were God's

fucking gift, which most of them were, since you measure a flyer by his groomed looks, his attitude, his build,
and the size of his cock, which every Joe knows, always
side-glancing in the showers, sneaking peeks for the biggest cock of the walk, always hoping you won't be the
peewee. Not that anybody ever said anything. Except
about Big Boyd, who was hung so big everybody talked,
like once a cock gets to be a certain size nobody's embarrassed to talk about it. There wasn't any Flying Ace who
wasn't sort of in awe of the size of his 13-inch gun.

"If I had me a dick like that, I'd screw me Rita and
get my roll in the hay-worth, I'd gobble Betty Grable,
and I'd show Lana Turner a few new turns. And they'd
all die with smiles on their pussies where my dick went
in and grins on their mouths where my dick came out."
We were nuts. We were young, with scores of our last
high-school games still stuck in our heads. We were
American warriors. We were on a charted deadset bomb-
ing mission. Berlin or Bust!

Anyway, that hour before dawn, those other
dickheads were still tucking their pricks away in their
skivvies while Boyd and me, strutting down the run-
way, all suited up in our sheepskin-lined brown-leather
flightsuits, coveralls they were, both of us laughing because of our wild fuck the night before, crawling this
morning out of the secret rack we'd hidden in the back
of the hanger, skipping our showers to make the sweet
smell of our sex last longer, sucking the taste of cum
from our tongues, and of sweet ass from our moustaches.
He was so blond and hairy I felt I ought to comb my
teeth.

Boyd pulled me up short. Not hard to do, me being 5-
7 with a 8-inch propeller. We stood alone under the dark
shadow of a B-52 wing. He grabbed me by both shoulders and looked down at me from his full 6-foot-3 and
220 hard pounds. The squadron had nicknamed us "Mutt

and Jeff." I confess we were both easy on the eyes. Everyone said so. I was fair and ruddy with red-brown hair. Big Boyd, well, Big Boyd was the blondest Polack I ever did see.

He squeezed me in tight with his big arms, real romantic, and kissed me, tubing his big tongue like a second cock through my lips, dribbling his sweet saliva that tasted like my cum he had sucked off, one last time, only minutes before, in the maintenance room behind the latrine. God! Was I in love with him! Me, 21, a cracker lieutenant from Little Rock, A-R-K. Him, 26, a crackerjack captain from Pittsburgh P-A's Little Poland. Without a war we'd have never met. He sucked hard on my tongue. My dick hardened. His was always hard. Polish sausage. *Kielbasa*, he said. It rode hard. He carried it hard. It showed hard even through his thick leather coveralls.

"Hey!" He held me out at arms' length. His voice was deep and smooth like blond honey poured over warm gravel. "Don't sit under the apple tree with anyone else but me!"

"Till I come marching home," I said.

That song was our secret code those days when no one talked about how easy, and how natural, sex, and, sometimes, real and abiding love, could come to lonely soldiers who, faced daily with sudden death, dared to sleep with other young soldiers. Thank God, I knew passion. Thank God, Big Boyd was my one great passion.

In my life, I never regretted what I'd done, only what I didn't do.

If it hadn't been for that war, we'd have never met.

If it hadn't been for that war, I'd never have been killed.

Without that war, I'd have had to live my whole life managing the Woolworth's in Little Rock, serving my three never-to-be-born kids free Cokes at the soda fountain, not knowing what I missed, never having fucked around with the XYY-likes of Boyd Grymkowski.

Don't be cynical. TV networks make series out of being dead. Only I'm not dead. Not anymore. I'm as alive as you are. This day. This year. But, whoah! I get ahead of myself. Heaven can wait. Ask Warren. Ask Shirley. When a man like Boyd Grymkowski tells you to sit under the apple tree, you sit, obedient as Adam in Eden. And you wait. Anyway, we're all old souls in a new life who turn and turn again, and if you don't believe that, they won't let you drink vegetable smoothies in Southern California, Venice, precisely, where Boyd after the war...

The weekend after that morning, when I nearly got my balls blown off in the ball turret, which is maybe why the bastards call it that, our squadron barracks was empty. Unbelievable. Luck. Chance. Destiny.

The military's more perverse than fags, because war is first of all having to live with too many guys in too close a space for too long a time. So far so good. Not a shabby concept for shitting, shaving, and showering with every Tom, Dick, and Harry. Voyeur's heaven! A 100 guys times, what, 6-inch to 8-inch, shit, say 7-inch, dicks, equals 700 inches of cock, or 58 feet of meat! Fuck privacy! Give me any day hundreds of young soldiers' buck privates, cocked, blue-veined, hung, dangling right or left so you knew how the guy jerked off when he was a growing kid. Pricks tenting under sheets at night. Skivvied meat hardening at the mere mention of blowjobs. Buns, hard bubble-buns. Athletic pecs. Lean hard chests. Nipples rosy, flat as quarters, erect as Hershey's Kisses. Shoulders broad as gun racks. Armpits dripping drill-sweat through red and blond and brunet hair. Hard arms. Proud biceps. Some tatted with "MOM" or "Betty" who'd long since sent her "Dear John." The bitch.

Corded forearms of handsome mechanics. Sculpted hands. Long fingers. Grease-crescent nails. Lucky Strike Green hanging from lips surrounded by Barbasol shaving cream. New cookie-duster moustaches. Old Spice after-shave. Cornfed farmboy thighs, ah, yes, high-school football thighs, wrestling thighs, varsity-letter thighs. Flat sit-up-till-you-throw-up bellies. Torsos lightly upholstered tit to tit. Hairy butts. Farts lit in the night. Screams of jackass laughter. Hairy legs. The sinewy curve of instep on a hard foot spied under a john partition. Beautiful, suckabilly toes. Anonymous hard cocks porting through wooden gloryholes into anonymous warm mouths. Every manjack among them in full bloom. Too young, too fresh with semen, to give even a hint of going to seed, to pot, to rack and ruin, and every one so ravenous for sex that given the right time, the right place, and the right liquor...

Boyd loved my lust for life.

I loved his.

It nearly killed him when I died.

At dusk that Saturday evening, he returned to the barracks covered with grease from working on "Booger Boy," and soaked with sweat from a hard workout in the squadron gym. I don't know who he had been wrestling, but I could tell the other guy hadn't won. No one beat "The Grymko." Ever. Victory turned Big Boyd Grymkowski on. (Pit him and Hitler in a ring....Fuck!) Boyd's 10-inch shaft, plus its 3-inch bulb-head, was hammocked hard in his tight red-wool wrestling singlet.

What a combo! The grease of a mechanic and the sweat of a competitive grappler. He stripped slowly, teasing, wiping the back of his hairy blond hand across his mouth. He dropped the thin straps of his singlet down. He reached his big arms behind his neck and pulled his teeshirt up from the hairy-ape nape of his neck. First his navel appeared on his belly like a button on a washboard. Then the line of thick blond hair that ran up to his twin-pack pecs peeled out of the teeshirt he pulled over his unshaven, greasy face. Finally he husked the teeshirt off his head of short blond hair.

He grinned and his blond moustache spread golden as dawn's first light flat along the horizon. Shit! He knew what he did to me. His blue eyes. His rosy nipples like twin islands in the sea of his blond-haired pecs. He laughed. He hawked up a luger—we were all sport-spitters—and spit it end-over-end toward me. A perfect shot. The flume, white as cum, landed on my hard cock and hung like a juicy rubber band.

"Bull's-eye!" he said.

I lubed my tool with his spit.

"What you got there, kid?" he said.

"My cock," I said.

"I mean what you got in inches?"

"I got," he wasn't trying to humiliate me, only tease me, but I was a sass-mouthed match for him, "maybe 16 inches."

"Sixteen! Why that don't look like more 'n about 8 to me."

"It is 8. I was just planning on fucking you twice."

"Right after Helen Keller crowns Eleanor Roosevelt Miss America."

I savored each hardon fetish word: "You ever going to strip off that...sweaty...red...wool...wrestling...singlet?" He knew I liked kneeling on the floor in front of him any time, every time, he stripped. He always peeled real slow, the way big-muscled guys do who, sometime before, in boot-camp locker rooms figured out that normal-sized men couldn't take their admiring eyes off them while they stripped off their uniforms, showered, and dressed, never in much hurry. Boyd was born cock of the walk.

He spread his broad shoulders, ran his hands up and down his hairy arms, palmed across both his furry pecs, and slowly slam-dunked both hands down his hairy belly, sliding his fingers into the red singlet. I beat my cock watching him, with his tongue between his teeth and his eyes fixed on his crotch, as he started the slow roll of the red-wool singlet down from his steel-belted waist, down his hips, toward the revelation of his huge blond cock. His fingers outlined the full shape and length and circumference of his 13-inch piece of work. The muscles in his linebacker thighs corded into groups like soldiers in V-formation. I wanted his cock. He wanted his cock. I adored his dick. I loved it. But no one loved it better than Boyd himself. It was big, handsomely shaped, heavy-veined, Polack studcock.

I knew what was coming.

"Lay back on the floor," he said.

I looked up at him, 6-3 and 220 pounds of him, as he walked up the length of my body. His huge hairy legs dripped with sweat. His bare feet smelled rich from wet leather boots and damp wool socks. Standing, he straddled my chest. His pecs were beautiful. His shoulders...his face...I loved him.

"You ready?" he said.

I rubbed my hands up his hairy legs to wet them with his sweat and, wet-palmed, started salt-stroking my cock.

He leaned over me and tongue-funneled a long stream of spit from his mouth that ran Niagara to mine.

He smiled. I swallowed. Finally! Finally! Finally! He rolled the red-wool wrestling singlet down to mid-thigh. His porcelain-white cock, studded with blue veins, rose from the matted sweat of the blond hair in his crotch. His big bullnuts dropped loose and free, rolling in the play of his big palm like two billiard balls cupped by a hardstick pool stud. His dick turned like a gun turret, heavy firepower, standing straight up and straight out.

He looked down at his big rod over the mounds of his

pecs. This night I knew he was putting on a special show to pleasure me. He laughed. His blond face broke open, the way sun at 3,000 feet breaks through fog over Europe. Nothing lasts. Not in war. Even the best is bittersweet. I was determined to beat the odds. I wanted to remember forever, so I could find him again, his sparkling blue eyes, massive chin, big grin, and the kind of white teeth peculiar to born jocks, big white perfect teeth with spaces between them like pickets in a fence around a yard where you'd like to live. Alone. With him. Worshipping forever his big cock.

"This one's on me," Boyd said.

He was a born exhibitionist. He dropped to his knees over my chest, his drayman thighs triangled across me, below my nipple line, leaving me space to reach one hand through his crotch to beat my meat. My other hand roamed across his pecs, down his belly, juggled his balls, and wrapped around the base of his 13 inches. I squeezed. The veins purpled up under the blond skin. A big drop of clear bubble pearled in his piss slit. My tongue darted for it. My lips stayed put on the mushroom head of his meat.

He toyed with me. Slowly face-fucking me, rimming my lips with his cockhead, planting the knob-end of his 3-inch cob in my mouth and slow-stroking his 10-inch shaft, taking pleasure in himself, giving pleasure to me, who was received like a guest into the personal pleasure he found in his own masculinity. He was like that, I knew. He liked having sex with anyone who liked to be part of him having sex with himself. Like me. Like Lorraine.

That thought, after I was dead, saved my life.

With his dick in my mouth, I was never more alive. His cock was so big jutting out in front of him, he was like the rider of one huge stallion which he took from trot to canter to gallop, flogging hard flesh deep into me, ramming inch after inch deeper into my mouth, sliding over my tongue, breaking through the glottis, burrowing down my throat, hard, proud, yet so graceful that his insistent force seemed gentle for all my choking, salivating, and gasping for air around his sweet blond studcock. He face-fucked me deep and hard, falling forward over me, 220 pounds of hairy Polish beef, counting cadence push-ups, his dick divoting down my throat, my nose buried in his redolent crotch hair, then on the upstroke, the wild suction of his dick pulling up and out of my tight throat like a plunger pumping a john. He push-up-fucked me to fifty, then seventy.

"Ten more," he said. "Hard ones."

Eighty.

"Give you something to remember me by."

Ninety.

"The last ten," he said. "Animal fuck!"

He gave me what I wanted as he headed to a hundred. How much is 13 inches times 100? My lips were splitting. My tongue was tangled. My throat was bruised. Blood came from my nose. Yet he did not cum. On the hundredth stroke, he pulled his slick dick from my face and leaned over and kissed me.

"Love me, Mutt? Ya love me, Booger?"

He took his cock in one big meathook. He was a southpaw. He held his 13 inches like a boy's ballbat. He rubbed his right hand across his big pecs, flicking his nipples, while his left began the beguine on his enormous cock. He knelt directly over my face, over my open mouth, bringing his fully hard rod to full bore, cocking the trigger, pulling the piece, shooting his sperm-luger load all over my face, into my open mouth, up my nose, down my chin, on my nipples, on my chest. He scooped up a dripping load of his cum on his big fingers and fed me. I sniffed the smell of his seed, tasted the sweetness of his sperm.

"You swallow up all my little babies." He was talking like a daddy, sticking his big hairy fingers down my throat. He dropped down full weight on top me and kissed me. "Jeff loves Mutt," he said.

My heart took off for the wild blue yonder.

Which brings us back to that kiss before dawn on the tarmac. That mission was my last. This ball-turret gunner bought the farm without ever seeing Paree. Big Boyd nearly died my death grieved him so.

Later that spring, VE Day changed everything. Boyd, his uniform dripping with medals, stopped off in Pittsburgh to see his family and to marry Larraine, crossed swords and all, which seemed the right thing to do, just as right as him taking her and a couple Samsonite suitcases and moving to Southern California, where a lot of other vets were toodling around like wild ones on motorcycles, still restless from the war, not ready to settle down. But Boyd, already settled with Lorraine, always wanted everything, thank God, both ways. So Lorraine, who was no fool when it came time to worshipping 13 inches, didn't mind too much when Boyd rebuilt an old Harley better than new, didn't mind it as much as the tattoos he got on both his hairy arms. Plus she had to admit she had been bored shitless with Pennsylvania, so anything "California" that Boyd wanted to do was okay with her, except have a kid, not too soon anyway.

I watched all this. My lover, Boyd, pumping up on some iron, becoming a blond-bearded 235-pound biker, pretty sexually straight those days, with always a little playing on the side, mostly with guys who liked to worship and adore his muscle. Somethings never change. (Can you imagine being dead and jealous?) I still loved him. I still wanted to be around him. One thing I know some folks don't. They think we all just come back as somebody anonymous. No way. I know smart old souls

can put in an order and wait. So I did. And any fool can
guess what it was.

The fucking Santa Ana winds were blowing, the
winds that make all LA crazy, making Lorraine crazy
for Big Boyd's big dick, but this time I knew he wasn't
planning on cuming in her face. He fucked her hard and
deep till she was screaming and climbing the wall and
the more she bellowed the more of a big rutting, fucking,
blond biker beast he became. They were wrecking the
bedroom, and all of Venice Beach could have heard them.
It was what I wanted. It was what I'd been waiting for.
It was passion. I wanted to be a son born of his lust.
When he grunted deep and low in his throat, "I'm
cuming!" And she screamed, "Cum in me!" And he threw
back his head of long blond hair, raising his face up, I
zoomed faster than the speed of light like a bullet through
his forehead.

I lodged in his pituitary where I took first car in the
roller coaster of his cum that exploded in a starburst of
energy, partly me coming in, that shot down under the
blond bristles on the back of his thick neck, down his
well-muscled spine, straight through his prostate, picking up other seed all along the way, me picking the best
one to attach myself to, then rocketing around the double-
8's inside his big bullnuts, and finally, launchtime, I hit
the first micrometer of his 13-inch cock, poised, perched,
ready like a shot in a sling, when his toes curled under,
his big butt tightened, his thighs hardened, his pecs and
belly bulged, his powerful arms flexed, and the column
of his neck stood corded like a huge cock.

His orgasm tore me at about a million G's as I shot
down the inside cannon of the 13 inches of his cock. Not
only did I have to beat out a couple million other anonymous sperm, I had to hit the target with Lorraine bouncing like a bitch in heat. But what's a ball-turret gunner
good for, if he's not a hot shot?

So, for one brief moment, I was sailing along inside the 13-inch cock of my lover who, I knew, still grieved for me, but, *Bingo!*, not for long, not when nine months later he held me in his big daddy arms and said to Lorraine, "We'll call him Mutt."

"His name is Michael."

"So we'll call him Mutt."

"No."

"Then we'll call him Booger."

"I'll call him Michael."

"I'll call him Mutt."

The way he said the names I knew he recognized me. He kind of crooned under his breath and noodled my chin singing, "Don't sit under the apple tree."

And that's how my lover became my dad and we were the first ones on motor scoots and surf boards, and everything was very California because I was no fool. I made sure that his sperm I connected up with was genetically XYY-coded to be built big and muscular, blond, hairy, and hung like my old man with a 13-inch dick.

He always got off on himself so much, he liked me even better when I grew up looking everyday more and more like him.

"You're Boyd all over," Lorraine always said.

There's nothing better than when the lover becomes his beloved. Or close to it. His beloved's son. I had quite a boyhood, a better adolescence, and when my old man hugged me on my 18th birthday like he'd never hugged me before, well, what goes round comes round, like father, like son.

Would a man with a 13-inch penis lie?

Everybody Lives in Hubbub, Texas.
When You Need Advice,
Ask Dr. Strangelove!

WAIT TILL YOUR FATHER GETS HOME!

Dear Dr. Strangelove:

I saw your column in *Man2Man Quarterly* when I was on a business trip to San Francisco and I would like to ask your advice for solving a problem in my situation. I live in Hubbub, Texas, but was raised in the Midwest and then in Texas in a Christian home. For the last few years I have been a practicing homosexual. I have also had sex with women, but, in total, I have had more male encounters. I did not have sex at all until I turned 23 because I was taught that it was a sin outside of marriage. I repented many times for masturbating when I was a teenager.

I masturbated in constant fear of being caught and punished severely by my dad, as he was strict and believed in corporal punishment for a lot more even than masturbation. I don't know if you whip your sons, but my dad was quite a disciplinarian. My three older brothers and I were paddled on the buttocks with a board for minor infractions and given severe whippings for anything serious.

Dad had a wooden paddle about ten inches across and an inch thick with drilled holes, made out of oak. He also had a thick strap of cowhide attached to a wooden handle. He made these himself and he kept them locked in his tool chest for the purpose of disciplining. Sometimes, he'd grab whatever was handy—his belt, a boot with leather laces, a rod, birch switch, length of hose, or even a board, and give us a licking.

For minor infractions like talking back, not doing chores properly, low grades, arguing, lateness, discipline reports from school, bad sportsmanship, he made us bend over and grab our ankles. He'd swat us hard on the buttocks as many times as we were old, and he didn't mind doing it more than once a day if it was called for. He used a wooden paddle or shaved 2x4.

The worst fear was being taken to the basement or out to the garage for a whipping. This was for something serious like disobedience, fighting, swearing, lying, getting in trouble at school or somewhere. Then he bawled the hell out of you and left welts with the paddle or strap or whatever.

He was a big man and could hold me down over his lap until I was 16. I had reached my full height of six feet and weighed about 145 at the time. Now at 31, I'm 170. I have always been athletic, trim, and health-conscious.

The worst time for me was when I was in Junior High. I don't know how old your sons are, or whether they cause you any trouble, but I got into a hell of a lot of trouble for about three years there, and dad was on my back a lot. When I was 14, dad was mainly a disciplinarian. I feared him, but kept behaving badly. I was a discipline problem at school where it was common to give licks on the buttocks if you couldn't take detention. Dad pushed sports, and if you didn't go out for them you had to work for him after school. Either way, I couldn't sit in on detention, and so had to bend over for licks from whatever teacher was working out his frustrations. Dad, who was never frustrated, repeated these at home.

I sneaked off from school one day with some other guys and got caught shoplifting teeshirts. We were taken to the juvenile hall. The cops called our dads and when our dads got there, the police chief strapped each of us five times on the buttocks with a hefty leather strap while our dads watched. They had an old poster at the police department encouraging the use of corporal punishment at home. The poster was a drawing of a sad-looking father, standing in a woodshed, holding a big exaggerated strap on which the artist had printed the words, "Parental Responsibility!" Staring up at the father was a regretful-looking boy. The father was saying, "This is going to hurt me more than it hurts you."

Personally, I believe corporal punishment is a good thing and sometimes wish that dad was still around to put me in line. Talk about whipping "the devil!" That same year, dad found out that I was skipping church school on Wednesday nights and made me strip out of my Sunday suit after church and tanned me with the licking strap. I had to sit in my jockey shorts until he finished breakfast—then he returned to the garage and gave me a second whipping, strapping my bare back and shoulders and legs. I was welted from top to bottom before he was finished.

Dad gave his permission for other men to discipline us if we were in their charge. He and mom used to go fishing in northern Minnesota and I'd stay on a ranch here outside Hubbub with a friend. And, yes, my friend's dad frequently beat me on the bare buttocks with a utility belt. I complained to dad, but he approved.

Dad was certainly strict, but even though I hated the punishments, I'm glad he was tough, because I don't think I would have ever gone to college. After the shoplifting incident, dad talked to the police chief and then to the principal and one of my coaches at school and they agreed to administer severe lickings if I misbehaved or didn't pay attention in classes. With parental permission, they could give you a licking like your dad—even more than the prescribed five swats allowed by the Board of Education.

They didn't have to count. Paddles were made in shop class. They'd take a ball bat and shave it down. This was the instrument they'd use for spanking. For the rest of the school year, because dad gave the principal and the coach the okay, I was sweating like crazy, fearing these punishments. Any bad report from a class, and I was taken to a store room in the gym where they kept the equipment apparatus, mats, etc., and held down over a table. One of the men would paddle my buttocks and thighs until they were black and blue. I would holler, but no one could hear you there.

Dad kept the swats up at home too, and made sure I studied. Most of the punishments I received were administered on the buttocks and thighs, even though strapping and switching often included the back, shoulders, and legs.

Dad was not troubled by disciplining me in front of others. Several times I was switched outside in front of others with my shirt off. Once, on a fishing trip, he made my brother and me lie over a log for a switching in our swimsuits. This was in front of other guys' dads. We had been fighting, and dad wanted to set an example. He dipped the switches in water and whipped the hell out of us—welting our backs, butts, and legs. Another time, after disobeying a friend's dad, the guy complained, so my dad offered the strap to the other guy who gave me a hell of a beating in my jockey shorts.

Both my older brothers are married. My oldest brother has seven kids. He uses a wooden paddle with holes, just like our dad used to do. My other brother raised his wife's nephew in Fort Worth. I was present once for a severe beating he gave the kid. The garbage had caught on fire due to the kid's negligence, and my brother used a large wooden bed slat on his buttocks. The kid was fifteen at the time, but howled his head off. It must have hurt like all get out since my brother weighs 185 and is built like my dad.

If you're from the Midwest or South, then you must know that corporal punishment is still practiced both at home and in schools. This probably has something to do with the more Christian attitude in those places. I continued high school in Fort Worth where discipline records were kept and sent home to parents. Right up to the last minute before I graduated I was taking licks on the butt from somebody. Dad gave me my last severe licking with a fan belt in the garage when I was 16. He took the hide off me for not returning the car when he said. He used the fan belt from the car, because he liked to make the kind of whipping instrument fit the crime. You can bet I yelled on that one.

I think that whipping is a good discipline both physically and spiritually and mentally. I was forced to work a lot harder knowing dad or a teacher or a coach would whip my butt. I also think it's good for raising boys to have a manly character and backbone even if they're queer. Learning to take the discipline of corporal punishment helps develop the body and the mind as well as the soul. Dad knew what he was doing. He was not being abusive, but really raising a son. Lickings are part of that.

I'd be interested in hearing from men who like to beat ass. It's been a long time since I've taken a whipping. Getting that regular attention again might be good for me.

—Waiting for a Licking,
Hubbub, Texas

Dear Waiting in Hubbub,

Any man who wants to oblige you on your terms can write you with details c/o "Ask Dr. Strangelove," PO Box 193653, San Francisco CA 94119. The letters will be forwarded to you.

—Dr. S.

P.S. Meanwhile, Dear Waiting, you might consider the possibilities of the following Email Doctor Strangelove received late last night regarding "Born-Again Whipping."

Dear Dr. Strangelove,

Born-Again Family Man, 32, married, athletic in body, and strong in soul, father of three sons, offers to whip the devil from homosexualized men desiring first steps on return to repentance, and return especially to fundamental natural family sex. Whipping of shoulders/ back only, stripped to waist. Will tie sinner up if necessary for salvation. None of your Sodom & Gomorrah lifestyle nudity, sex, drugs. Absolutely no touching. I am sincere family man attempting to bring back normality, through discipline of the body, to men habituated to sinning with their flesh.

After Hours in the Jockstrap Gym,
Pumping Jack Lumberjack!
So Whatcha Gonna Doofer Me?

BIG DOOFER AT THE JOCKSTRAP GYM

You want to hear about the 10-inch *doofer*? At the Jockstrap Gym where I work out is this guy who's, you might say, a bodybuilder except he doesn't look like the guys you see in contests all real huge, too big maybe, if not for Krypton, then for this daily planet. Anyway, he's muscular, hard-built, a no-nonsense kind of guy with dark curly hair cut short like he was in the military not too long ago, because he's only about 25, or 27 tops. Clean cut. Lotsa chin. Handsome black moustache. Kind of an air of authority. Maybe a former MP.

After his face, I first notice his thighs, how big they are, then I notice his arms, how nice they are. So is his chest. But what knocks me out is the bulge in his gray cotton gymshorts, like his jockstrap is a slingshot for about ten pounds of raw meat I want slung at me *en brochette*. But what can I do except look? Turns out the guy's attending the Police Academy so he can be a deputy sheriff for the county.

A forbidden object of desire!

Perversely, I want him more. I respect men in authority, and the evening I finally see him step out of the single shower stall at the gym, drying off his hair, with the towel ends dangling down over his face and eyes, I act on my vow to get him. Someway. Somehow. The way our kind always gets what we want, because desire is smarter than a 10-inch cock.

In high school, I played every sport, not because I was much good, but because that was the way I got to hang out with the jocks, and hanging out you become buddies, friends, and more than friends. You become secret-sharers.

That's how I set my baseball cap for Deputy John Wilson who is coming walking dripping toward me, naked, with the towel over his head, and his big dick swinging thigh to thigh. Hairy thigh to hairy thigh. I make my move. I duck my head down to do a real cool gymstyle loose-tie of the laces on my carefully scruffed white Reeboks, and, like a heat-seeking missile, he bumps his cock into my hair.

I raise my face straight up the length of his dick, sniffing his soft-hanging pud every inch of the way, and say, "What the fuck," and he says, "Jeez, excuse me," and then we both laugh like it's the funniest thing that ever happened, which breaks the ice, and leads me to say, "Hey, I'm going to Don's Cafe for a protein smoothie," and would he like to come, and he says, "Why not," and that's how I found out all about him and the Police Academy and why he wants to be a deputy sheriff, because he intends to become a private investigator.

"Like Magnum, P. I.," he says.

"A private dick," I say.

He looks at me curiously, then we both break up laughing again. Good. Everytime you get a potential trick to laugh you chalk up one more klick to *yes*. When they don't laugh, leave; you'll never lay them. His big fingers toy with the length of his smoothie straw. It's plastic, not like the old-fashioned paper straws where you can play "He-loves-me/loves-me-not." He says he likes me because I talk about things, about stuff, which he pronounces drawled out like *stough*, like for him his *stuff* is tough. He says I don't just ask *doofers*, as in the kind of questions bodybuilders get asked 90 times per day at the gym by other guys: "What do you *do for* your biceps, or *do-fer* your pecs, or *doofer* your shoulders?"

An hour and six cups of hot, black caffeine later, we're laughing so much I put my hand on his knee under the table and he doesn't pull away. So I move my hand to his crotch. His hard rod feels like 2 inches short of a foot. Real fine. Total silence. Our eyes lock. This is *stough*.

"So," I say, without moving my hand, "what do you *doofer* that?"

"I shove it down your throat."

Hyenas. We laugh like fools. Half the cafe looks our way. I like being seen with handsome guys.

"Let's go," he says. We grab our gymbags. I figure my place. He insists on his condo efficiency. Cop stuff is everywhere. Soon-to-be Deputy Sheriff John Wilson is kinky for police work. Everywhere: night sticks, handcuffs, service revolvers, rifles, uniforms, pictures, actual Al Antuck photographs from the police-only bodybuilding competition called Mr. New York's Finest, recruiting posters, *Police* magazine all stacked nice and neat next to his physique mags. His place is totally cool.

We slow-strip each other. He gets me naked first. He strokes my 8 inches. I launch from the hard pad of his strong hand. His big cock hangs massively thick. He pulls on a pair of tight-fitting red nylon police running shorts that display his 10-inch rod like a nightstick behind the PD insignia. His muscular build is perfect. Not too much. Just right. His wrestler thighs are in perfect proportion to display his big dick. He tells me to kneel in front of him. The bishop orders his tomb at St. Praxed's. I go down eye-level to his cock. He towers over me. He strokes his meat with his hand. He spits in his palm. He adds baby oil to the spit and soaks the red shorts. The wet nylon glistens so sheer the veins show like rope laced around hard flesh.

"So," he says, "what are you gonna *doofer* me?"

What I do is rub my hand down the slick wet nylon length of his cock. His stomach is tight. Hair spirals out of his navel. He smells clean. I pull the nylon shorts down his hard hips. I cup my palms around his perfect ass. I watch his cock, free of the shorts, rise drooling toward my mouth. He's got big hairy nuts.

"*Doofer* me," he says.

Holding the base of his rod, I tongue the tip. His piss slit is already oozing white stuff. I wrap my lips around the head, tasting it, savoring the sight of the 10-inch pipeline from my mouth to the hairy base of his bod.

"That's it, baby. Take it easy." He locks the fingers of both his hands behind my head and starts slow-pumping my face. "That's it. Let your daddy do the driving."

My heart races. Sex is one thing. Nasty talk is another. The jock in him is turning into a daddy and the daddy into a deputy and the deputy into a cop, all my favorite kind of each. I'm working my dick with one hand and rubbing his thighs and belly and pecs. I finger-flip his nipples and he moans.

Suddenly I know this cop's trigger.

He pumps my face slow and easy, enjoying the ride like Dick Tracy fucking holes into the mouths of FBI Wanted posters. I suction him, tongue him, hold the head of his cock prisoner in the O-ring at the back of my mouth, at the top of my throat. I'm impaled on his cock. His cock is locked-down in the back of my throat. In sex, sooner or later, someone surrenders. Not this time, boy-o! Unspoken, we work out a truce.

He jamfucks my face till the snot runs from my nose. He feels great. His big body bumps his boner down my chuckhole. I choke. I gag. I feel pretty. Oh so pretty! He holds my head tighter. I almost cum. I stop jerking my cock. I reach both hands for his big pecs. I find his tits hard as hood ornaments on his Corvette pecs.

"Don't," he says, "Stop. Don't. Don't stop."

You know the litany.

He is a man whose cock is driven by his tits. His big 10-inch revolver revolves ramtough down my throat. I feel his spasms start. I try to catch my breath for the big blow, knowing he's gonna dump a load to remember. Sure as the weather obeys the TV weather news, he tornadoes his load. A funnel explosion of cum. Trees bend in the wind. Dogs howl. Crops fail. Trailer parks twist into wreckage.

I'm choking, licking, sucking, pigging it all down. Eating cum. Yeah. Sucking sperm out of his 10-Inch Saturday Night Special. He's slamming my face tight into his crotch. The slight sweet taste of blood from my lip. His throbber keeps pumping out the juice until it doesn't. He eases me back on the floor, straddles my chest, drops his still drooling Big Dog K-9 dick into my mouth, and says, "This is what I'm gonna *doofer* you."

I look up. Handsome brute. I jerk my dick. He pokes his tasty cock, now hanging in at 9 fat inches on the peter meter, farther into my mouth. My eyes feast up at him.

Always a titman, he plays with my nipples, shoves his cock deep down my throat, and nasty-talks me how he's gonna sit on my face, blow me farts, and feed me fudge, all of which together makes me shoot my load all over his hairy ass.

"How'd you know about me," he says. He lays back and lights up a fine cigar. Just like a lawman. Attitude for days.

"Outside shot. I hoped more than I guessed. And you. How'd you know about me?"

He laughs. "You don't quite believe I'm going to be a

real private investigator. Now you can. I checked you out two weeks ago. I been prick-teasing you ever since. You think you bumped your head into my dick tonight at the gym? No way. I rammed you, fucker." He takes his cock in his hand, takes a hit on his cigar. His cock starts rolling, rising. "If this gets hard again, I'm gonna have to arrest you for good."

"Yeah," I say, "Do it to me one more time."

That's how I broke into the inner circle of bodybuilders and just plain jocks at the gym. Just like in high school: once I sucked off one of the team, the rest came running with "*doofer*-me" hardons. Deputy John Wilson is any man's hot ticket. When we started working out together, I suddenly became somebody. His buddy. His training partner. Even though my body's only medium gym-muscle. I'll never be Mr. America, but women cruise me as much as guys, so I must be doing something right to get through the doors I want open to me.

Anyway, my deputy is my entree who gets me into some *stough*. Oh yeah! Like this one night, after 10, after the gym closed, for some after-hours horsing around, post-workout posing, muscle challenging, tape measuring, that leads to a nude posing, cock display, dick pumping, circle jerk of four or five guys studying each other in a muscle-line-up in the mirrors. Fuck, yeah. A guy hasn't lived till he's been locked into a gym, sucking in air saturated with the sweat of men pumping iron for hours.

So this one night's contest is down to my deputy who sports this husky semipro football build, plus the drop-dead blond manager of the gym who's won—I'm talking competition BB here—his share of contests, and another severe dude, hard-muscled, yeah, but lean, and tall, built like a race horse, who trains in logging boots laced up to the knees on his gray sweats, wearing one of those classic male fetishes, a wool plaid Pendleton shirt with the sleeves not torn, not cut, but rotted off at the steaming armpits. Its buttons were long ago ripped off to expose his hairy chest and furred abs. The look fits his bushy beard and big moustache. His black hair is long, the way excon bikers wear it long, when they grease-comb it straight back from the widow's peak on the forehead. He's known as Jack Lumberjack.

"So," my deputy whispers, "what you gonna *doofer* them?"

"I never been locked into a gym before. It depends on the rules."

"A man's gotta *doofer* what a man's gotta *doofer*," he says.

So I play it by ear. I figure I'm the odd man out, the new kid on the block, them having obviously been here before, together doing gym-time after-hours, because I feel something brewing in the air.

My deputy and I are getting close to each other. Emotionally. The fucker's setting me up. Either to clinch me or dump me. I don't know which.

The three men are pawing their way around the gym, kicking weights, dropping their butts and torsos suddenly under a Universal machine, bench-pressing up a quick pump on the pecs, wrapping a leather belt around the waist, with a chain hanging down the crotch of their sweats, and 90 pounds of weights clipped to the chain so they can grind out a set of wide-grip chin-ups that pressures the chain tight against their big hard-packed dicks.

The blond BB stands on a 3-foot length of 4x4, bending over 90 degrees, holding onto the weight rack in front of the leg station. Jack Lumberjack with the rotted Pendleton shirt climbs up on top the BB's butt, mounting him like a muscle horse, adding in the swaying rider-weight the BB needs as he starts his bent over calf raises. In the mirror, they look like one man, two torsos.

I know the long animal dick of Jack, the bearded muscle-rider, can't help but be hardening against the beautiful blond bubblebutt. They are silent, intense, breathing hard, serious, exhibitionistic. This is what my deputy wants me to see. The nonsocial side of the Jockstrap Gym. The secret side of manhood. What hard muscle really means. Why some men train so ferocious, so hard. The late night side of iron pumping when men engage each other wordlessly, and, what happens, happens, and no one of them after the wordless private pleasure ever speaks of it, maybe even knows its real name.

The blond BB completes his set. Sweat drips from his moustache. In the mirror I see his square jaw tighten. Jack Lumberjack meets the blond's eyes in the mirror. He slides slowly off the butt and down the haunches of the big-thighed manager who, without moving his feet, stands straight up, butt back against Jack's dick, shoulders against the taller man's chest. Jack pulls the BB's baby-blue tank-top, torn to the tiniest shreds across his shoulders, up from the waist, across the bat-wing lats, and up the mighty upraised arms of the blond watching himself be stripped naked to the waist in the mirror.

His big blond cock tents in his sweats. The sight of his own muscle makes him hard. He is a stud born big, made bigger by diet and workouts, made massive by steroids. Jack Lumberjack sniffs the sweaty tanktop, holds it in his sharp, feral white teeth, and runs his hands over the blond's shoulders, then down, cupping his massive pecs, vise-gripping his thumbs and forefingers down on the twin nipples tanned and shaped like perfect blond chocolate chips. The BB raises his arms to a double bicep shot and grins at what he sees bulked and defined and vascular in the mirror. Jack leans down, spitting out the tanktop, and licks the BB's 22-inch biceps, diving under to clean out his sweaty unshaven pits, those two damp dripping caverns where chest and shoulders and lats and arms all tie in together.

My dick is creaming in my shorts. I see my deputy

standing off to the side working his 10-incher in his hand. That's cool enough for me. I strip off my shorts and take my 8-inches hot in hand.

The stud pair at the mirror turn face to face. Jack Lumberjack pulls the drawstring on the BB's sweatpants that slide off his edible butt, getting caught on the upraised hook of his hard cock.

Jack wraps his hand around the cotton-covered cock. I see 10 inches, maybe 11, looking like 12 inches wrapped in the gray sweats.

The BB flexes his abs, rolls his shoulders, pumps his arms, squeezes his butt, reaches out and peels the Pendleton shirt down the long-muscled hairy lumberjack. He strips him to the waist. He wolfs down on Jack's hard pecs and harder nipples, raking his teeth through the thick hair on his chest. Jack pulls a leather thong tied around his neck. He grabs hold of the gray sweatpants tent-pegged on the BB cock. He stretches the sweatpants to the base of the cock, outlining the head and the shaft through the worn cotton. He starts at the base of the BB cock. He wraps the leather thong around the base of the sweatpants blanketing the cock. He cinches and ties the whole length of the bull-steroid muscle dick with the leather thong inside the funky sweats. I expect a gusher of piss to soak the cotton.

My cock aches to see the pair of bones hung on these two. My deputy, stripped down to his cop utility-belt of cuffs, keys, and gun, nods. I get the wink from Jack and a look from the blond manager. They know why I'm here. I know they know why I'm here. My deputy told them I know how to suck, swallow, and worship dicks, big dicks, really big dicks, really big muscle dicks. I crawl on my knees between them.

"Suck him," Jack says.

I go down on the huge cock wrapped in sweats and webbed with the black leather thong. My mouth dries out instantly. Jack laughs. The BB pisses and floods my face. I gulp all I can drink. I try to look thirsty, hoping for more. All three men laugh. Jack Lumberjack takes his hunting knife out of its sheath. My heart skips a beat. He slashes expertly through the tip of the sweats exposing the hard cockhead. The blond stands perfectly posed, his cockhead purple and bulbous from the lacing, as if some overhead light from some eternal physique contest shines grace down on his handsome face, his regal muscle, his monster cock, his radiant blondness.

"Peel it," Jack says to me. "*Doofer* me what I want you to *doofer* him."

I waste no time. I peel it. The blond bodybuilder's big dick reveals itself fast as I unwrap him: bulbous 150-Watt head screwed into a long blond shaft wired with purple veins, skin popping, ready to blow from the palpable thump of his pulse throbbing along the ever-ready 12 inches. His dick is magnificent enough. I look up at his muscular symmetry and I figure to deserve the body fluids of this man that somewhere in my youth or childhood, I must have done something good, or else I sold my soul.

"Kwitcher stallin'," Jack says. He pushes me, mouth first, down on the BB's dick. The circumference of head nearly splits my lips, but the smell of salt-sweat, chalk, and iron lifting-bars on Jack's leather workout gloves inspires me, especially when he stretch-jams his fuck-fingers into the corners of my mouth and butts the back of my head with his own hard cock bundled in his jock, pushing me smack down on the blond's pole. Vlad the Impaler has nothing on this guy. He likes rough-fucking my face on his buddy's cock, holding my head like a bowling ball, jamming, "Oh yeah, we were jammin'," the blond bombshell's monster cock like a long ramrod through my mouth and down my blowhole. I try not to cum. My cock likes rough stough too.

"That's the way," Jack said. "Take it like a man."

The Weiderkind BB pulls his dick free, holds its base in one hand, with two handsful protruding like a billy club, and beats my face. Hard. Spit from his piss slit drools across my eyes. The hardness of hard flesh always amazes me. Jack drools down some spit of his own. Cocksucker. He's packing a pinch of Copenhagen under his lower lip. The BB laughs and they grab each other's tits, flat-hand slapping of chests, rough, the way you figure big built guys like it, feeling up biceps, licking armpits, hugging shoulders with big arms so tight their mighty pecs grind into each other.

They need me like a hole in the head. I'm a bell, a whistle, an add-on. I try to move, but they lock me in place, menaced, jailed, by four powerful thighs. I'm wrong. I'm no add-on.

I'm the cocksucker.

I do the one thing they don't.

The deputy nods for me to play my part. They need me the way exhibitionist bodybuilders need an audience.

The BB slugs me with his dick. A mean streak. "Unlace Jack's sweats," he says. He dickwhips me again, then again, a muscle gangster with a cock blackjack, size 12. I turn. More piss. More hot piss. Jack's dick wets his gray sweats. The yellow gurgle of his hose darkens the sweats. The BB pushes me into the foaming wet that smells sweet as a porcelain trough off the Green Room at a bodybuilding contest behind the door marked MEN. I swallow the head of his fountain cock through the filter of his sweats. He should've been a fireman. I choke. The fuckers like it.

The blond unties the string around Jack's waist. His wet sweats cling to him like a second skin. "Fuck," Jack says. He slowly rolls his sweats down. He smiles. He reveals his cock. Shit! Shoot! Shinola! A matched set. The logger pairs with the BB. Another 12-incher. Pig heaven. Bodybuilder ironpumpers with 24 inches. The deputy with another 10. That's 34 inches. Plus my 8 is 42 inches of cock. One yard and 6 inches of dick.

"Take me," Jack says. "*Doofer* me!"

The blond BB guides my head down the log protruding between the rag of the plaid wool Pendleton tied around his waist. His dickhead is pointed, not like the blond's round mushroom, more like a warhead. He's down from Oregon I find out later. Works as a logger. Did some hard time. Excon. Then Exxon. It figures. He's a hard fuck. He slaps me across the face.

"Watch your goddam teeth, if you want to keep your goddam teeth."

I drop my jaw, open the O-ring at the back of my throat, and he jams in. I choke. My eyes are running tears. My nose bleeds from the strongman pounding of my face into his crotch. They flip me around between them, taking turns with me, rough-fucking my face, talking about their big cocks, bragging about their prowess, taking real pleasure in digging in me deep as they want. They smile at my deputy.

"You weren't lying, buddy!"

They motion him toward us, me caught in a sandwich between them, and he triangulates the couple with his 10 inches. They make me suck him while they pump out muscle poses for each other.

"Let's get him," Jack says.

They pick me up bodily.

"Let's finish him off."

They put gravity boots on my ankles and carry me to a high chinning bar where they hook my ankles to the top, hanging my head cock-level.

Then they put it to me.

"Hit it," Jack tells the blond BB.

The blond's big trophy-winning thighs approach my face. His big cock rams my face. His force sways my upside-down body. He rams in deep every swing back I make toward him. My dick is hard. He slaps it once. The next time I swing toward him, he goes down on me. He's a cocksucker too. I nearly cum. His golden-blond muscle-mouth on my stiff cock. He feels my throb, pulls off, laughs, and fucks my mouth, my head swinging like a pendulum.

He is loaded with seed and ready to shoot it. He says so. He does. Grabbing me on the inswing with his massive arms and fuck-pumping my inverted throat. His cum explodes deep inside me. He squeezes me, a "Most Muscular" shot, with all his might, like a lost brother, his whole huge physique squeezing me, his big dick still creaming in my mouth. He lets me go and yanks his dick from my throat, the suction pulling out my breath with great globs of his cum that drain down my face.

No quarter is given. No quarter is expected. Jack Lumberjack plants his big boots square in front of me. His dick. My throat. He teases his cock into my mouth, bends over and takes my balls into his mouth, biting down on them hard enough to make me shout. I fall for his trick. When I shout, my throat opens, and he rams his dick full bore down the length. He's a deepfucker. His strong fingers grip the cheeks of my ass. His hips slam into my face.

"You want heavy-duty muscle pump jerkoff workout, huh?"

He intones the verbal sex-litany that turns him on.

"You're getting muscle dick, big 12-inch, fucking muscle cock. You got some buddy who'll get you what you want, asshole, but you get it my way, hanging upside down. I'm a fucking face-banger, fucker, and I'm banging your face."

His 12-incher grinds in my throat. He augers me deep, never pulling out, ordering me to tighten my throat, the two of us swinging together, his 6-3, 225 pounds, clinging monkeylike to my hanging body, almost his full weight hanging with mine from my ankles. I can feel his paroxysms start. He plans to choke me with his cum. He plans to make me pass out. He can kill me if he wants to. I'm already in heaven.

His mouth comes off my balls. "*Doofer* me," he says, and he slides my dick into his mouth. Fucking closet cocksucker! His beard in my crotch! His warm mouth around my cock! He feels my body cuming. He feels my dick about to cum. He slams his hips into my face. We both begin to howl at the same barbaric moment, both with our dicks full of cum, shooting, shouting, shivering together. I feel my body, my soul, my aura, my being, my becoming, my transfiguration. I swallow cum. His cum with the blond's cum. I'm groaning for joy.

The two of them cradle my upside-down head in their hands. Their muscular arms are pumped and veined. Their pecs like God's chest.

"One more *doofer*," Jack says to the deputy. "Cum on this sorry fucker's face."

My deputy pulls his service revolver from the holster at the small of his back. He parts my lips with the cold blue steel. I suck the gunsite. His dick is in his hand. My head is held by bodybuilders. My mouth is arrested by a husky muscular cop. He takes his 10-inch cock and strokes it. Three times. No more than three times. He jams the gun between my teeth. He leans between the two panting bodybuilders and fires point-blank his seed into my face. I lap. I lick. I suck. I swallow. The gun tastes cold, oily, mixed with his warm cum.

My own cock shoots volcanic sperm that runs hot rivers down my belly, down to my pecs, down to my chin, down to my mouth.

They raise me up, the three of them, gently, easily, and lay me on the floor, kneeling in a circle around my face, fantasy men, but real men, men of our tribe, men who do the things you pray men will do, if only, as I learned in high school, you know how to crack the inner circles of their secret society.

"How's that," the blond BB gym manager says, "for a total *doofer?*"

Hey! I'm spinning!

Photo Op at Walt Whitman Junior College

Swimmer's Bodies.
Long, lean, hardmuscled.
Water Jocks. Sunfreckled shoulders.
Chest and arms built by lap after lap
of backstroke, crawl, and butterfly.
Clean chlorine smell of 'pits and crotch
and sunstreaked hair.

Robed, they mill on the breezy pool edge,
toes curling, hot for competition,
28 young men on two college teams,
handing off their robes
for a test plop
into the flat blue water's roped lanes.
Stretched nylon trunks, brief, pouched.
The warm assurance
of a quick unconscious self-grope.
The feel of a buddy's cupped palm
patting encouragement
on a wet nylon rump.
The swimmer's jockstrap:
lightweight, cotton banded
around muscular collegiate waist,
strapped down
around symmetrical moons

of golden undergrad butt.
Grab-ass, towel-snapping
naked horseplay in the showers,
but serious
at the water's edge. Intense.
Water animals.
Fresh wet hair tucked
with long-fingered hand
into tight latex cap.
Bright eyes, goggled.
28 young men,
splashing and dripping with sun.
28 young men and all so...manly.
They hardly douse
whom they know
with spray
when to cheers they raise victorious fists,
pulled triumphant from the pool,
walking barefoot
past the bleachers,
leaving wet prints of perfect feet
and dripping Speedo trunks.
Eyes reach out
to feel
what applauding hands may not touch.
Love's lust
makes the swimmers' bodies
loved all the more.

Overhead,
above their nearly naked brotherhood,
a long-muscled diver
takes golden flight:
bouncing,
then launched,
tucked, rolled,

knifing downward
through the crystal air,
slicing through sun into deep waters:
a dove
breaking the surface of the sea,
a god
in graceful descent,
a man
in full plunging dare.
Cameras click.
Telephoto touch.
All their warm wet images,
single-framed,
for magical conjuring,
late
in the private one-handed night.

**Girls Sighed. Geeks
Trembled. But I Had...**

THE ASSISTANT FRESHMAN FOOTBALL COACH

Once upon a time I was a college professor, back during the war in Nam and the war on the campus. The complete cliche. I had exchanged my 3-piece Yves Saint Laurent designer suit for my Ken Kesey jeans, cowboy boots, and tie-dyed teeshirt, all of which fit tight-and-snug in all the right places. I was 28 and toned. I worked out and showered in the campus gym, trading weight benches with the university team players, the varsity squad, and the pencil-necks trying hard not to be geeks. I had me some arms and some pecs, and was determined to keep them, because without pecs, you're dead.

I was far from buffed like the real jocks, but back then I looked more athletic than your usual North-Midwest ivory-tower academic. I was the youngest member of the English department. My "Film as Literature" classes were packed. I was teaching peace, love, sex, and violence in cinema. My chairman thought I could do no wrong. "Nice touch," he said one day after a class. He had walked in and seen me lecturing, sitting cross-legged like Allen Ginsberg on the desk, pontificating Timothy

Leary theory, with everything but flowers in my hair and incense burning in my navel. "You can get away with murder!" He patted me on the shoulder. "Just keep packing them in. To save our department budget we have to keep the body count up."

General Wastemoreland couldn't have said it better. The only body that counted sat in the first row. He could have been Ryan O'Neal's younger, bigger brother. He was a senior who'd mistakenly taken all his "electives" his first two years. Now he was stuck with all his "requirements." He was a sweetheart, more bored than pissed.

You want to know all?

He was also the assistant freshman football coach.

He was a blond knockout. All he owned were faded jeans and teeshirts. His jeans fit him like Levi Strauss used his butt and thighs for a mold. His teeshirts, always white, hung loose on his tight belly, but stretched like Saranwrap around his big pecs and big biceps. Old Levi never had an inkling what his jeans would do for a tight box of big blond balls and 10-inch sausage-roll cock.

He had quite a rep at his frat house. When his house bros let those "certain" campus undergrad girls in late at night and let them walk door to door, a hetero-whore version of exactly what the gay baths used to be, the most beautiful coeds headed straight for his room where he laid out stripped to his massive-packed jockstrap, legs spread, arms up, hands finger-locked behind his head, smiling, flashing his perfect straight white teeth, under his bushy blond moustache that all young men had in those days of "Hair, the political statement."

He held the documented house record for best body count.

Get the picture? A stud. And studs are always out to prove something. His name, like many boys born during the WWII 40's and 50's of the idolized great American father-figure Dwight David Eisenhower, was David. But anybody who called him "David" risked life and limb. When I first called his name on roll, his deep voice interrupted me politely but firmly, "Call me 'Dave.'" Girls sighed. Geeks trembled. Good. I was one step closer. These were the university days, remember, when students weren't trying to be like their teachers as in the old traditional days. Everything was opposite: the teachers were trying to be like the students. That was the beginning of the end of American higher education.

Anyway, something clicked that semester. Dave and I got close in the classroom. Sometimes I felt I was talking only to him. It was his corn-blue eyes that mesmerized me. He never said much, but he listened like no student I ever had before. I gave him, he said later, his "intellectual awakening." Too bad he hadn't gotten it freshman year, but better late than never.

He showed up at the front door of my home near the campus late one snowy February night. I was a little bleary-eyed from grading papers, the curse of the teaching class. He didn't say, "Hello." He said, "Wanna scrimmage?"

Be still my foolish heart. "Warm up by the fire," I said. "Wanna beer?"

"How 'bout some wine?"

Was this massive boy talking to me in code? Beer was for bull-shitting man-to-man. Wine was for romance. "Mateus," I said. It was the current undergrad wine of choice. "So what's happening," I said.

He got straight to the point.

"You're always doing stuff for me. I figured it was time I did something for you." He sat on the floor next to the fire. I plopped cross-legged opposite him. He didn't say what he had in mind exactly. It took three more glasses of wine. "I thought," he said, "you might be getting tense grading papers and all, so maybe I could give you a massage."

A log popped, cracked, and tumbled in the roaring fire.

"You don't owe me anything."

"We all owe each other something," he said, like a line he learned in one of the new sensitivity-training classes where the instructor had students draw their version of their real faces on the inside of brown grocery bags and then put the bags over their heads. I'd still love to have a snapshot of that: a whole classroom of students with sacks over their heads, meditating, while the teacher walked around, invisible, checking out groins and loins.

I never argue with sensitive, blond, muscular, handsome, senior-class assistant freshman football coaches built like brick shit houses.

"Turn around," he said.

He put his big strong hands on my shoulders and kneaded my neck. He rose to his knees and slid them along the outside of my thighs, planting his crotch against my butt. Was this foreplay? Or was he just a jock, trainer, coach, who regularly touched men's bodies to salve their bruises and ice their strains, and nary a sexual thought crossed his mind? This BMOC, after all, was known by coeds and frat bros alike as the campus studmaster.

"Feeling better?" he said.

"Better than what?" I said.

"Turn around," he said.

I faced him directly. Our knees touched. He put his hands on my shoulders and stared directly into my face exactly the way I'd seen him stare into players' helmeted faces under his intense coaching.

He was the most beautiful young man in the world.

"Since I was in grade school playing ball, and on up through junior high and high school, and now in college, and maybe some chance at some semi-pro ball after I graduate, I've been being touched by men. Like, you know, crashing into them. Getting rubdowns from coaches."

I wanted to say, "Getting your fanny patted," but I didn't.

"And I touch them. I put my hands on them. I feel them. Can you imagine how good it feels to be 6-2 and weigh 225 pounds and be all suited up and crash into another dude built about the same? The impact is like nothing else in the whole world. Except maybe two armored tanks. You come crashing down together, rolling end over end, like you two are one person and then you untangle helmets and pads, slap butt, and turn your backs on each other."

"Like most gay romances." I didn't say that either.

"Why don't you take your shirt off," he said, "so I can rub you the right way."

"I will if you will."

His pecs were a mass of blond hair eddying around blond nipples. The heat from the fire ran rivulets of innocent sweat from the hair in his armpits. His belly was the sportster belly that's halfway between the hard-disciplined ball-playing jock and the beer-drinking fraternity party animal: hard-muscled underneath, but sheened over with a tiny layer of soft keg-beer roll. He was all of 21. He'd been born a jock to a jock father who raised him right until the school coaches took over. He'd be a jock all his life. Some jocks' athletic masculine sex appeal blooms early and fades, their glory days gone forever with high school or college. His early bloom, I could tell, would last his lifetime—if the draft didn't get him—changing, maturing, with the decades, but always in dominant bloom.

My cock was hard.

His massage of me turned into my massage of him. I followed his lead. We were like dancers. His hands, more powerful than he realized in his innocence, started soft on my shoulders and grew stronger on my chest. He gripped my pecs like he'd found something he'd lost or looked for forever. Maybe deep down he just really liked men's chests. I palmed down his hairy chest savoring the texture of fur over bulging muscle. He massaged me harder. "Easy," I said. "This isn't the playoffs." I flattened my palms on his pecs, gripped medium hard, and for the first time, instead of athletically massaging him, erotically massaged him, not unlike a sex-coach, and said, "Like this." I knew what he was after, even if he didn't know what he was after. I could only jump-start him. I placed my fingers on his nipples. Startled, his eyes opened and looked directly into mine. The tiny mounds of flesh on his pecs burst to life. He tossed his head back in a new-found ecstasy as I finger-rolled his virgin nipples in my fingertips calloused from the iron-weights at the gym.

"Can we get naked?" he asked so sweet, this boy who had fought his way for years across the gridiron.

If I ever drown, and the soundtrack of my life flashes by my ears, I hope the last thing I joyously hear will be him asking, "Can we get naked?"

We could. We did. I unhitched his belt. His cock was at full staff in his jeans. God! Was he hung! He was totally unembarrassed. He trusted me. Like the quick study he was, he reached for my belt and peeled me, free of my undershorts, springing my hard cock to full view. We both smiled, like a student and teacher breaking taboo in a war-torn time of broken totems; and he hugged me in his powerful arms.

"You know everything," he said.

"Not everything," I said. "But this I know."

We stood and stripped off our jeans. He dwarfed me, only 175 and 5-11 to his 225 and 6-2. We stared at each other in the blazing firelight.

"I love you," he said.

"I love you too," I said, meaning it the way we meant peace and love back in those horrible war years of nightly news of grisly combat footage and the lies of Watergate that led young men like him to doom. We both had draft numbers. His was active. No wonder with so much death we wanted to hold each other. Our love was real. I think at that instant the general love and respect I had for him turned to a specific love that to this day I cannot forget even though he is long gone, and that only makes me romantically love him all the more in memory forever.

That night, I remember, his hard cock did not embarrass him.

"It never goes down," he said.

I had seen him in the gym shower room. He spoke virtual truth. His cock did, in fact, go down, enough for decency's sake, but it always hung thick, fat, long, and raring to go. No wonder he had a rep as a stud. He sported one of the biggest documented pieces of visible meat on campus. One drunken night, his frat bros measured him in at 10+ inches. Word that good gets around.

With studs like him slumping wide-legs open in my classes and stripped in the gym, it was no wonder I had a taste for big beefy college boys with built chests, hot nipples, b-i-g d-i-c-k-s, sweaty buttholes, fast cars, faster cycles, daddy's money—all of them driven fuck-crazy by the danger of death in a very dangerous war. Gloriously golden. Inviting. But untouchable, forbidden, tempting. Once, when no one was looking, I had dived like a true fetishist, sniffing Dave's gym gear, chewing his jock that he had dropped in a sweaty pile on the dirty floor in front of his locker.

The maze of gym locker rooms, and showers, made galleries of exhibition and horseplay. Big wide feet stomping wet out of the shower. Big toes. Thick-haunched thighs. First-string players. Wet white towels dropping carelessly off their hard athletic butts. Me, pretending to take forever to tie my laces, bent over, eye-balling their young stud equipment. Big nuts. Big dicks flopping, curving right or left, betraying the hands they used since boyhood to beat their meat. Some pud thick-veined, long. Some dicks thick, fat, and juicy. Big hands, like his big hands, toweling dry big young bodies. Big. Big. Big. Big everything. The goal of every power athlete. Their muscular arms raised, buffing the towels across broad shoulders beaded wet with shower spray. Lickable armpits rampant. Fresh and dripping. Powerful arms rooted in thick shoulders crowning strong chests and staunch backs. Naked. Horseplay. A flurry of white towels snapping across the benches at bare butts. Big hands cupping dick and balls for protection. Jumping. Laughing. Grab-assing. "Cut it out, fuck-face!" Bull-shitting in the locker room. Wild. Fuck-crazy. Absent-mindedly scratching their naked crotches the way they do standing talking serious to each other.

The locker room air was always boiling with their heat, spermy with their smells. The movie in my head remembers him, exactly him, him exactly, Dave, the way he planted his perfectly formed foot squarely on the wooden bench next to me, drying himself slowly toe by toe by toe, his square-boned hand rubbing foot and calf and thigh and crotch dry, 10-inch dick and balls and asscrack, dropping the towel like some careless gift that fell seconds later wet and redolent of him into my own casually open gym bag.

The blaze from my fireplace lit his cock from below throwing a huge dick shadow up his body and across the ceiling.

"You're a big boy," I said.

"So are you."

"Ha! My cock's only a Fellini." A reference to the film we had discussed that afternoon's class.

"*8½*," he laughed. "You always crack me up."

"How about me—cracking you up—tonight?"

"You're the coach," he said. "I mean, the teacher."

I knew he was a tight-end virgin. I poured him some more wine. He pulled out a rolled doobie flown in from Columbia, the country, not the university. We drank and smoked and necked. To show him we were equals by then, I spread his linebacker thighs and went down on his 10-inch trophy dick. His meat was fine stuff, a hard-veined column of manhood, I kissed, lipped, tongued, and swallowed, inch by glorious inch, going down on him, slowly, taking him down my throat, like a wide receiver running the ball for a touchdown past the 50 yard line, the 40, the 30, 20, and 10, straight into the TD end zone.

He moaned. "Nobody's ever swallowed me whole." His voice came from the ozone. "Be careful. I always cum too fast."

With 10-inches down my throat, I could hardly warn him not to. He grabbed my head tight as a football caught in his hands, and held me down, jamming his cock farther down my throat. He raised his hips. His body locked down. I felt his cock build to spasm in my throat. Oh shit! He came. His hot sperm exploded from the tip of his cock.

With the shock, came the thought that I had just swallowed somebody's older brother, because our one night, I knew, for him was just an undergraduate sensitivity experiment before he took his diploma in Phys Ed and ran off and married some Peggy Sue who, full of some later night's sperm, would give birth to his first baby. Fuck Peggy Sue. And he would. But I got there first, and Peggy Sue, who'd probably think cocksucking was lip-kissing the head of his penis, would never be able to chow down on his 10 inches.

"I cum fast," he said. "But I can cum four or five times a night."

Things were looking up. I rose up his body with my mouth full of his cum. We were both blissfully, transcendentally stoned. He stared straight into my eyes, not at all afraid I was going to kiss him. I didn't. I dribbled his cum back and forth across his pecs and down his belly and onto his rockhard cock, glazing him like a meat pie. The rest I swallowed. I wanted him in me. I wanted his cum to be digested in my body so that forever he'd be part of my flesh.

"You are what you eat," I said.

"Far out."

We took a break. His cock stayed hard. I stoked the fire. He lit the joint. He wanted more. So did my hard cock. Small bottles of baby oil were planted in drawers all around my house. He laid back and I squirted the oil on top of the cum and with both hands rubbed his square pecs and hard belly straight down to his big hard cock and hanging balls. My fingers reached under and oiled his buttcrack. He moaned. He didn't say any words, but the moan, when I fingered his asshole, sounded like *yes* to me. What the fuck? The politically correct fascists were yet to be unfortunately invented. In a permissive age of campus revolution, who needed to ask for permission when everything was permitted? Besides, free, white, and 21, he, unannounced, uninvited, but most welcome, rang my doorbell, standing there, his football shoulders covered with snow, asking for he didn't know what, but wanting whatever it was, and trusting me to deliver.

I took his wild-red penis in my hand and masturbated him up to the point of another fast cum, just to keep him willing, but I didn't let him shoot. Instead, I spread his upturned knees with my shoulders and scooted my Fellini under his balls and planted the head of my cock against his virgin pucker.

We were 4th down and goal.

I decided to punt.

His blue eyes grew wide as saucers. He wanted it.
He didn't want it. He wanted it. He wanted sensitivity
training. "That may be a little too sensitive." He was getting a feel of what all those coeds felt when he came at
them all 10 inches rampant, hard, veined, cocked, and
ready to fuck. He sighed, "But maybe it's not." The movie
playing the Campus Theatre was *Myra Breckenridge*,
and he was Rusty Godowski.

"Hike up your butt." I chose the word *hike* deliberately. He slid down on his shoulders, his head resting
against the couch. If there was apprehension in the
stoned brain cells huddling behind his eyes, his eager
rockhard cock was already six plays ahead. Cocks do
that: betray conscience, intellect, and bourgeois morality. I had me a future All-American butthole up against
my present faculty cock. "Go Panthers! Push 'em back!
Push 'em back! Way back!"

I eased my cock head against the blond rosebud of
his immaculately showered hole. He flinched, but smiled.
His eyes never left my face. My eyes feasted on his hard-
muscled body and his hard-veined 10-inch keeper. It was
time to shit or get off the pot. I punted, slowly driving
my 8 inches, an inch at a time, deep inside the furnace
of his ass. He took it like a man. I don't mean like the
cliche. I mean really like a man.

I felt something mystical, the wine and grass
notwithstanding. I felt I wasn't fucking up his ass, but
that I had entered through his ass and my cock had de-
toured up inside his big cock. I swear I watched his 10
inches grow to 11. He must have felt it too. "Make it
bigger," he said. At that, I knew I was being too gentle
with this virgin. His whole life had been spent, from third
grade to college, slamming as hard as he could into boys
and men slamming into him as hard as they could. My
gentle penetration had excited him, but he wanted what
he was used to. He wanted it rough.

He squeezed his big cock and I could feel him squeezing mine inside his. He jacked his hand up and down. "Don't cum yet," I ordered.

That winter night, like Frost's "Stopping by Woods on a Snowy Evening," stays forever in my mind. The fire had died to brilliant coals. The cold full moon spilled through the window in a rectangle that framed his body. I fucked him hard and long. The rougher I fucked, the more passionate he became. I realized we weren't exactly making love; more like I was coaching him, me his teacher again. Big built as he was, he was light as a feather when I hitched him this way and that. His big cock bobbed, oozed clear pre-cum, and throbbed when I took it in my hand.

He had said he had trouble with premature ejaculation. I was teaching him how to hold it back. I greased my hand, all the while fucking his hole as hard as I could, and jacked his dick, slapping it hard when I felt it throbbing toward cuming. To my surprise, and his, the slap made his cock jump another inch. A foot long. 12 inches. Grown longer and thicker because he had another cock inside him, up his ass, up inside his cock.

"I'm gonna shoot," he said.

I slapped his dick, said, "No," raised his legs like goal posts, punted, and rammed my full shaft deep inside him, not once, but a hundred times, getting what I wanted, every football fantasy, because sometimes life gives you only one shot and you have to grab it. He loved it. His hands ran all over his hairy chest, down his belly, back up to his handsome face, feeling himself up, sucking on his long thick blond moustache. The moonlight haloed his blond ringlets he wore as long as the Football Department would allow its players in those long-hair days.

I pulled out and rammed in again, like working out at the gym, pumping at least 10 sets of 20 reps. Over and over. He was moaning, groaning, crying out, never saying "Stop." Even though I could have taken it forever, I couldn't take it anymore. The look of that boy grinding his big body in ecstasy impaled on my cock triggered the click in the back of my head that fired like a starting gun down my spine into my loins, clicking the chambers in my balls, and shooting my load deep up inside him. He felt the force and came at the same time. I stuck deep inside him in awe. His 12-inch cock shot a massive load and then, the big surprise, he convulsed again, and shot a second load, that I feel to this day was my load that I had seconds before shot up inside his cock.

Six months later, he called me. "I'm engaged," he said. "I wanted to be totally honest, so I told Kristie about you. And me with you. She said she wanted me to see a psychiatrist."

"What did he say?"

"He told her I was a normal American male."

"You're better than normal."

"She says, if I want to marry her, I can never see you again."

"Not even as friends?"

"No," he said. "But I had to tell you."

"I'll never forget you," I said. "And I don't mean just that night."

"I've got a job coaching high school wrestling near South Bend," he said. "I'm playing some semi-pro football."

"You take care," I said. "Hang on to your true self."

"You were the best teacher I ever had."

That was the last I ever heard from him. Teachers get used to that. You know students so well for a semester or a year and then they graduate and marry and march off into their new lives and leave you standing there with memories in your heart and a hardon in your hand.

That Summer. That Camp.
The Father. The Son. The Cousin.
They Were the Gene Pool's Greatest Hits!
32 Inches of the Taggart Clan!

FATHER AND SON TAG TEAM

I woke up in this fish story suckling his big dick. When you're 18, and still in your wonder years, like I was that summer, you do strange things in your sleep, like kick off all the sheets and dream buck-naked with your prick up hard and straight as a stick. Older counselors like Taggart, who was 19+ (as in *plus 10 inches*), love to pull tricks on younger guys. You know, when you're out playing counselor at some "Camp Gitchygoomee" and it's the last week of the season, after all the campers have packed up their sweaty little jockstraps and nylon Speedos and headed back home. I missed some of them: the best of the cool young dudes all tanned and buffed and trained for their football, wrestling, and swimming teams back home. The camp was deserted. Quiet. More beautiful than ever. We had maybe a week's more work to do. Almost alone. Me and Tag.

I kept sucking, my eyes tightly closed, pretending I was asleep. I felt Tag's big blond thighs straddling my chest. Maybe I was dreaming. All summer long, I'd lusted after him. He was a diver, 6-2, 185, lean-muscled, and handsome. A dreamboat. When he practiced his approaches on the diving board, his long defined toes striding the length to the tip where he bounced up and down on the edge, my eyes never left his crotch, the tight wet, big bulge of his red trunks, the famous nylon Speedos I once stole and sniffed and shoved into my mouth to suck out the taste of his big cock.

Tag hung 10 easy. Eyes closed I knew that. I felt his soft dick hardening in my mouth. I worked my lips around the velvet head, almost afraid to open my eyes, for fear I'd wake up and he'd be no more than an early-morning piss-hard dream vanishing in the late-summer dawn. But his dick gelling from soft to hard in my mouth, the taste and smell of him—hey, I knew the real thing.

So I opened my eyes, and, shit! It wasn't Taggart at all!

Well, it was, but it wasn't the Taggart I thought. It was, I swear to God, the other Taggart! It was his dad, who had been a big stud at 16, had fathered Young Tag at 17, and was still married to his wife, Verna Taggart. They all ran Camp Gitchygoomee with Verna knowing everything, especially bookwork and her place.

The night before, we had celebrated Big Tag's thirty-sixth birthday, telling him the truth that he didn't look a day over twenty-six. You get the picture. He was the coach, the daddy, the husband, the stud. The Taggarts, father and son, were a special breed of the biggest cocks I ever saw. So I looked real surprised, and twice as pleased, when I opened my eyes and found Big Tag threading my throat. I'd worshipped Big Tag from afar all summer: *him* swimming naked in the pool, endless laps of backstroke with his long cock cutting the water, sluicing its own wake; *him*, in Fort Cobb, which is what we called the main toilet, flipping his big dick over the gray sheet-metal piss trough; *him* groping himself in his nylon shorts around the evening campfire. I saw where Young Tag, who no one ever dared called Little Tag, got his size and I knew why Verna hung around her men smiling no matter what went on.

Between his thighs, Big Tag sported a real handsome piece of blue-veined meat. I'm talking 12 inches of blond cock, maybe 9 inches circumference, which I think is about the exact circumference of my mouth stretched open to its widest cocksucking ring. The mushroom head, I could tell when he pulled it out of my mouth and with both fists waved it back and forth across my face, flushed that juicy hot purple peculiar to blond cocks.

He smiled and said, "This is your wake-up call, Sonny."

I remember everything exactly.

"Are you surprised?"

I grinned like the cocksucker I've always been and shook my head *no* and stretched my tongue for his lubing piss slit.

"Are you disappointed?"

I snorted one of those you-gotta-be-kidding laughs and he drove the head of his cock right straight through my smile and laid pipe down my throat.

When a good-looking summer-camp director who stands 6-4 and weighs in at a solid 225 spreads his jock-thighs across my chest while the morning sun spotlights the blond hair on his pecs and forearms, I know, like the joke about where the 2000-pound canary can sit, that any man that much larger than life can, if he wants, sit on my face and peddle my ears till the cows come home. I worship big dick and Big Tag loved adoration. His cock played my vocal chords like the devil plays fiddle.

"You want it, huh? You little cocksucker."

Beat me, daddy. Eight to the bar. Obviously, father and son, probably playing "tag" together, had pillow-talked about me behind my back, and that's always the best kind of talk. Besides, I'd read some of the graffiti written on the walls of Fort Cobb.

Big Tag spread my jaws and drill-pumped me inch
by inch, working deeper, bringing tears to my eyes, and
choking sounds to my throat.

"Your throat's too tight too soon," he said.

He worked me loose so he could go deeper. Six inches
was easy to handle. I slurped him like a pro. Inches 7
and 8 came harder, but not that hard.

Early that summer his son had broken the deep-
cherry back in my throat where a hard cock exits down
and out the back of your mouth and passes through the
first gate leading to your guts.

I worried about inches 9 through 12. Like, could I
swallow that much cock. I'd never quite got fully impaled on his son's 10-incher; but then Young Tag was
rougher getting his nut. Big Tag, was smoother, more
experienced. He talked dirty to me—I'm a sucker for
verbal sex—almost hypnotizing me, fuck-talking, building my passion for the triumph of swallowing his total
manhood down to the root. He was so intense a talker
he convinced me to go for it, to dare to take it. He slipped
me inch 9, then pulled out, real slow and gentle, and
immediately drove back in, knocking off inch 10, surprising me, smiling a small sneer that curled up under
his bushy blond moustache. The sweet blond hairs of
his crotch were still 2 inches from my face, and I knew
he wouldn't shoot till my nose was buried in his groin,
and he was in me a foot deep, his full 12 inches.

My own cock was bouncing fast in my hand. Big Tag,
who always kept a neat pinch of Copenhagen under his
lower lip, turned and spit slow sweet tobacco drool down
on my dick.

"Beat your meat," he said. "You'll find room for my
last 2 inches in your own cock. When your own cock gets
cock-crazy, you'll let me in."

He wasn't forcing anything. I mean this wasn't a rape
fantasy. It was real. It was the greatest thing two men

can do. It was 6:30 in the morning. He had his horsecock planted 10 inches down my throat, and he was coaching me, like the summer coach he was, to take more of what he had to offer.

My daddy never raised me to be nobody's fool. I know now what I learned that morning. There is one sin in life: when a man offers you a hard 12-inch cock and you do not take it all. I didn't need much coaching. I was such a cock pig, I wished that Young Tag was there, son and father, 22 inches of cock between them. But it wasn't that fantasy either. It was reality. Sweaty sheets. Dripping armpits. Nasty talk. Bouncing bull balls. Hairy chest. Dropdead looks, blond hair, three-days' unshaved bristle. His big cock pumping my face, slowly, his lean hips and waist rocking over me, my hand working my cock, knowing I could cum for the first time in my life with 12 inches of big blond cock pistoning my tonsils, if only I could split 2 more inches of ch-ch-cherry throat.

Life, my daddy told me, is mind over matter. Thanks, dad. My cock beat on the cusp of cuming. I looked up at Big Tag. The brilliant morning sun hit him, lit him, over me like a golden stud. I realized the most private part of that man was deep in me, and I wanted him deeper. I groaned guttural sounds and looked up at him and wrinkled my forehead and nodded. That was all he needed. I beat my dick. He drove half-inch by half-inch into my mouth.

At 11 inches he paused, then began not to penetrate, but to fuck my face. From slow to hard, he toppled from gentle persuasion to bucking passion. He fell over my face like a jock doing push-ups and pinioned my arms on the pillow above my head. I thought I'd choke or die, but I didn't. I did what he wanted. What I wanted. I opened and swallowed. He face-fucked me past 11 inches to the full 12.

I felt his blond crotch slam solid against my lips. He was home. He fully holstered his rod in my throat. He worked me wild. I felt his cock throb and expand in the sheath of my throat, and feared I'd drown if he shot his load into my lungs, but I didn't care, cuz he'd give me mouth-to-mouth and hold me in his arms, and at the precise moment when he blew, my own cock, untouched, shot across my belly, sort of like his huge cock was inside my cock, and his white cum came boiling up out of my nose, my mouth, and, yeah, out of my cock. His cum shooting out of my cock. His cum that turned into Young Tags with 10-inch dicks. His 12-inch cock, seeming inside my dick, stretched my own rod out a full foot so my dick skin strained like a rubber stuffed to bursting with a studbull cock. I could feel what it felt like to pack a 12-inch rod!

Oh, God. You get the picture. I did. I do.

That summer I had more "Tags" on me than a Blue Light Special at the Kmart. Young Tag had a cousin, Big Tag's brother's son, Lawayne MacRory Taggart, who everybody called "MacTag," because he said so. He was tough and streetwise and he liked to wrestle, freestyle, slam-banging and clowning like the pro wrestlers on TV. He'd gone beyond his once-beloved Hulk Hogan and was idolizing the muscular Billy Jack, the buffed and blond Kerry Von Erich, and the outrageous tag team, the Road Warriors.

He fed the campers a liar-liar-pants-on-fire line about how he wrestled on TV, billing himself the "Masked Counselor." The campers loved it. Especially when he pulled a black wrestling mask over his blond head and climbed into the ring with one of the tougher, huskier, older ones, both of them stripped down to nylon briefs and wrestling boots, bouncing off the ropes, MacTag picking the kid up, throwing him across his shoulders and spinning him around, slamming him to the padded canvas, flopping across the kid, fullbody, pinning his shoulders, while the crowd went wild screaming, "Next! Next! Me next!"

MacTag was their chance to act out a fantasy. I know. One night that last week after camp, I stood in my Speedos in the door of MacTag's cabin. I could feel the full moon falling warm on my shoulders and back. MacTag looked up from the table where by the light of a Coleman lantern he was reading *Leaves of Grass*, buck naked, playing with himself.

"Next!" I whispered.

He smiled, closed the book, and stood up. He was a Taggart alright. He had the dick. He slow-walked toward me in that hip-ball-and-joint walk that athletes with powerful thighs and bubblebutts take as their trademark stroll. His dick swung easy between his legs, halfway to his knees, soft yet, but with the swelling blue veins that are sure-fire prediction of the cockquake to come. He walked straight up to me. He stood so close I smelled the sweet summer sweat glistening on his chest, running down his armpits, beading on the hair of his muscular arms. "You sure you wanna be next?" His smile had that kind of killer sneer that Maxwell Caulfield smiled in *The Boys Next Door*.

"Anything you can dish out, I can eat."

He snorted a laugh, but I could tell he appreciated my bluff of trying to talk tough like wrestlers do between matches on TV when they scream at the camera about what slime their next opponents are and how they're going to kill them with a metal folding chair.

"Can you eat this, Sonny?" MacTag wrapped both hands around his rising cock. "You want it here in the cabin," he said, "or do you want to go out to the ring and get beat up a little? You know, just a little punishment. Nothing serious that a 10-inch hot-beef injection can't cure. Just maybe a little fantasy in the squared circle to

make things hotter. A knee to the groin. A half nelson...."
"A full nelson." What was I saying? *Half nelson. Full nelson. Ricky Nelson.* I wanted him. I wanted every inch he had. I wanted his fantasy inside my fantasy. "Yeah. Good. A full nelson too. Maybe even a little choking. I mean I can tell by the look in your eye you want me to be the Bad Guy. You think I can be the Bad Guy?"

MacTag raised up his arms and flexed. His biceps popped like Teenage Mr. America. Blue veins ran down to the blond forest in his juicy armpits. He crunched out a Most Muscular pose, like a wrestling warrior taking center mat. His chest and shoulders pumped big, his abs rippled, and his dick, excited by the full flush of his body, cantilevered another inch up toward total erection: straight up his belly past his navel.

"You are definitely bad." My cock tented my Speedos. Faced with his 10 inches, maybe more, I reached for my cock knowing my secret I never told anybody, that every inch of big cock I sucked made my cock grow that much bigger, slowly but surely. At 16, I measured 6 inches all by my bonesome lonesome. At 18, I was 8+. These encounters were working. Some cocks make you larger. By the time I was 30, I projected I'd be hung at least....

"You fuckin' little Size Freak." MacTag said it in the appreciative way a big-hung guy says a line like that when he knows he's on to a cocksucker who won't waste his time sucking down anything less than 8 inches. Believe it or not, some cocksuckers won't do big dicks. Or can't. Or worse, tongue-and-lip only the tips like most of those lipstick dollies do in straight suck films.

Go figure.

MacTag, faster than I could think, picked me up bodily, throwing my legs over his shoulders, just like that statue of ancient wrestlers, hanging my head upside down facing his big juicy dick. "Suck it, fuck-face!" he said. He knew from the walls of Fort Cobb I liked to hear bullies talk nasty. "Suck it! "Or I'll body-slam you to the fucking floor."

Upside down, I took the flared head of his cock into my mouth, figuring its circumference more than 7 inches. He bounced me on his shoulder with one hand, banging the back of my head with the other, kind of dribbling my noggin like a basketball down on his rod. He was teaching me a whole new 69. Then he flipped me up over his shoulders and swung me in full-circle airplane spins.

God! He was strong. His dick stuck out, proud of his performance. Sex-wrestling turned him on. Suddenly he raised me, pressed me, by the sheer strength of his upper body to arms' length, high in the air, above his head.

I whipped my dick. This was new! This was sexplay! This was what the big boys do!

Then like the surprise thrill on an E-Ticket ride in an X-rated park, he slam-dropped me like a feather to the floor. As crazy as it was, everything seemed in slow-motion. He threw his big thighs across my chest, took one of my wrists in each hand, stretched my arms out, and slid his drooling cock across my pecs and towards my face where he buried it head-first in my mouth before starting the snake's slow slithering down my throat.

Everything felt awful comfortable. I realized I wasn't on the hardwood floor. I was pinioned on a mattress on the floor. MacTag was a class act, but how did he do that?

I heard a loud slap. The kind of slap one strong flat palm makes striking another when two men slap five.

"Tag team!" MacTag said.

"Tag team!" Young Tag said.

I tried to say "Oh Shit" around MacTag's pumping cock.

Young Tag had been napping in one of the upper bunks while MacTag read. He'd tossed the four single mattresses to the floor.

"Tie this on," he said to MacTag. He handed him a camouflage green bandana folded to a head band. "We're the Blond Mercenaries," Young Tag said. "We got plenty between us because we got 20 inches between us! Whoa!"

"He wants a full nelson," MacTag said.

Young Tag obliged. From behind me, his strong arms slipped under my armpits and he clasped his hands behind my neck, positioning my mouth perfectly for a straight-on fuck from MacTag who never took his dick out of my mouth. Young Tag's dick was rockhard between my shoulder blades.

Was I in heaven or wha-u-u-t?

MacTag was shorter and stockier than Young Tag who himself, being a swimmer, was leaner and not quite as tall as Big Tag, who, I mentioned, was 6-4 and 225. They were like three studs in the same gene bank and all of them hung like sonsabitches with 32 inches among the three of them.

The Tag Team worked my legs, squeezed me in bearhugs, double-teamed me, both of them working their own hard cocks, standing over me, talking dirty to me about their big animal cocks, dropping down with one knee across my chest, showing me the dick I wanted, teasing me with their huge pricks, then raising me up with aerial tactics, hammering me into the canvas like pro maniacs, always pulling their punches, squeezing tight on the choke holds, taking turns beating my face for real with their 10-inch cocks. I crumpled under the "brutal" bull-dogging; but I wanted more.

This was a championship bout of inches.

We must have brawled off and on for almost an hour, which is a really long time when you're wrestling or being mauled by two strong young cousins acting out on you the pro-wrestling fantasy they've played so often together.

Finally, they pinned me. Again. Their weight on me felt like an avalanche of hot young jocks. Their dicks ran stout, stayed hard, pulsed for release. They slap-tagged each other's hands and knelt up over my face, taking turns fucking my mouth, the taste of each distinctive, with yet that undertaste of the sweet, sweet, sweet Taggart genes.

As much as they liked my mouth, they liked the mirror they were to each other: the heavier-muscled blond wrestler and the lean-muscled blond swimmer, so much alike in their sunny good-looking faces. Kneeling over my face, my mouth tonguing their furry balls, they sucked tongues and fingered nipples and beat their meat, building their passion to a climax.

Down between their thighs, I watched their studplay: kissing mouths and licking tits and rubbing biceps; both pairs of blond balls beginning to swell, rolling and rising, left nut over right, then back again, with the dorsal veins on the underside of their almost-twin cocks growing thick with potency, both cousins totally into one another, talking dirty in short one-word grunts, saying, "dick," "big dick," "big blond dick," "beat it," "big fucking arms," "sweat," "dick," "juicy hard dick," "lick," "suck," "gonna take you on the mat, motherfucker," "gonna cum," "gonna cum," "on his face," "shoot it on his fucking face." And they did, both cousins, locked in their embrace of arms and chests and faces, beating their meat over my face, squirting the loads of their young, blond 10-inch dicks into my mouth held open wider than a choirboy stuck on the fourth note of "O Holy Night."

I came without touching myself. I was 18 too, remember, and this was summer's end, and nothing, I was certain, would ever be this much fun again. Not if we became grown-ups.

We fell together into a pig pile of sweat and cum and cock. MacTag and Young Tag dozed with me sandwiched between them. The only sound was the buzz of the Coleman lantern and the crazed moth that circled it.

I heard footsteps come the final three steps up the cabin stairs. The cousins' two pairs of sleeping blond arms wrapped around my head kept me in traction. The footsteps, heavy even in Reeboks, stepped directly behind my head. I looked up over my eyebrows, and I gulped.

It was Big Tag grinding his 12-inch keeper in his hand. I could tell he was on the last ten strokes of cuming. He had been watching us all along. He raised his fingers to his lips to keep my silence. His fine big body arched back, displaying his massive cock, one hand working his nipples left and right. Then he stood almost at military brace, and with a silent tremor, holding in his cumshout, wanting to shoot the surprise of his load on the pair of unsuspecting, dozing blonds, gritting his breath, blowing air between his teeth, he shot the load of the father on his son, his nephew, and me, thick blasts of cum splashing down on us three boys like hot rain in August.

I don't need to send you a fish-camp postcard. You get the picture. I have the pictures. Like, I still have them. In my head. In my dick. In my scrapbook. One picture in particular: the four of us, Tag and Big Tag and MacTag and me, standing nearly naked, our big dicks half hanging out of our Speedos, all in a line, with our arms around each other's shoulders like we would always be together.

Verna, I remember, snapped the picture. "Now you'll have a snapshot," she said proudly to me, "to remember how it was this summer with you and my three big guys."

Tomorrow on TV Talk: Consenting Adults Who Wear Leather

5 or 6 times a day I strip myself
to check if under my cruising clothes
I'm still in 1 piece, pulling on/off
socks & jocks
shirts & shorts
leather & Levi's
boots & suits & ties.
Located mainly in my head,
on top the clothespile,
I unclench my fist
to make a hard hand
to oil my
belly & balls
pecs & pecker
thighs & feet & ass.
I check with good reason:
once some cannibal doctor
took my tonsils
and, worse, my 4skin,
but he can keep—the fuck!—his rubber
gloves
off my goddam gonads.
And off my head: through it
I breathe think taste talk rim hear see
smoke lick eat & suck.
My head suffers no failure
of perversatility.
For instance, you hire me
to suck your hairy pecs
to light wooden matches

to blow them out
to lay them hot on your wet nipples
to hear the steam pop
to hear you scream.
I know you're in there somewhere
inside your cotton clothes
inside your leather clothes
inside your rubber clothes
inside your athletic clothes
inside your burning body
inside your fantasizing head
inside the 40 bucks you pay me.
Man!
I laughed
the day I found out
you and I
were the people
we'd been warned about.

In the Gay World, Everything Is Always
Reversed Through the Looking Glass,
and Over the Rainbow.
He Was Looking for the Face of God
at 18th and Castro.
There, at the Other Foot
of the Rainbow Arch from Oz, He Found...

RAINBOW COUNTY

On the last day of spring, June 20, 1973, at high noon, at the corner of 18th and Castro in San Francisco, Robert Place found the Face of God in a pornographic photograph. Not that he was given to dirty pictures. Rather, he had been drawn, by some—what?—*thing* to this neighborhood, by some *thing* he had vaguely heard or read or sensed, that had nothing to do with the corner barber shop where he had sought refuge, but had everything to do with whatever was intersecting the intersection which was inventing its flamboyant self even as he watched.

He had parked his 1957 Chevy BelAire with the candy-apple red body, tuck-and-roll upholstery, and the white "Says-who? Says-me!" top, and then he had walked all four of the single-block arms reaching out like a cross from the main intersection which was more like ground zero than anything he'd expected even in California. Everything rushed oingo-boingo right up at him: the omelet-brunch cafes with cake made out of, go figure, carrots; the dandy little flower shop near the corner kiosk where a one-legged ancient eye, maybe the world's oldest newsboy, hawked the call, "*Chronicle!*" like the last screech of a dying species; the loud beer bars with slender young men in white tanktops and baseball caps posing and partying in windows open to the street; the chic boutiques selling nothing anybody would ever need after a nuclear attack.

All of it was alien to him. Or he was alien to it. He had entered foreign territory. Fear—not so much the fear of the unknown, but more like the human animal's fear of his own kind—bristled the shorthairs on the nape of his neck. The unexpected thrill of temptation put him on edge. Seeking sanctuary, he spied a revolving red-and-white barber pole. He bolted past the blue arrow pointing up the stairs. On the landing outside the barber's door, he stopped, catching his breath. He was a young man in need of something familiar, and what was more solid than a good old-fashioned barber shop?

Until that bone-bright noon hour when Robert Place actually witnessed what looked like the campus of the world's most flamboyant boys' college, he had little more than a tourist's curious Kodak hope that there, at that world-famous intersection, he'd see people unlike any of the people back home in southern Illinois, people stranger and more festive even than the hippies he'd seen on TV in the Haight, people, who, rumors persisted, had always existed, the way bohemians and gypsies and magicians, all of them outlaws, had always existed, even before the Druids, but had never been seen before, at least not in broad daylight, in such visible numbers. So he had come to see for himself.

Because of his uneasy feeling that he already recognized these new people even if he did not know them, Robert Place immediately affected toward them a distanced attitude which he knew camouflaged his ground-glass fear he might, in fact, be one of them, whatever they really were. After a grueling four-day cross-country marathon in his car, he had come to California for what? A trim? Yeah. Sure. That was it. A little trim and some talk. A simple visit to a quiet barbershop. The best place for some local gossip. Some shaving cream hot around his ears. The scrape of the straight-edge razor across the thin skin over the hard bone of his skull. That was all.

Only a few days and many miles before, he had been driving aimlessly through his small town where he knew every street and every house and everyone who lived, or who had ever lived, in those houses, when one of those almost religious, certainly reckless, transfiguring impulses no one can ever deny had possessed him. He had thrown one suitcase into his Chevy, left a rose on his mother's fresh grave, and headed west. He had driven from Canterbury, in Green County, in southern Illinois to the San Francisco crosshairs of 18th and Castro where, in the heart of lightness, of the California sun at high noon in June, almost the solstice, the day of the year's longest light, the most familiar thing to him, the only thing he understood, man-to-man, as his father always said, was the gold leaf spelling out LLOYD'S BARBER SHOP. His hair was not long and he had not even felt in need of a haircut; yet why else had he pulled his Chevy to the curb in front of the shop, traipsed back and forth three or four dizzying blocks, and then run from his car up the flight of stairs leading to the door of Lloyd's Barber Shop that looked down directly on the corner of 18th and Castro?

Lloyd sat customerless in his single green barber chair. He wore a white puckered nylon barber's smock. Across his lap were spread the guts of a player piano he was working over with a screwdriver. He looked up at Robert Place. "Come on in," he said. "I have to do it, otherwise I spend all day looking out the window. Take a look. You'll see. What a parade. It looks like half of Noah's ark.

The stag half if you catch my drift. The neighborhood's changed."

Robert wanted to ask from exactly what to exactly what and was it good or bad or neither, but he kept silent, not wanting to tip his hand, because he figured it didn't matter where he'd played before: California was a brand new game.

"I'll be with you in a minute," Lloyd said. "Hope you're in no hurry."

Robert checked his watch against the clock on the wall. One of them was ten minutes fast. Inside himself, the clock of his body, the only clock that really mattered, began to slow. He felt the speed built up on the I-80 freeway descent from Reno and Truckee down to San Francisco slowly recede from himself. Time zones like tide in the Bay ebbed from him. He jingled loose change in his pocket. Nickels and dimes from back home mixed through his nervous fingers with quarters and Kennedy half-dollars he won in less than an hour playing the slots at a filling station somewhere in Nevada.

"I hope you're not in a hurry," Lloyd repeated.

Robert remembered his appointment book on the front seat of his unlocked car. Never had he ever left his car unlocked. He peered through Lloyd's gilt-lettered window. At the parking meter he had forgotten to feed, a white-helmeted metermaid ticketed his windshield. She turned slowly from the Chevy toward Robert as if she could feel him watching her every move. The noon sun glinted from her helmet. Robert could not see her face. He did not want to. He did not need to. Back home he could drop a deer at a hundred yards. She was a dead bitch in his book.

"No," he said, "I'm in no hurry. I was late for the last appointments I made four days ago. I sell, I mean, I used to sell Fuller Brushes door to door." He was warming up, trying to feel like himself again. "I can tell you more than you'd ever want to know about natural bristle brushes for your hair and your bottles and your carpets and your drapes and your dog and your cat." "That a fact?" Lloyd said. More than once he'd been told his droll roll of a phrase reminded the teller of W. C. Fields, which only encouraged him, despite his efforts to speak naturally. "And the women!" Robert presumed that Lloyd, same as all barbers, liked to talk about women, when he should have known only most of them like to talk about women, but they all love to talk about sex, except the Seventh Day Adventist ones who were always closed on a Saturday when a man was most likely to get his hair barbered. "Let me tell you," Robert said, "about those little housewives. Those lonely ladies sure do want to talk, talk, talk. Always saying, 'Well, Robert, enough me talking about me. What do you think about me?' Do you believe the utter conceit of women?"

"Much, much less than I believe," Lloyd said, "in the unutterable conceits of men."

"Those girls were always giving me coffee till I thought I was going to drown. Always asking me if the coffee was sweet enough and how they could make it sweeter, shaking their hair down, trying out the sample brushes, teasing me, asking me how I thought they looked. I tell you. More than once before I left, I had to comb my teeth. It was murder. Door-to-door can kill you."

"That so?" Lloyd fielded like W. C. "I'm what you might say interested in hair brushes too. Being a barber and all, it's natural."

"I bet you've heard everything too," Robert, doing his best Holden Caulfield said. "At least twice."

"Frankly, I never hear the half of it. In one ear. Out the other. I'd go crazy if I really listened. We're all maniacs except when we're not. I must confess music's my mania."

"Is that right?"

"Right as rain."

"What kind of music? Grateful Dead? Judy Collins? Lawrence Welk? What?"

"Piano. I play the piano. But not with these hands. These are the hands of a barber. I always play piano with my feet." He surveyed Robert's puzzled face and grinned. "I catch me one everytime with that," he said. "Player piano, of course."

"I knew that," Robert said.

Lloyd gestured to the plaster-of-paris busts sitting awry on a shelf over Robert's head. He had saved and bought each one of them from Silvestri's statuary company in South San Francisco. "There you see them." He pointed with his screwdriver. "Bach. Mozart. Schubert. Beethoven. Liszt."

"A whole shooting gallery." Robert stared straight at the barber. Lloyd was a man dragging age forty-five like it was sixty. He combed his graying hair into the stiff part and pomp he had learned as a boy thirty years before. His glasses were as thick as binoculars. Robert liked that. He liked the way some older men and older women kept on with the styles they got locked into when they were young, like they were fixed in some time warp, instead of changing with the fashions and looking ridiculous in clothes that were too young for them, or too modern, or too ugly, like the new uniform for the old, polyester leisure suits for the men and polyester pant suits for the ladies, topped off with a frizzy reddish short perm, or worse, one of those Dynel wigs that catch the sun like orange copper wire. If he got old, which he doubted, that's what he planned to do. Sort of stay just like he was. Not change a thing.

"Turn around and look," Lloyd said. "Bach and Liszt. I like them best."

Robert panned his head to the figurines. They were each ten inches of white plaster with the names chiseled into the bases. "Nice," he said. "Really nice." He surveyed the rest of the room.

This was not the first barber shop, waiting room, or bookstore that Robert Place had cased. In fact, it was a matter of police record that Robert Steven Vincent Place had been found guilty of at least one misdemeanor: slicing articles and smuggling magazines from the Green County Public Library. His mother had paid his hundred-dollar fine, but his year's probation was not half up, and he was on the run.

He had confessed to the judge that he had started with laundromats, that one day he had ripped one article from one magazine in one laundromat. The judge didn't bother to ask his motive, and Robert could hardly have volunteered one. He didn't know exactly why he coveted certain pictures like the first ones he had ever stolen, photographs of blond bodybuilders on Venice Beach hoisting even blonder starlets high onto their broad shoulders in the brilliant California sunshine.

From stray magazines in laundromats and doctors' offices, he had moved on to the neighbors' mailed magazine subscriptions, and from there on to harder cover stuff, to the *pieces de resistance*, the photo-books on reserve at the public library. He had moved from a noisy tearing the pages to a quieter slicing them with a single-edge razor blade, and he had cut out for himself quite a collection of classical Greek athletes. His most prized theft was from a portfolio of reproductions of Lumiere's 1903 photos of the legendary strongman Eugene Sandow in an appealing variety of masculine, but modest, figleaf poses.

His satisfaction with his secret addiction had given him a false confidence that he figured out later had made him greedy and all too careless. He constantly needed more pictures to satisfy himself. Sometimes the actual tearing felt better, bolder than slicing.

Pleasant little dangers thrilled him.

It was his own fault when Miss Ollie Thomas, the head librarian, and his mother's cousin, had herself pinched him red-handed and called the sheriff. She had caught on to him, because he never coughed except when he was in the library, which, as his second cousin once-removed in a family inclined to TB, she thought was worrisome, but then she divined that he only coughed when he was, of all things, tearing out pages, and the louder he coughed the more pages he was tearing out at a pull. She was, of course, incensed, even when she apologized to his mother for calling the law.

The week after his sentencing Robert had returned to one of the two laundromats he frequented with a half-filled basket of clothes. He disliked washing his laundry in machines which he suspected harbored the curlicue hairs of strangers. He added his soap and extra bleach, dropped in his quarter, and settled back to pass the time reading.

Unexpectedly, as he leafed through an old 1964 issue of *Life* magazine, he came across the ragged seams of the pages he had ripped out the week before. The photospread had featured what they termed a man's-man kind of motorcycle bar called The Tool Box in San Francisco. Oh, he'd ripped that one out right away! Yessir! He liked cars and motorcycles both! And now he had the same gutted issue in his hands again. He looked neither to the right or left in the laundromat. He grinned at touching the evidence that he had ever before been in this place at the scene of the crime. Getting caught once was bad enough, but better was the thrill of returning to the scene of an undetected crime.

In his switch of his clothes from washer to dryer, he stuffed the evidence, the rest of *Life*, unnoticed by the hawk-eyed manager, into the bottom of the basket on whose canvas he had carefully marked with a red felt-tip pen: "If found, return to R. S. V. Place." He didn't need to put his street address, not in Canterbury where everybody knew him.

"I don't really play piano," Lloyd said. "I'm not a pianist. I'm a mechanic of the piano."

"I don't really sell Fuller Brushes," Robert said. "But I did. People like to meet me. I like to meet people." He reached for a small stack of magazines that lay next to him on the burgundy leatherette seat.

"Why don't you flip through a few of those," Lloyd said. "Being from back East, you might never have seen those kind of pictures."

"I'm not from back East. I'm from the Midwest. The southern part of the Midwest. New York and New England's back East."

"It's all back East here in San Francisco which has nothing to do with California which has nothing to do with the rest of the country, if you catch my drift." Lloyd adjusted a wire and a screw in the board across his lap. "Nossir," Lloyd added, as if he were changing the subject to answer a question Robert had never asked. "I never get lonesome up here looking down on the boys and girls in Rainbow County."

"Is that a bar?" Robert asked.

"Nope," Lloyd said. "It's the other foot of the rainbow arch from Oz. It's just a teeshirt I made up. It's a state of mind. What size do you wear? Maybe I should give you one."

"Hey, don't injure yourself doing me any favors," Robert said. "I can pay."

"I got a hundred of them," Lloyd said. "A man has to be enterprising."

By the late Sixties, Lloyd had nearly gone under. He had standards. He had tradition. He figured men and boys should be groomed a certain way. He hadn't been able to see himself as one of those fancy-nancy men's salons that other barbers changed to when nobody wanted Princetons or flat-tops or, his favorite, crewcuts anymore. He figured to ride out the long-hair fad. But here he was forty-five, with a one-chair shop and a steady but small clientele of older balding gentlemen of the sort people once kindly called "born bachelors" as opposed to "eligible bachelors." His trade kept him comfortable. The brisk pace that had once been Friday's and Saturday's had fallen off taking with it the strain from his eyes and the pressure from his varicose veins.

"I been closed for four months, yeah." Lloyd said. "Just a second and I'll have all these wires tied up. Out for four months. Back for three."

"Vacation?" Robert asked. He was vaguely bored. The magazines were nothing to write home about.

"Operation," Lloyd said. "Eyes. Yeah. Wouldn't be able to see today but for those two operations."

He smiled with such a general gratitude for his health that Robert, who in his own life was grateful for nothing, felt uncomfortable. Robert wished for another customer, preferably a mother with a small boy who would have to be hoisted to a kid's chair inside the big one. With commotion like that he could easily slip one or two of the crummy nudist magazines into the sleeve of his jacket.

"I always figured," Robert said, "that little boys always understand the world earlier and better than little girls."

"Why's that?"

"Because little boys get taken younger to barber shops. You sit them up on that little chair. You wrap that big cloth around them. All of a sudden they see what it's like to be a disembodied head caught between two mirrors. That's why little boys cry at the barber shop, because, all of a sudden, they're scared. They're face to face with the secret how we're all just curving off into infinity."

"I like that myself," Lloyd said.

"Maybe that's why you barber."

"Could be." Lloyd looked up at a hundred mirrored images of himself.

"To tell the truth," Robert said, "I think everybody ought to have two full-length mirrors facing each other in their house."

"Why's that?"

"So in case you ever need to escape for any reason, like, you know, to get away from whoever's after you, you can just stand yourself between the two mirrors and walk right out of space and time into some infinite dimension."

"That sure is another reason to be able to see," Lloyd said. "If I was blind, I'd never know if you were telling me the truth about mirrors or not."

"You are so right," Robert said.

"Of course," Lloyd continued, "more practically speaking, if I was blind, I couldn't barber. Whoever heard of a blind barber?" He thought a moment. "Guess it's possible to have, you know, the touch without the eye for it." He paused lost in the thought. "Me? I got the eye and the touch. Mmmm. Must be a blind barber somewhere."

"I figure," Robert said, "if the human mind can think of it, somebody somewhere is doing it. You should hear some of the things my human mind thinks about."

"Damn!" Lloyd shifted his piano tools hand to hand. "That sure would take a trusting customer."

"What would?"

"A blind barber."

Robert began a careful roll of the magazine next to him.

"I can see now," Lloyd said. "Good as you."

Lloyd kept his eyes on the piano board, but Robert felt accused. He flipped the magazine away casually. The guilty flee, he thought, and he meant not from the barber but from back home. For crissakes, what am I doing here?

"It's funny," he said.

Lloyd looked up with a vaguely cross expression.

"That I came up here, I mean. I came into your barber shop not wanting or really needing a haircut and I'm not getting one. I came into your shop and I'm not getting what I didn't want."

"Oh," Lloyd said. He folded his tools into a felt bag. "I thought you meant that I could see was funny."

"Oh no," Robert said. "I guess I came up here looking for something else. Barbers always know what's going on around town."

"I mean," Lloyd said, "it would be funny if I couldn't see and I was a barber. But it wouldn't be funny if I couldn't see and I was a pianist. You see them on the TV all the time. Pianists who can't see. They say it helps them play better. They feel it more. But you never see a barber who can't see cutting hair on TV."

"I guess not," Robert said. "Too bad for you that good old Ed Sullivan isn't on anymore. He eyed the morning's *Chronicle*. A sensational murder, one of a series of murders by the Zodiac Killer, spread across the front page; he was fascinated, but the paper itself was too bulky to smuggle under his clothes, and he was too shell-shocked from his arrest in the Green County Library to tear out the long article that continued to the last page of the first section. Instead, he tried to memorize the interesting, livid details of thirteen apparently connected murders and six other persons missing.

"Even if I couldn't see," Lloyd said, "it wouldn't make me any better a pianist." He lifted the wired board off his lap. "This here's like I always rebuild." He carried it across the shop and drew back the curtain on an adjacent room. "You remember player pianos? I get them from all across the country. Bought one in Nebraska for twenty-five bucks. Sold it in Sausalito to Sally Stanford for you wouldn't guess how much." He pulled the curtain closed. "Nossir. Seeing or not seeing would be all the same to me pumping at one of my players with both feet."

Robert looked out the window. Down in the street the ticket left by the triumphant meter maid flapped in the ocean breeze sweeping down 18th Street to Castro where men, he never would have thought it, walked arm in arm. They were strangers, maybe dangerous strangers, but he recognized them all the same. "I should've locked my car." He thought of the .22 caliber handgun stashed under the seat and he laughed because it's impossible for someone on probation to get a permit for a handgun, but it's no way impossible for that same person to get a handgun, especially when that person's daddy dies and leaves it loaded in a bedroom drawer. "Damn," he said.

Lloyd moved to the window, wiping his hands. "That your Chevy?"

He admired the Chevrolet gleaming all red and white with hardly a speck of any road grime Robert had wiped off every time he stopped to gas up. He had bought it, brand new and cherry, the day he turned sixteen, paying for it with insurance money his mom had given him as his share of his dad's policy. Those had been the days! In 1957 the draft had been lenient to neglectful. By 1973, the draft was carnivorous for redblooded all-American boys. He told Louise Yavonovich, the gray-haired lady who ran the Green County Selective Service Board, that she couldn't draft him because he was leaving for California.

"For school?" she asked.

"Yes, a school" he said, "for becoming a minister, a Quaker minister," but his *yes* revealed itself for the lie it had always been before he had driven the first five

hundred miles west. He knew he'd never sit in another
school in all his life. He knew enough to get by in the
world. And more. Even though he was no way, José, one
of those spineless conscientious objectors, he vowed he'd
never let anyone take him to some hellhole place like
Vietnam, or even to prison for dodging the draft. By no
more than impetuous instinct, he had hopped into his
car that day and worked out his plan about heading toward the coast, with its beaches and sex and drugs and
rock 'n' roll, leaving fat old ugly Louise, no more the wiser,
and a little the worse for wear, sitting on her cellulite in
the sprawl of her manila alphabetical files. Even before
the fierce rainstorm he had sat out in his car west of
Omaha he had laughed. He was just another missing
person out of millions. The old bitch would never catch
up with him. He had no way of knowing that Louise had
rather fancied him, and had let him make good his escape, because, in her heart she knew the war was a sad
cause, and that Robert was all that was left of the Place
family, his dad dead all those years, and his mother gone
six weeks.

With Lloyd looking down with him at his Chevy
parked at 18th and Castro, he saw every mile of the
89,787.3 reflected back at him in the late sun of a thin
Pacific afternoon. A wave of depression suddenly washed
over him. It always did, right after he felt good about
getting his own way. He wished to God he had been
drafted. They'd have given him a uniform, an M-16 rifle,
and his own chopper, and then turned him loose so he'd
have had no choices to make about anything, but shoot
it and screw it!

"Nice car," Lloyd said. "And nice arms. You got real
nice muscular arms."

"Thanks," Robert said.

"You work out a little?"

"Naw. I'm just naturally strong." Robert pulled up

his sleeve and flexed his right arm, cocking his fist near his face. "You want to feel my bicep?"

Lloyd rubbed his hands together and cupped his right palm over Robert's peaked arm and his left under it.

"Is that okay or is that okay?" Robert said.

"It's better than okay."

"You can let go now."

"So," Lloyd said, "whyn't you drive your car over to my place? We can work us out a deal. You do something for me. I'll restore it for you."

"Restore it?" Robert said. "You said you weren't blind! Are you crazy? That car doesn't need any restoring." He climbed into Lloyd's barber chair. "Just trim it."

Lloyd fastened the striped barber cloth tight around Robert's neck. He folded the tissue strip down neatly over the cloth. Wrapped and swaddled, Robert felt his body become subject to the barber. His mother had spent the entirety of his boyhood diapering and scarfing and lacing him in and out of clothes. One fall she had taken him after school to find a winter coat. She had wanted to shop at Penney's, but he had fast-talked her into a better buy at the Army-Navy Outlet. She had thought of her husband, a strict man Robert did not know was not his father, who had said the boy's last year's parka would fit well enough this season. Robert thought only of the brown leather bombardier's jacket he and his buddies had stared at through the plate glass window. They had pledged to form their own squadron. His blood-buddy Stoney named himself command pilot. Robert was to be head bombardier.

"This is the size," Robert had said, handing the jacket to his mother.

"That's too large, I'm sure."

"The boy's probably right." The clerk, whose name tag read *Nigel*, had spoken archly over the perfect knot of his stylish silk tie. "He really ought to know. He came in here several days ago with a gang of boys who disturbed the manager no end. I remember your boy especially. We caught him wearing this very jacket in the shoe department."

"I was trying it on."

"As a mother," Nigel the clerk had said, "you ought to know. We don't favor unattended young boys roving through our store."

His mother had been cowed. "Thank you," she had said. "I'll talk to his father."

Robert had ignored Nigel. He pulled the desired jacket down from the clerk's tight hand. He slipped in his arms and pulled the zipper. "I like it."

His mother had looked nervously at the clerk. "It does have windcuffs." Then making an unconvincing counterattack, for a moment she stared the clerk in the eye. "Well, Robert," she had said, "we'll take it. That's what we'll do. We'll buy it right now. No sense shopping around and then coming back right where we started." She looked Nigel the clerk dead on. "I think this will be fine," she had said. "Do you take charge cards? I'll have to put it on my charge card."

Back in the neighborhood, though the evening was warm, Robert wore the brown leather jacket out to show his buddies.

"Take it and shove it," Stoney had said. "Who needs a crummy leather jacket."

Robert Place could have taken them, maybe, one by one, but all of them together were too much. An older boy with light-blond down on his upper lip knocked Robert to the ground. Stoney picked up a piece of broken glass. He straddled the small of Robert's back and cut up the shoulders of the new leather jacket.

Robert escaped and ran and ran until he could run nowhere but to his mother's kitchen.

"I'm furious," she said. "After all I went through for

you with that pansy clerk! Just you wait till your father gets home!"

Robert's father took one look at his bruised face and sent him to his room, shouting after him: "I'll be up to take care of you, sissy-boy!"

Robert sprawled across the bed. His head throbbed from the kicking. Angry voices rose and fell in the kitchen below. He dozed in pain and missed the tread of his father's boots up the stairs. He started when his door opened and light from the hall thrust an awkward rectangle across his bed.

"Take off the jacket," his father had said. "It goes back."

Robert wrapped his arms tight around his chest. The leather was warm.

"Take it off."

Robert glared up at the big man silhouetted in the doorway. "No," he said. He folded his arms tighter, holding on to himself as he had never held on to anything in his life.

"Then I'll take it off for you." His father pulled at the jacket.

Robert would not surrender.

His father pulled off his belt. He was a short, powerful man whose veins rose in anger as he twisted the buckled end of his belt around his fist. "Don't tell me *no*, you goddam kid." He lashed out. "No goddam pussy-boy is going to tell me *no*." His belt struck across Robert's chest and arms. The boy rolled defensively to his stomach. His father saw the scuffs and tears on the jacket. "Sonuvabitch!" he said. In fury he tore Robert's corduroy slacks down below his slim haunches. His left hand shredded his son's worn cotton shorts. The blows from his belt welted across Robert's flesh, until finally, his father, hardened in rage, fell across him. His breath had the copper tobacco smell of Camels. "You tell your ma any of this," he whispered close into Robert's ear, "and next time I'll kill you. Make it look like an accident and kill you. Just hang you up by your neck in the attic and kill you. Just knock over a chair like you did it yourself, and kill you, you little sissy suicide, just like all faggot suicides. Send you straight to hell!"

"My old man was a real bulldog lady-killer," Robert bragged to the barber. "Everytime I come into a barber shop it reminds me of him. The way he used to smell once a month of all that Fitch Hair Tonic and rosewater. Once a month I could smell him coming."

"You don't say," Lloyd said.

"He got himself killed in a fight on an oil rig in Louisiana."

"That a fact." Lloyd combed and clipped at Robert's head. "Getting kind of thin in the back."

"Yeah," Robert said. "So it goes."

Lloyd clipped at one small hair growing in Robert's left ear. "Do you suppose," he said, "that they put out their eyes when they're kids?"

"Who?" Robert looked up from the magazine in his lap.

"Those pianists on TV. The ones that can't see because it makes them play better."

"I don't know," Robert said. "Most people'll do most anything."

"Sometimes in India they put out a kid's eyes so he can hustle more from the tourists. Hear the Mex do that too."

"Sounds to me," Robert said, "something like the boys who sang soprano for the pope. I got an article I tore out of some magazine at home on that. They'd take these altar boys and, you know, sort of spay them, operate on them, you know, down there, so they'd keep their real high voices. Their families were happy. Even the kids were happy. A kid with a real high voice could make a fortune in those days."

"That a fact," Lloyd said. "Maybe then that's why they do it. Just so 'Mr and Mrs America' can sit at home in front of their 'T and V' and watch those black boys who can't even see play the piano." He reached for the talcum. "Dagos really did that stuff, huh?"

"Lots of people do lots of things that sound cruel to us but not to them. Anybody who's not an orphan knows that." On the shelf, between Bach and Liszt, Robert spied a fresh half-eaten deli sandwich. He shifted nervously in the chair.

"Hold still," Lloyd said. He reached for the shaving cream. "I'm finishing up around your ears."

On the end-table next to the chromium-and-leatherette couch lay a second half-eaten sandwich. Blood sausage, the same color as the burgundy couch, hung bitten out of the white bread. In a Coke with no more than two swigs out of it, small bubbles fizzed noiselessly to the top.

"One of your customers left his lunch."

"Some customers leave stuff. Some take it. There's losers and there's claimers. You want it?" He arced his razor in a smooth crescent above and behind Robert's ear. The downstroke scrape flourished into a fast, thrilling swoop down his neck.

"I feel like my life is in your hands," Robert said.

"It is," Lloyd said.

"I don't know if I like that." Robert hated the nervous laugh in his own voice. "I only started back to barbers about two months ago. Before that it was nearly five years, being a hippie and all I had hair down below my shoulders. Then something, nothing really, happened, and this guy, this judge, made me cut it. When I was a kid, barber shops always gave me a headache."

"So. Just a little scrape with the law," Lloyd, W. C. Fields, said. He swooped his razor over and around Robert's other ear.

"I never liked anybody fussing over me that much. Besides, this barber shop my old man took me to had pin-up pictures of really big girls and I wasn't a very big boy. I mean now it wouldn't matter."

"The bigger the better, huh?" Lloyd rinsed his razor. He knew enough to humor his customers ambiguously. He met all kinds at the corner of 18th and Castro. "Never kid a kidder," he said.

"I kid you not," Robert said.

For years Robert had been titanic cruising among icebergs of females in his hometown. At the age of four, innocent of all need for cover, in the driveway between their homes, he had compared himself to the lower half of a giggling little Judy Esterbank. One month later, a modern doctor, new to small-town practice, had sold his mother an introductory twofer on the latest big-city hygiene and had wheeled him through white double doors to pull out his tonsils and slice off his foreskin.

He never really trusted her ever again.

At the age of ten, playing Lewis and Clark, he had tripped over a tent peg catching the strapless halter of twelve-year-old Joyce Gillette. One flawless white breast popped pert and eager into view. He stared and she smiled. He stepped forward and she stepped back tucking herself away as neatly as she packed her camping equipment. He stared at the veil of her halter. She stepped to him and cupped his groin in her hand. It felt good. "I ought to kill you," she had said. But her hand felt warm through his jeans. Three years later she kissed him there. Repeatedly. Up and down.

"Indeed I do love the little ladies," Robert said to Lloyd. Screw Judy and screw Joyce. He hated himself for continuing the elaborate lie he had intended to leave back in the Midwest.

"And that's why you moved to San Francisco." Lloyd dusted Robert's neck with clouds of talcum. "That's why everybody moves to San Francisco. They say it's the weather. They say it's the restaurants. But it's the sex that brings them. San Francisco's the place where when you go there you get laid."

"I'm interested in that Coke," Robert said. Brown air bubbles rose in slow chains up through the mocha cola. "It's second-hand and half-dead," Lloyd said. He handed Robert the bottle. "Just wipe the cooties off the top."

Robert toasted Bach and Liszt. He wished Lloyd's magazines were better. Even a *National Geographic* with naked natives would help him swallow the dying Coke and the whole afternoon a lot easier. "You know," Robert said to distract his train of thought, "that a '57 Chevy is the best car GM ever put out. That's why I got it new. That's why I still drive it."

"That a fact," Lloyd said. He unwrapped Robert's neck, took two swipes with the talcum brush, and flapped the green-striped cloth with a whipcrack. "Being's we're finished, let me show you something."

Robert remained seated in Lloyd's chair. Now maybe he would find what it was that had caused him to pull the Chevy to the curb, forget his meter, and endure a haircut and a Coca-Cola he had not desired. Lloyd disappeared into the piano repair room. Two single swipes zithered across a dusty piano harp behind the Fifties' floral-print curtain.

Robert waited for Lloyd as he had waited beside his mother's hospital bed. Her name was Isabel and his father always kidded her, saying like it was the first time, "Is a bell necessary on a bicycle? Is a bell necessary at all?" And she always laughed even though she hated him making fun of her.

For months she had lain wasting away with cancer in the depths of white sheets. He looked down at her remembering how all through his youth she had sized him up and encouraged him saying, "At least you're tall."

She warned him that no girl likes a short man. "Short men," she had said, "are impossible to deal with." She should have known. Robert's father was short. But Robert had felt tall, standing next to her shrinking form. For an hour at the beginning of her last week, he had stood by her bed with the plastic tube of the intravenous fluid pinched tight between his thumb and forefinger. Mercy or no mercy, he had hoped to kill her, but his hand had cramped even before the nurse almost caught him.

In Lloyd's piano room a large cardboard box grated heavily across the gritty floor. Robert heard Lloyd say, "Ah, there it is."

"I suppose they do," Robert called to Lloyd who was dragging the huge box into the shop itself.

"You suppose who does what?" Lloyd panted with the exertion, but his face was triumphant.

"I suppose they do put out their own kids' eyes." Robert had read more than he even wanted hanging out in libraries, slicing pages out of magazines. "There's all those operas about Greek plays where the kids get turned into mincemeat. Some parents kill their young. Maybe they're no more cruel than nature is cruel. People wouldn't pay good money to go see that sort of thing if they weren't naturally interested."

Lloyd began to dig into his box. "Now, don't you laugh at me," Lloyd said. He was matter-of-fact. "I have these treasures I don't share with everyone."

"I understand," Robert said. But he did not understand as much as he thought he did, and he was about to understand a whole lot more.

The box was neatly packed with magazines, picture albums, and loose photos of the kind most adult men keep to themselves. At first glance, Robert Place knew, almost faster in his groin than his head, what kind of illustrations these were. They were the kind Robert had tried all his life to avoid, but could not. They were the kind who called to him, from the flat pages of magazines, to breathe into them his life. They were seductive, attractive, flowers of evil. They were, somehow, an occasion of sin. They were young men more stripped than dressed who posed as sailors and athletes and construction workers. They were the kind of pictures of men Robert had sliced from certain physique pictorials in St. Louis bookstores to take home to lay with him on his bed, until he blacked out, saying, "Whoever you are, I want to spend eternity with you," waking up as if coming to, jumping from his bed, furiously destroying the evidence of his love for this kind of thing. He would crush the sticky pictures into tiny paper balls and burn them and flush their ashes down the toilet. They were bad boys and worse men and he was not one of them,

"Take a look at this," Lloyd said. He offered a magazine to Robert.

"Very nice," Robert said. He fanned the pages from the back cover forward and made bits and pieces of bodies flip in crazy motion from the last page to the first. Couples began in orgasm and ended in foreplay.

"You know," Lloyd said, "when it comes right down to it, your Chevy and my pianos show up for what they aren't." He scooped up a stack of magazines.

"What do you mean?" Robert asked.

"It's a lie what everyone says. That there's other things in life besides sex and money. Your car and my pianos aren't a hill of beans when it comes to getting laid. Down there at that intersection it's all bodies and sex. You could have the hottest car in town, and I could have the grandest grand piano, but unless you have a face and a body, which you at your age certainly do, and unless I have some extra cash, which at my age I have a little, no one's going to touch us."

Robert studied Lloyd's pinched face. "What about love?"

"What's love got to do with it?"

"Hell if I know," Robert said. "I don't even care. I never loved anybody and nobody ever loved me. I'm not even looking for love. I got no expectations except of the worst kind."

"I'm a realist," Lloyd said. "The only thing to be in life is twenty-one. Forever. After that, it's all hustlers. Everyone who comes through my door is selling something. Don't ever grow old."

"I've always looked young for my age," Robert said.

"So you don't know yet what I'm talking about."

"Yes I do."

"The devil you say!"

Lloyd thrust a dozen magazines named *Young Adonis* and *Mars* and *Physique Pictorial* at Robert who immediately judged their covers. They made him covetous. He wanted three or four of the magazines, contents sight unseen.

"I'd really like one of these," he said, holding a copy of *Tomorrow's Man*.

"Money can't buy them. Some of these I've had for fifteen or sixteen years. When I page through them, it's like with dear friends. When I'm eighty, they'll still be the same age, the same dear friends, and I'll still have them and they'll be a comfort."

"They're a comfort right now," Robert said. As he paged the magazines, he felt his spirit rise inside him. He was in the room but he was not part of the room. He sat between the mirrors. The men in the magazines sucked his very essence into themselves, coming alive to him, whispering secret words he could not make out. He gasped for breath like a man being dragged down a drain.

Lloyd pulled the yellow shade down over the glass door. Two years before he had painted in orange Day-Glo the words SORRY CLOSED on the shade, and the paint had not faded at all. He had some rising hope that his strange customer was hinting, the way first-timers so often hint, that he wanted to become dear friends with him. Robert, in fact, sat helpless in Lloyd's barber chair. He made small gurgling noises as he turned the pages. Back in Canterbury, he had only imagined what he would find out west. But he had not found it; it had found him. His hand clutched his throat as his breath finally, totally, slid out of him. He suddenly saw how life was going to be with him. Really be with him. Really in control of him. The thought took root like mandrake in his heart. He had never considered until that minute that everything he was about, had always been about, had masked the slow flowering fact that he was not different from all those men and boys cruising arm in arm in the street below. The same wild lemming call that had summoned them from everywhere had summoned him from the south-midlands to them, to this city, to this very intersection, to this catbird seat in Lloyd's Barber Shop looking down on something that was totally new to him, but also totally known.

He was not sure he liked the convergence.

What the fuck was Rainbow County?

The summer before, when he had fled south on a trial-run from Canterbury to St. Louis, Cleo Walker, with her brilly bush of flaming red hair, had walked right up and taken control of him. She had spied him sitting at a small table in an outdoor cafe in Gaslight Square and after she had scooped him up, she stripped him down in her sunplashed studio on Delmar Avenue near Forest Park. He had not felt awkward standing nude before her. For years, naked exposure had been his urge, so he had slipped, a true exhibitionist, easy and erect from his clothes. Without meaning his words, he apologized for his thing, his *thing*, standing at attention. Cleo refused to dignify his apology with the benefit of a real reply, so he had stepped toward her, reaching for her breasts. That was the script, wasn't it? But Cleo had refused his advance for reasons he could not fathom. Wasn't painting only a high-toned excuse for getting naked and looking at nudes?

"I want," he stammered low, "I want...I want...."

"Don't reach for something," Cleo said, "you don't know you want."

"What do you mean?" he asked.

"You're a virgin, aren't you?"

He said nothing.

"I'm not a virgin," she said. "So I know things."

"You mean it shows?" he said.

"You're a book with no pages," she said.

"I like the way you talk."

"Fuck!" Cleo said the word he had never heard a woman say. "You have an excellent body and an interesting face. You have a sexual energy I don't care to release. I only want to paint you."

He was crestfallen. "You can see faces like mine hanging in the post office."

She felt a sudden sorrow for him. "Look, Roberto, caro Roberto, there's nothing wrong with you. I'm a painter. I want to paint you. I don't want to have sex with you."

Yet, in Cleo's studio, he stood insistent, his pouting mouth silent, his lower part as straight and to the point as a declarative sentence. "I'm sorry," he apologized again, this time half-meaning it. "It doesn't have anything to do with you."

"I didn't think so," she said.

"This always happens when I take off my clothes, or think about taking off my clothes."

"It's no big deal," Cleo said. "I'm a painter. I look at you. I don't see your precious dick. I see light. I see shadow."

"Light and shadow," Robert said. He tried to concentrate on a pile of littered art magazines; but even they, so far across the studio, could not slow the excited flow of his blood. He had never shown himself naked to anyone, and he was embarrassed at how much he liked it.

Cleo ignored his excitement. She poured him a small glass of blood-red wine, and squeezed white and tan and browns across her glass palette. "I'm in my sepia period," she laughed. "I'm glad I'm no devotee of Freud, who I wish had been otherwise employed. Who said that?"

"Mrs. Freud?"

"Lean against the wall, Robert. Relax. Move your head to the left. Fine. Hold it. Just relax. I'm brushing in your basic line today. Later on I'll work in the tension."

He had leaned motionless against the doorway and then, finally, leaned against her for the next two months, because, one rainy August afternoon, when she had lost the light, and poured them both some more wine, she had said, "When I told you I didn't want to have sex with you, you silly goose, I didn't mean I didn't want to fuck you. At least once."

Go figure, he thought.

Their love-making confused him. All love-making confused him.

"Was I okay?" he asked. He had not been able to keep from asking that question even he knew was ridiculous.

"Who were you thinking about?" Cleo asked.

"You," he said.

"Lying bastard!"

He could have cheerfully killed her. She had him pegged. She polarized him the way all women did. She was all women. He knew he was supposed to desire them, but he had no feeling for why. They filled him with an empty want they could not slake. They took his coloration and line the way Cleo's sidelong look, her brush-hand resting on her mahlstick, had day-by-day transferred his face from his head to her canvas. He was the primitive and she was the sorceress capturing his spirit. Transfixed, he could not move from the pose into which she had enchanted him. His naked body trembled visibly.

"Get it together," Cleo had said. "Take a break."

She handed him a book of prints and text. Absently he leafed through page after page of what seemed to be the *Life and Hard Times of Andrew Wyeth*. Not one of the reproductions tempted him to pull his single-edge razor blade from his wallet and start slicing.

"That's why I like to paint you," Cleo said.

"Why?"

"Your face hides nothing. You're bored. You're light years away. From here. From me. From everybody."

"I don't care for cartooning." He tossed the Wyeth book to the floor and resumed his pose.

Cleo strode across the studio and retrieved the book. "Wyeth isn't exactly Norman Rockwell," she said.

"Same school." Robert hated the nasty sound in his voice, but he didn't care.

"What would you know about art anyway," Cleo said. "It's about order. You're all chaos."

"Is that so? I know plenty. I've read articles."

"So don't throw Wyeth down. Read it," Cleo said. She shoved the book hard against his naked belly. "And you better not tear a goddam page out of it."

"I confess my secrets and you refuse to forgive me?"

"Fuck you and your sins." She said it flatly and marched back to her life-size canvas. "Tilt your head to the left."

Robert obeyed. The Wyeth book hung in his right hand. It felt cool against his thigh. Holding his pose, he raised it and fanned once more through the pages. Print after print of paint-brushed faces peopled Wyeth's decaying afternoons. One painting, an immense field, contained a solitary male figure. Everything was brown and dead and spun out of sorrow. Wyeth had painted it the winter of his own father's death. The editor's note explained the painting as an exorcism of sadness. Robert stirred slightly from his pose. He caught the sense of the painting, but he could hardly see the face of the man in the field. Somehow Wyeth had lost his own face along with the lost face of his father. The canvas was full of nothing so much as his own grief.

Deep inside Robert that thin tensile strand of generations snapped. In a moment of his own infinite sadness he realized that he too had lost the face of his father. In the stead of the man who pretended to sire him, and had really abused him, stood only shadow images and half-remembered sounds of the sweet times: the wet-lipped kiss from that unshaved face in the dark over his bed. It was all reduced to that: the memory of his father, home from the late shift, leaning over to kiss him goodnight. As if he were again half-asleep in his little boy's sleep, Robert could feel his father's ghostly kiss on his face. He could not forget his father's love, but he could not forgive that one night of his father's drunkenness.

Robert realized that he had been losing everything despite his desperate collecting of folders of stolen clippings and magazines purloined from under the eyes of cheery dental receptionists. In the glory days of the large magazines, he had tried to save the images of the week by swallowing up the sleeves of his school jacket whole issues of *Look* and *Life*. Finally, when he had been caught with his single-edge razor blade in the Green County Public Library, his mother had said, "I hope you're satisfied. You now owe me a hundred dollars more." Her face looked screwed with pain that he thought was no more than her embarrassment at his conviction. "Bobby, Bobby, Bobby. What do you expect me to live on? When will you ever grow up and settle down?" Six months later, she was dead and he had fled to San Francisco. He was fed up to his eyeballs with personal relationships. He had a need for a city of strangers.

Lloyd, like most barbers, could hold a one-sided conversation with a corpse and was finishing up his long monologue when Robert remembered where he was. "Old Sammy Davis, Jr.," Lloyd said, "only got one of his eyes put out. That's because his folks wanted him to dance. Be kind of hard to poke out both your eyes and dance too. Might fall off the stage. But before long, you'll see, someone'll show up and try it big as life on network TV." He handed Robert another magazine.

"And they'll be tapping out something in code, those dancers will." Robert took the magazine and laid his line on Lloyd. "That blind guy you say'll be dancing on CBS will be tapping out in code something everybody ought to hear. Something like SOS." Robert considered his words. "Just like SOS," he repeated, and he wanted to cry out, not for help, but for something else, "because we're all in danger and we have to save our souls."

"That a fact," Lloyd said. He passed a perplexed look up through his thick glasses. Should he make his move? Was this guy wanting it, or was he all talk and no action? Were the magazines, dragged out to arouse him, missing their mark?

"But not everyone will understand it." Robert slowly turned the pages of the last magazine.

"Maybe you shouldn't bother trying to understand what you do. Just do it," Lloyd insinuated.

Robert looked up straight into Lloyd's eyes through his thick glasses. "I have a gun," he announced. "A .22 caliber handgun."

"You don't say." Lloyd backed off.

"Does that make you scared of me?"

"Do you have it on you?"

"No."

"Then you don't scare me. Your gun scares me. I don't like guns."

"Sometimes you have to scare people. Terror's the only thing they respect. If you scare them, you get their undivided attention."

"Whyn't you finish up," Lloyd was changing the subject, "reading that magazine."

"Sure," Robert said. "So far I like it fine. It's your best one yet."

Lloyd took a last few snips here and there around Robert's ears, then tried to gentle him down, and sidle on in, seductively rubbing Robert's neck with an electric massager. He was surprised to find very little tension in Robert's neck and shoulders. "You're a cool customer," he said, "as cool as a cucumber."

Suddenly, Robert sat bolt upright in Lloyd's barber chair. He held it in his hands: a black-and-white photograph on an unnumbered magazine page. It was the picture he had spent his life looking for: magazines in one hand, razor blade in the other. The photo was of a man seated alone. On either side of the photo were separate single shots of athletic women. The one on the left held a golf club. She was set to putt and her breasts hung down between her stiffened arms. The naked woman on the right held a jaunty tennis racquet. But it was the naked athlete in the middle photo who mesmerized him as much as if he'd found a snapshot of his real father, the original missing person, whom he had never seen.

He was seated, stretched slightly back straddling a locker-room bench. He was a little older than Robert, and bigger, very blond, with a fully developed chest over his washboard abdomen. His thick wrists connected his athlete's hands to his powerful arms. He wore football pads across his broad shoulders, and a football helmet, and, between his casually spread legs, he was erect. His eyes looked directly from the helmet into the camera and directly out of the page into Robert's face. The face-guard on the helmet covered his mouth. No New Testament word of mercy could spring from those Old Testament lips that Robert knew were set, mean and hard and without mercy. He looked directly out at Robert. He was erect and Robert knew he faced the powerful, inevitable Face of God.

"I must," he said to Lloyd, "have this." He rose out of the barber chair. "Ask any amount, anything. Only let me buy this from you."

Lloyd thought to press the trade for sex, but the young man seemed too volatile. Besides, a quick flash of looking down the barrel of a handgun made him think better of it. "That one you can have," he said.

"I can't just take it. I learned my lesson about that the hard way."

"Then trade me something, anything," Lloyd said. "I won't take your money." He stared into Robert's ecstatic wild eyes and suddenly, more than he wanted him, he wanted him very much gone.

"I don't have anything," Robert said.

Lloyd laughed nervously at him. "Everybody's got something."

Robert mentally searched his car. He had his clothes. He had the loaded handgun. "Nothing," he said.

In the room, he seemed volatile.

In the mirrors, he looked vulnerable.

Lloyd, fighting his rising lust, chided himself for being a cautious old fool. He threw risk against the wind. The boy was right. Danger was aphrodisiac. He put his hand on Robert's knee and slowly smoothed his palm up the inside of his thigh.

"Not that!" Robert watched the hand slowly advance up his leg like a giant spider. "Not that!" Robert said.

Lloyd's heart jumped with a rush of adrenaline. "Then

what?" Lloyd stood straight up. "You said I could have anything for the picture."

"Not that. Not here. Not now. Not you."

"See what I told you about your car and my pianos?" Lloyd worked the only logic he knew in situations like this. "What if I pay you?"

"For what?"

He thought to say for sex, but he said, "To take the picture. I'll give you money to take the picture," Lloyd said, "and then you can leave."

"Don't go inverting everything."

Invert? Invert. Lloyd had psychology books from twenty years before when *invert* meant only one thing.

"Then take the picture for godsake and get a move on."

"I told you, man! I can't take it for nothing."

"As far as I'm concerned, you can," Lloyd said. "This is getting old. I want to close up shop."

"Wait," Robert said. "I got it." He pulled out his wallet and reached inside. He handed the folded-up paper to Lloyd.

"What's this?" Lloyd asked. "The number of your Swiss bank account?"

"No, you asshole," Robert said. "It's the combination to my gym locker."

"I'll bet."

"Go on. Read it!"

Lloyd unfolded the smudged slip of paper. "I need my reading glasses."

Robert stared down at the picture of the blond athlete, but he barked his order at Lloyd, "Read it."

Lloyd hooked his half-lens bifocals over his ears and read the word "Postmark."

"That's the title," Robert said. "It's a poem. A short poem."

"Good," Lloyd said. "Short and sweet." The afternoon

had not gone the seductive way he had hoped and he regretted missing lunch as much as he missed lunching on Robert. "I have low blood sugar."

"Read it, please. No one else has ever seen it. I wrote it on my way out here. To send back home. To everyone back home."

"'Postmark,'" Lloyd read. "'Dear God: You created me, then you hated me....Dear Folks: You conceived me, then deceived me....Dear Teacher: You taught me, then you fought me....Dear Boss: You hired me, then you fired me....Dear Lover: You painted me, then you tainted me....Dear Death: You embraced me, then erased me.'"

"Well?" Robert asked.

"It's not...bad."

"Not bad?"

"It's pretty good."

"You think so?"

"Yeah," Lloyd said. "I like it like really a whole lot."

"Good," Robert said. "We just made a trade. My poem for your photograph. Strange, isn't it? I came in here not knowing why I came in here. I didn't want a haircut and you cut my hair. I got a parking ticket. You handed me a magazine and I found a picture of the face that's always been in the back of my head."

"What's that?" Lloyd said.

"Never you mind. You wouldn't understand."

"That's three bucks for the trim," Lloyd said.

"Here's four," Robert said. "Keep the change."

"Don't insult me," Lloyd said. "You never tip the owner."

"I do."

"Suit yourself."

"I'm leaving," Robert said. "It's been real."

Lloyd slipped full into his W. C. Fields routine. "Never give a sucker an even break. Here's your hat. What's your hurry? Don't let the door hit you on your way out."

"You calling me a sucker?"

"No," Lloyd said. "Take it easy. Where you headed?"

"To the beach," Robert said. "Land's end at Land's End." He walked to Lloyd's cash register counter.

"It's been a slow day moneywise," Lloyd said nervously.

"Hasn't exactly been a stampede, I'd say." Robert pulled the single-edge razor blade from his wallet and expertly sliced the magazine page so that the athletic girls disappeared, leaving only the 5x7 of the handsome football player. "Tonight's the full moon and the summer solstice. I've never seen the Pacific. I'm taking this picture and I'm going to watch the sunset and the moonrise."

"You want maybe instead to use my john?" Lloyd slipped the four bills directly into his white nylon pocket.

"What for?"

"What all little boys use it for when they've stolen daddy's dirty magazines."

"I never did anything like that."

"No one ever does, according to them, when it's always the thing they do most," Lloyd said. "Do you have anyplace to stay for the night?"

"What's it to you?"

"Nothing." Lloyd backed off. He slept single in a double bed. "It's nothing to me."

"I'm going to the ocean. I'll roll up my jeans and I'll walk in the surf and I'll listen."

"To what?

Robert held up the photograph. "To him," he said.

"To him?"

"To him. I'm old enough to see if he'll ever speak to me."

Lloyd wanted to roll his strained eyes back in his head. All these people, all these immigrants to San Francisco were getting stranger than strange. "So," he said. "What if he doesn't speak to you."

"He'll speak to me alright."

"But what if he doesn't?"

"Either way it makes no difference since he never has anyway."

"So if it doesn't make any difference, why you so hot to go?"

"Because that picture is the Face of God."

Lloyd stopped W. C. Fields from cackling: "The Face of God. You don't say." He didn't say it; instead he said: "You got to be kidding."

"He'll tell me, if he wants to, everything I need to know."

"What's that?"

"Ways to keep me out of hell. Ways to get me into heaven."

"What ways?"

"Ways you could sell like Salvation Coupons the night before Judgment Day. Ways those men and boys down in the street probably know. Old ways. Ancient ways. Ways so secret only a few men, and maybe a few women, know them. But there's more of them out here that know than back home, or anywhere else ever before in one place on this whole earth, right here, I figure, in your Rainbow County. They know the ways. I know they know the ways."

"You mean sex," Lloyd said.

"Sex?" Robert said. "Sure, why not? Sex must be one of the saving ways, but the way has to be right. Just right. Or else sex is just like everyone says, the way to damnation." He bored his stare hard through Lloyd's thick glasses. "And guess what else?"

Lloyd guessed what else was he had himself another one of those religious sex nuts trying to break out of his shell. He wanted to take a step back, but he was too proud to show Robert any fear; he remembered Robert bragging that terror was the only thing most people respected once it got their attention.

"Besides sex," Robert said, "guess what else."

"I can't guess."

"Damage."

"Damage?"

"Just a little damage."

"Why damage?" Lloyd said. "What damage? What to? Who to?"

"To you," Robert said. "To me. To everybody."

"What kind of damage?"

"Big damages," Robert said, "and little damages."

"I could call the police."

"By the time they got here, my razor blade could cut your face. I could make you blind so you could go on TV. By the time they got here, I could cut my throat. Slice right through my jugular. None of it would make any difference to anybody but you. I don't care. I might die or I might go to jail, but you'd still be blind, trying to cut hair and play your pianos."

"I get the picture," Lloyd said.

"No," Robert said. "I got the picture." He held the photograph up and out at arm's length. "He'll tell me what to do. In my life I know life does damage to you." He looked down at the swarming men in the street. He had his looks, he had his car, he had his gun. "So I figure I might as well inflict a little of the damage myself."

"I never quite thought of life that way."

"Well, you sure are the slow one. Everybody else thinks so. Doesn't that explain the evil that people do to themselves, smoking and drinking and whoring and taking drugs and driving fast and fighting and killing and raping and molesting, because that's the only way they can make the world that damages them everyday make any sense is if they do some of the damage themselves. Everybody but a fool knows when you can't beat it, you join it."

"You expect him, the guy in the picture..."

"God."

"...God...to speak to you and tell you what to do?"

"I expect he'll tell me if I should do any damage for him and if I should, to who. Maybe to you. Maybe to me. Maybe to anybody he tells me to. Nobody ever went to hell for that." Robert smiled and took a step forward. "Take it easy, Lloyd. Relax."

Lloyd pasted a smile on his face but his heart was racing.

"See what I mean about a little scare getting your attention?" Robert broke into guffaws of snorting laughter.

"You were putting me on?"

"I bet I had you so scared you had a bone on."

"You were putting me on!"

"If you think so, Lloyd, ol' buddy! You should've seen your face, a hundred times over, scared sure as hell, curving off in those mirrors, which, by the way, could stand a bit of washing. Shoot, I was just kidding you, wasn't I? 'Don't kid a kidder,' you told me, but I did and you took it hook, line, and sinker. You wait awhile and you'll get to know I got a real killer sense of humor."

"Never mention killing."

"Hey!" Robert said. "That's a figure of speech. Nothing is what it seems. It's all mirrors. One thing's always meaning some other thing besides what a person thinks it means. You know that, being a barber, standing between your mirrors in all those parallel universes. I'm not dumb, you know. I've spent most of my life in recent years reading all kinds of the strangest things so the inside of my head's like an encyclopedia. My second-cousin, Ollie Thomas, who's madam librarian back home told me so."

"Perhaps you have," Lloyd said, "low blood sugar. I myself often experience strange mood swings."

"Naw. My blood's fine and my sugar's better." Robert winked the way his father always winked. "If you catch my drift."

"Sounds like," Lloyd pulled his ear, charading, working Robert toward the door, "like we've circled back to sex."

"Have you noticed that too? How everything sooner or later always comes back around to sex?"

"You are sure going to have a good time down there on 18th and Castro," Lloyd said. "That intersection is laying on its back with its legs in the air just waiting for you."

"I ain't done it." Robert's face reddened with anger. "I told you I ain't done it! I ain't never done it when it was my will. But when I'm good and ready, I just might, and I just might be the best at it."

Something, some *thing*, in the room ground suddenly to a halt between them.

"What?"

It could only be one thing. Lloyd wished he'd carried a little hand fan, something petite and operatic from the eighteenth century, to hide the smirk on his lips.

"I ain't done it. Not yet."

"Done what?" Lloyd was intent on forcing Robert to say it. I love it, Lloyd thought, all this talk and no action has been the braggadocio of a male virgin with very blue balls. "Done what?"

"You're going to make me say it, aren't you?"

"Robert, I bet no one could ever make you do anything."

"My mother always said that." Robert's eyes kind of crossed in his head.

"You haven't done what?"

"I haven't had sex. Okay? So laugh."

"And risk another wrinkle? Never. My God, as it is, look at my face. If wrinkles hurt, I'd be screaming."

"I'm serious, goddam it. I haven't had sex. Not really. Not ever. Not unless you count the time I didn't want to,

and the time I thought I had to, but I never count those
two times and I never talk about them."

"Some experiences are too painful to recall," Lloyd
said, "but I can't recall any."

"Shut the judas-priest up. I'm not dumb. I can do
sex. I know what goes on out there on those streets. I
told you I've read and forgot more stuff than you ever
even thought of." He held up the picture of the blond
athlete. "I know what he's going to tell me, but I want to
hear it from his own lips, me lying in the dunes at twilight feeling the warm breeze from the ocean."

"This is summer in Northern California," Lloyd said.
"What warm breeze? You'll die of exposure."

"He'll tell me. And they'll tell me."

"Who?"

"The fellows down there in that intersection. One at
a time. And I'll listen. One secret at a time. That's how
to make sense of it. One after another of the men who
know the secret ways. One after the other. They'll all
whisper to me and when I've heard them all, I'll know
all about life and damage and death and the ways to
stay out of hell."

"Are you sure, really sure, that's what he wants?"

"I don't know what he wants. That's why I'm taking
his face with me to the beach. So maybe he will talk to
me first the way the others will talk to me later."

"Maybe you should forget him and them and figure
out what you want."

"I just want one SOB and one SOS one right after
the other. I want some of the pleasure of all of the danger if I'm going to suffer the damage anyway."

"You're talking crazy," Lloyd said. "You're going to fit
right in with all the fruits and flakes. You're a nut."

"No, I ain't," Robert Place said, "but so what if I am?"
He held up the picture like a holy icon. "Only he can tell
me."

"Sure," Lloyd said, "you've got that pornographic picture."

"It's the Face of God!"

"I've seen London," Lloyd, W. C. Fields, said, "and I've seen France. I've seen the queen in her underpants."

"Are you making fun of me?" Robert said.

"I wouldn't dare make fun of you," Lloyd said. "My blood sugar's too low to keep this up. My prescription for you is to get laid twice before bedtime, and don't call me in the morning."

"What does all that mean? Everything means something."

"It means," Lloyd said, "you've come to the right place. It means, Welcome to San Francisco. Welcome to Rainbow County."

"That's better," Robert Place said. "I like that attitude much better."

"Have you ever thought," Lloyd said, raising his SORRY CLOSED shade and opening the door, "about maybe swallowing something you can buy on the street to lay yourself back some, about letting your hair grow long again?"

"Why, Lloyd," Robert said, halfway down to the first landing, "You surprise me. I would never have figured you to be one to turn away business. I'm going out and I'm staying out..."

"You're coming out."

"...until he talks to me. So you'll see me again. A real regular. Plan on it. I intend to show your Rainbow County a thing or two. I intend to stay a close-cropped soldier until all of them down there in that intersection talk to me, and you're going to keep me ready for him and for them, groomed like I just stepped out of a bandbox."

The Real Cowboy

Looking into a cowboy fella's face
man-to-man, you can read him complete:
how hard his Levi-thighs feel;
how his crotch rides in rough-out chaps;
how his salt-sweat gloves taste
when he bites the leather fuckfinger
in his strong white teeth
to pull the glove off his hand;
how rough his hands must feel,
because every one of those cowboy faces
has been real familiar with rope,
and quick with knots,
since he was a kid
in muddy boots with undershot heels;
what he smokes, chews, snorts, drinks;
how his slightly bowed legs
stance for a piss in a dusty corral;
what kind of big-dicked livestock
he raises for stud;
how much he knows firsthand
about fist-and-arm's length
insemination,
about castration of big bull nuts
and stallion balls,
about branding irons and guns and
traps and trucks;
what his armpits, and rosewatered hair,
smell like, before, and after,

his bunkhouse hosedown;
how his feet set in his
dirty cowboy boots;
how cut, or *uncut*,
shows in the squint and look
of his cowboy's eye,
the devil with blue eyes
and blue jeans,
just sizing you up, rodeo-style,
mano-a-mano. Whoopy-tee-yi-yo!

North of San Francisco:
Male Rituals, Initiation,
Discipline, and Transcendence.
As in *Casablanca*, Sooner or Later
Everyone Comes to...

S&M RANCH

Foreman Dogg Katz was a young fox with a goatee, so Peter Eton-Cox made a phone call to S&M Ranch. Torture, he figured, is a relative pleasure. Some tortures please the tortured. Some tortures please the torturer. Only in San Francisco, Peter thought, are physical values consensually inverted. In the Midwest, pleasure causes religious guilt and pain. In California, pain is as sweet as the pleasure of tonguing on a loose tooth. Some pain hurts so good you just can't stop.

Such strange thoughts swam through his head as he drove north from the City across the Golden Gate Bridge toward Sonoma County. Peter had a good hour's drive to ponder why men like him preferred a place like S&M Ranch.

Fuck. Three topics about which people rally and march and lose their cool are: religion, politics, and corporal punishment. Odd. People argue religion and politics back and forth. Punishment by comparison was so taboo, that good old corporal punishment was rejected almost without argument or debate. Sometimes Peter felt like a voice crying in the wilderness. Corporal punishment was out of fashion with the social consciousness that coddles offenders. He wished America would return to corporal punishment: flogging, heavy bondage in solitary confinement, behavior modification, electroshock clamps on balls and dicks and tits and tongues, hanging by the wrists, branding, punitive tattooing, painful and invasive medical procedures involving sutures and catheters and probes and enormous enemas administered by inexperienced health care workers who would benefit from the chance to practice.

Delaware, Peter had noted in a newspaper clipping, had reinstated the whipping post for teenage delinquents. A young guy whipped by a burly guard in the semi-public setting of a county jail courtyard learns a lesson on his stripped back that no amount of probation or juvenile-hall time could ever teach. And he'd learn it without being corrupted by spending ninety days with worse bad boys who'd tutor him into the truly finer points of delinquency. In addition, a twenty-minute flogging is cheaper for the taxpayers who then do not have to support the juvenile delinquent for the term of his sentence. Peter liked the idea of swift and defined justice meted out in corporal punishment to the men and boys convicted of nonviolent crimes like bouncing bad checks, or offending the public decency, or hitchhiking.

For the violent criminal, Peter had other thoughts. Instead of executions that waste a convict's healthy body, he favored harvesting a criminal's body parts for transplants to those in need. Gary Gilmore, condemned to death in Utah, should not have been strapped into a wooden chair, hooded, and executed—wasted, literally—by rifle fire. Gary Gilmore should have been slowly harvested. First his eyes, then his inner ear mechanism, his kidneys and lungs one at a time, his skin, and finally his heart.

Once society fully adjusts to the morality of transplants, people must adjust to the desirability of Ultimate

Harvest as a legitimate corporal punishment where the entire body of the criminal pays off his debt to society.

The men at S&M Ranch, led by Whipmaster Dogg Katz, had left San Francisco with the cloning of the Castro. They were advance guard of the exodus north where same-as/same-as men could still pass as unlabeled men among the rough-and-tumble redneck straight breeders in their boot jeans, down vests, CAT caps, and 4WD trucks. The brotherhood at S&M Ranch had retreated away from the incestuous urbanity of City slickers whose horizon was no higher than the skyline of the Castro. They had returned to live among the kind of men who had made them prefer men in the first place. They had by choice abandoned the Castro to the clonies, the dronies, and the phonies who dressed and acted in ways you hoped you'd never see men dress and act.

With ritualistic intent, the men of S&M Ranch abandoned the City to live lives dedicated almost monastically to simple manly discipline—defined by absolute corporal punishment—in the northwoods of Sonoma County. Even the Elite Corps of "The 15" chose their S&M Weekend Encampments not far from the secret preserves of S&M Ranch where corporal punishment and discipline were a way of life.

When Peter called the Ranch, Dogg Katz told him to high-tail it up Highway 101 past Sausalito and on up through fastidious Marin County to laid-back Sonoma County. Dogg had two good-looking ranch hands—code-named "Rip" and "Strip"—and the largest toy collection in California. The working barns, noisy with cattle and sheep dogs, were fully equipped: hoists, pulleys, crosses, woodsheds, burial pits, hog pens, fence posts, wooden spools coiled with barbed wire, harness sheds with metal dockers to install rubber-rings for slow castration, and a four-holer outhouse set over a bondage board sunk so

deep in the cool Sonoma clay that a man tied down underneath that brick shithouse looked up spreadeagle at
a new understanding of gravity's drop, splat, and plop.
The three S&M cowboys, Dogg Katz particularly, offered
their services through the classified ads in various queer
papers. Their best encounters, they found, came to them
by word-of-mouth. Dogg had invited Peter for free.

The afternoon was bright with the spring light that
makes Sonoma County look like Ireland when the Cowboys met Peter at the top of the road leading back to
S&M Ranch. Rip and Strip and Dogg were strong, weathered, handsome workingmen in their early thirties. Their
bodies were as good as their heads. They ran on instinct
about what, and how much, and how heavy, were the
painful tortures and disciplines they could lay out on an
urban man driving to the county in need of corporal
punishment. With Peter, they had no particular script.
Even Peter had no idea where the afternoon at S&M
Ranch might take the four of them. They had all played
together before. Hitting and switch-hitting. Even Dogg
Katz, the famous top, balanced himself regularly with
heavy corporal punishment delivered by itinerant men
passing through. Peter was open to anything that felt
good with these men.

Dogg offered a joint they smoked in the sun before
heading up, north of the main ranch house, past one of
the corrals where a naked bear of a chunky man lay tied
down spreadeagle, face up, dick up, in the dirt. A mestizo Mexican man, cleaning his own toe nails with a buck
knife, sat vigil off to the side on a wooden box that had
once been Peter's prison for three days. Peter remembered the mestizo well. Along the trail, a sling hung like
an ominous sexual hammock between four large pine
trees. They walked past several small outbuildings, one
of which Peter recognized from an underground video
called *Woodshed Whipping*. Peter smiled when they

crossed past the Hanging Tree where, several weekends before, he had seen a slender naked man sitting astraddle a horse. His hands were tied behind his back. His dick stood up a full attention taller than the saddle horn. A noose was knotted tight around his neck. His eyes were stoned with sexual fear. Another rope was wrapped tight around his chest and back and secured under his sweating armpits to sustain most of his weight when the posse of five men, gathered around his horse, slapped the gelding into a sudden gallop that jerked the naked and bound man into a terrifying swing through the cool air. The noose pulled at his throat enough to make his tongue swell out and his wild eyes bulge in his young unshaven face. Peter noticed the cigar butts and cigaret butts still lying on the ground where the group of men had stood and smoked while the rustler hung dangling and twirling, with his dick at full throbbing hardon, for their amusement, until they all came and someone sucked the hanging cowboy off and cut him, sobbing, down.

The three Cowboys led Peter into their Whipping Stall. He pulled out a gram of MDM and offered some hits all the way around. Dogg motioned them to kick back on the blankets covering the bales of hay. A can of Crisco stood atop a Stall post. The mirrors in the Stall reflected the four of them back across the rack and the whipping horse and the leather-covered weight-lifting bench. They all smiled at each other. Easy. Measuring out the weight of the needs of each man in the Stall. One by one, led by the Dogg Himself, Rip and Strip turned to Peter who under the joint and the MDM had turned in on his own self. The Cowboys were sensitive men. They knew what unspoken thing Peter needed. They knew what he only then was beginning to realize.

Dogg stood up, long, lean, and lanky, to piss. He popped the buttons of his 501 Levi's and reeled out his big uncut dick. He looked at Peter. Then he walked deliberately across the Stall to a galvanized trough running the length of one wall and emptying into a metal pail. The sound of his dog piss was heavy as rain on a sheet-metal roof of a kennel. His yellow flow drained like a thick, slow waterfall off the end of the pipe into the bucket. Peter had seen that bucket lifted and tilted to fill an enormous six-quart red-rubber enema bag equipped with a long hose fitted with a double nozzle that was among the most corporal of punishments.

Peter had seen a man tied spreadeagle, face down in a sling, at S&M Ranch. His belly had hung free beneath the sling, and his furry butt stuck up in the air between his wish-boned legs. Dogg Katz, who liked butts inside and out, had held up the double nozzle like a prize. Rip shoved one big black fist-sized nozzle up the man's ass. Strip fastened the other big black dick-sized nozzle tied like a piss gag into the man's mouth. The Dogg Himself slowly released the clamp on the red-rubber hose, so that the slow, excruciating trickle of hot posse piss drained torturously down into the man's body, filling his butt to exploding with all the piss his mouth could not swallow. He was tied and plugged and connected into piss distending his hanging belly from both ends. Where it entered his body was his no-choice choice. What piss he failed to drink went down his asshole. Either way his belly and guts kept filling up, distended into a daddy-belly worth punching, till his mouth barfed and his butt spouted and the whole process started over again. Only worse.

Slowly the value came home to Peter of the generosity of three men turning their time and energy to shine on him. To refuse their touch would be perhaps a sin in a world where real touch is more often rejected than received. Was the touch of the Cowboys on him the invocation of some ancient male ritual? What would they do to him? And why did he have no strength, when they touched him, to resist them? On his truck radio driving up the Eagles had sung, "Some dance to remember. Some dance to forget." Peter wanted to forget nothing. He wanted to remember everything. He knew nothing finer than the deep, wild ways men play with each other.

The three Cowboys' rope-calloused hands began to remove his shirt. They pulled off his boots and Levi's. They dressed him in black leather chaps with the codpiece pulled off, leaving him naked with his crotch and butt framed in black leather front and back. His cheeks stood out, molded by the tight leather. They pulled on his boots and zipped the chaps down tight and locked the zippers closed with padlocks. They cinched heavy leather restraints around first one booted ankle and then the other. They tightened thick padded leather restraints around both of his wrists.

Peter stood bound in leather, inspected, in the middle of the straw-covered Whipping Stall. The four men studied each other. There was no pretense among them. No role-playing. No barriers. No masks. The stripping had been of more than clothes. They preferred aptitude to attitude. Peter had arrived, already naked, in the need the Cowboys saw in him. They coached his need and his feelings up out of him. They were not executioners. He was not one of the *Penitentes*. There was no guilt in all of this to be expiated. These men, instead, were concelebrating priests of a man-to-man ritual older than all the previous gods ever worshiped on Folsom. They were a quartet of men in perfect post-urban alignment under the watchful eye of Dogg Katz.

The Cowboys led him to the padded black-leather exercise bench. They fastened his body belly-down. His dick was cinched with rawhide. His wrists and ankles were tied to rings welded to the steel legs. His bare butt rose exposed defenselessly. A heavy powerlifter's leather belt was laid across the small of his back and cinched under the bench. He was tied tightly into place. He felt

Dogg Katz's huge unshaven chin and moustache push between his cheeks and he felt Dogg's tongue pierce his pucker and suck the tip of his fudge. Wordlessly they executed their sure moves. Peter knew the choreography. He thought to resist, but thought again about this almost unique chance to receive. Slowly, the men walked around his bound body. Studying. Gauging. Plumbing the intensity of the depths to which they all might descend together. One after the other, the Cowboys picked whips of gradual intensity. One after the other, they took turns flicking his butt, pinking his cheeks, reddening his white skin with light welts. Peter at first made small noises and then, growing used to the fine play of their belts and whips on his bare butt, fell into a rhythm of acceptance. He was on his journey to the land of corporal punishment.

The Cowboys played him: easy to rough. Had a stranger on a City street struck him a quarter as hard he would have felt injured. The smashing slap of their belts bit in like layers of their energy laid flat across his flesh. Could anyone observing have known the sensual truth? A young son patted on the butt by his father smiles up at the man. A young son, guilty of some disobedience and spanked no harder than the pat his father gave him earlier in play, feels the full sting and cries at the intent. With no guilt in this Whipping Stall, the beating was not one of atonement, but of pleasurable at-one-ment.

Peter's leather-bound dick hung beneath him, stretched through a hole strategically placed in the weight-bench. While Dogg, growling, crawled under the bench and sucked his rockhard cock, Rip and Strip were beating Peter. He was being beaten by them. They were in concert of celebration in one mind. By turns they whipped his ass. Each Cowboy choosing each time a different instrument of corporal discipline: hand, gloved hand, riding crop, belt, cat, cane. Varieties of each one

applied lightly, then rising sensually from the easy beginning to full thick-armed force.

This was corporal punishment, pure and simple: the
uncomplicated beating of a man by men.

After more than an hour's slapping, spanking, belt-
ing, and whipping, they released him from the bench.
They stood him on his feet and silently turned him to
view his glowing red butt in the mirrors. The shackles
stayed on his wrists and ankles. They laid him back on the
mattress and sat and smoked while they talked to each
other and he stared silently at the rafters in the barn.

Peter had not known this would happen. He had intended only to drive away from the City, fleeing Castro,
Folsom, and then-some, seeking some consolation among
some pioneer survivors who had left the City behind for
all their own reasons. And to Peter, a man's true reasons were the most important thing to his head. The
greatest treason, he figured, was for a man to do the
right thing for the wrong reason.

Peter understood the peculiar and upbeat New
Masochism. It was not the tired alcohol, tobacco, and
bar-leather masochismo ritualized by untherapeutized
guys who need to be kicked down twelve steps in order
to have guilt-driven sex. Peter could appreciate a good
Degradation Bottom. But he himself didn't need the degradation excuses of leather wannabes' abuse in order to
find psychic permission to bottom out to beatings,
cocksucking, boot-licking, rimming, and whatever *merde*
was *du jour*. His head permitted him to acquit his New
Masochism in a way that maintained his dignity as a
male. The heavy physical endurance of pain and discipline raised him to the noble league of jocks enduring
the rigors of practice under a serious coach, raised him
to the dignity of young warriors suffering for all the right
reasons the transcendental pain of the Sundance Ritual,
their chests and tits skewered and pierced and their

bodies suspended from their chests as part of their ritual passage from carefree boyhood into responsible manhood. Peter understood why a Boy Called Pony became a Man Called Horse. He understood the totem rituals of tattooing, piercing, scarification, and branding. He had not suspected these three Cowboys would take him into a scene his conscious mind had not known he needed. He, in truth, was no sexual S&M ingenue, but he had not really defined how much he needed this trip to S&M Ranch. He could hardly have prepared himself for the Cowboys giving him an unexpected gift, the best kind worth giving. He surrendered to their control. Openly, gladly, even gratefully he accepted their hard caresses. Peter, laidback, had that floating pure feeling that people have during out-of-the-body experiences. He had long ago forgot about this kind of special masochistic hunger in himself. Beyond the drug, beyond the pain, with these men, he was in a stage of rising consciousness grounded in absolute physical pleasure.

The Cowboys took him again: next round, next level. This time they picked him up bodily and hung him upside down by his ankles, face into the post. Six feet above, his booted feet were spreadeagled wide apart on opposite sides of the rough beam down around which came his legs. His dick and belly pressed into the wood of the post. His head dangled a foot off the straw-covered floor of the Whipping Stall. His face rubbed into the rough wood. He wanted to say something as they bound him with cinch-ropes tighter and tighter into totally immobile bondage. But he could not speak. He could not bear to break their intense sexual concentration. They were all four beyond words.

He hung silently upside down.

Their bondage forced him to hug the post. They took yards of rope and began to slowly cinch his spreadeagle ankles toward one another. They wrapped his legs in his chaps tight into the ropes. Suspended upside down and cinched bellytight into the post, he could not move. A moment of panic swept over him. He raised his head slightly. They moved around his inverted body. He could see only their dusty boots and the frayed heels of their filthy boot jeans. He could hardly believe they were wrapping more rope around his waist and torso. They pulled his chest and shoulders tight into the post. Dogg Katz took the first of three wooden dowels and inserted the wood into the rope web and turned it clockwise causing all the tight ropes to tighten even tighter. He repeated the clockwise turn-and-tightening with the other two dowels increasing the square-inch pressure of the bondage. The hair on Peter's chest and belly snagged splinters on the post. The inflatable penis-gag parted his lips, depressed his tongue, and filled his throat.

Peter was hanging, head down toward the barn floor, pressure cinched against a whipping post with his red-welted ass framed for beating by three serious men already credentialed with their serious intensity. S&M Ranch took men where they consented to go...and then one step beyond. "Abandon Limits, All Ye Who Enter Here." What more defined reality could a man ask for? For such moments, a man's place in the universe seemed quite clear. Hanging by his heels. Bound immobile. Deep-gagged. Whipped. To be whipped even more. His butt hung framed by the chaps, exposed at the exact height of their chests and whip-swinging arms.

Again, one by one, the Cowboys took turns beating him. One man laid into him. The other two watched, stroking their dicks, picking their next instruments from the footlocker full of whips, belts, quirts, bamboo, drilled and studded fraternity paddles, and a cat-of-nine-tails made from a stranded mix of rubber straps, leather thongs, and hemp rope. Peter dropped beneath words to guttural sounds. Their beating was penetrating deep into him, making everything civilized in the City fall away, until there was nothing left but the sound of the whip followed by the sting and the pain and the welt and the wait for the next crisscross blow. His own sounds, even to him, sounded as if they came from someone else, some inner primitive, gagged deep inside him.

The flat thwack of the belts made echoes resound off craggy nerve-cliffs inside his body. The quick cut of knotted cats scythed through golden underbrush in an uncharted wilderness deep inside him. The three Cowboys ganged up on him for a long and serious three-way whipping. Each took an identical whip. One after the other they alternated flogging him. In the geography of his body, he felt acres of primeval timber thrown into brilliant upheaval by bodyquakes trembling down the length of his completely suspended, bound and tied, immobile self.

Peter could not tell how long the Cowboys beat him. He cared nothing for clock time. He thought of nothing. No headlines. No job. No relationships. For now everything disappeared. There was only this beating. Only this purifying, simplifying corporal punishment. He was serious as an ascetic monk on the Western range. He had only to feel and receive. He trusted their judgement. He knew they would whip him more thoroughly than he had ever been beaten before. He was glad when finally he felt the pinking sting of his butt begin to ooze red and finally run with blood. He could feel with each blow the fine spray of his own assblood splashing hot across his sweaty back.

This was real. Unlike most encounters that seemed unreal, surreal, he was no longer living a jerkoff abstraction, talking of theories and fantasies of S&M over restaurant coffee. He was restrained. Immobile. He had once been the best little boy in the whole wide world and he guessed maybe he still was. The quality of the men whose company he kept convinced him of that. This was, he knew for sure, one of the ways men of a certain mind touched and evened each other out, so they never made the climb into the bell tower with an AK47. Their private intensity, judged perverse by the world, was antidote to a global village of breeders that was truly, madly, deeply, publicly perverse. Their passion kept them from going insane in a world of crazed ballot boxes, hostages, meltdowns, ethnic cleansing, gender blackmail, and bears getting in touch with their Inner Goldilocks.

Sailors, Peter had read, often had their backs tattooed with the Virgin and Jesus. They hoped that, if ever they were to be stripped for flogging, that the Whipmaster would show them some mercy out of respect for the religious picture tattooed across their backs. Peter had never felt his body to be more of a sacred vessel than at this whipping. If grace existed in the universe, then he was hanging suspended and open to the flow. The harder the Cowboys whipped him, the less nay-saying he felt, until, transcended beyond all negativity, on the edge of Total *Yes*, he heard the crack of the bull whip across the barn.

Dogg Katz, who had a reputation as big as the legendary whipmeister Fred Katz, warmed up his big arm for the final workout. Peter heard the bull sing through the air and crack louder each time Dogg Katz's arm repeated the stroke more vigorously in the warm air of the Whipping Stall. Rip and Strip, like an opening act for a main attraction, finished off their flogging and stood back sweating and waiting to witness the ultimate "Beating by Bull Whip" of one man by another.

In the silence, only boots shuffled under the heavy step of Dogg Katz warming up with the bull whip. Peter tried to raise his head. His body, with the beating, had tightened in, under the ropes and dowel-twists, ever closer to the whipping post.

Something had happened. Earlier, Peter's dick had

been rockhard. Now he was quiescent. The leather thongs tied around his cock had made his everhard cock feel like a coldcut laced out dark and purple. He didn't care about dick. This game had progressed beyond genital sex. Maybe it was the MDM that took the energy from his dick and shot it to his head. Maybe it was endorphins. Maybe it was God. He knew they had dared to go beyond games, turning his body into a medium for conjuring something up in the barn so raw and primitive it had no name and was rarely called for by men. They had left civilization now.

It was more than driving up to S&M Ranch. They were somewhere in the deep past and somewhere in the deeper future. This was nothing like the mindless highs of urban culture. This rush defined *rush*.

Around him, Rip and Strip greased their wet dicks in anticipation of this consensual blood rite. Dogg Katz licked his lips. Dogg Katz sniffed Peter's butthole. Dogg Katz licked that pucker, stuck in his finger, pulled out the stink, sniffed it, and sucked it down.

Peter had never been bull-whipped. He had witnessed lashings in old movies on late-night satellite-dish, and he'd bought those *Brute Force* whipping videos where that International Mr. Leather Joe Gallagher is whipped till he quivers, but he had never thought he would ever be tied upside down with his bleeding cheeks primed and ready for a Cowboy with a professional whiphand. He didn't know if he wanted it or not. Dogg Katz was a legend. This moment might never come again. He sensed it. He embraced it. He loved himself, yeah, and it was weird, but he loved these men, whoever they really were, and he loved this whiphand Cowboy Dogg more than he had ever loved or felt anything in his life.

Peter thought the first blow of the bull whip would never land. Then, cracking, the bull cut lightly like a small sting, tentative, into his cheeks. Dogg Katz timed his blows, layering each succeeding lash in under the burn of the cut before. Peter felt the rising intensity. He knew Dogg was clever enough not to go so far as to violate the integrity of his body and ruin the reputation of S&M Ranch. But he knew that long before that limit, there were marks he wanted that would last for weeks. The bull cracked and sang louder, faster, heavier. Peter felt everything. He felt nothing. He was inside himself. He was outside himself. He was one with them. He could feel the energy of the Whiphand Cowboy, Dogg Katz, flowing down into him. His blood ran down his back toward his shoulders. The clock stopped. He was screaming. The clock was running backwards. He was in ecstasy. The clock melted down. His body was quivering. The men were untying him, taking him down, lowering him, laying him flat out on the floor, standing him up to see their work on his butt, walking him to the mattress, laying him back, sitting together with him, and him with them, and all of them together.

Dogg Katz stuck his leather-dog-tongue between Peter's bloody cheeks and, to the victor go the spoils, ate the trophy leather-dog-hole that relaxed, tightened, pushed, pulled, and finally blew like a mud dam. Rip and Strip knelt in close to Dogg.

The beating had not exhausted Peter. The beating had been fine foreplay. The bull whip had opened him up: head and body. There was no resistance left in him. Even if they had taken him out to the four-holer outhouse, where men were kept tied to the bondage boards in the cesspit in the broiling Sonoma heat, he would not have objected.

Rip and Strip grinned shit-eating grins at each other. They reached over to Peter and secured his wrists, then raised his shackled ankles to chains hanging over the mattress in the straw.

Dogg Katz, licking his lips, was greasing up his fist.

The Old Shell Game

All these calisthenic nights,
olympic fun in bed,
in the red lamplight,
changing changling faces
fascinated by my decathalon sense of sex.
The old shell game, baby,
fricating flesh together,
tongues pretzeled into holes
no mother ever knew.
Musical kamady-sutra nightly
on the chandeliers.

Oh it's my body.
Without you, once again, it's my body.
And it's their bodies
in these shells so fit for games,
biceped, bearded, buttocked to fit
in two-fisted love,
reeling in the terminal encounters
of glorious flesh,
in the glorious encounters
of terminal flesh.

Wrestlers of perfect form
choreographed in classic holds,
ah yes, and yes again, to our bodies;
but behind their eyes,
but behind my eyes

the torch of passion lights, flares, passes,
so laid back together,
our bodies sated,
I wait for his warm hand
to cup my cool left cheek
in your old accustomed way,
but he is he
and I've sated him.
He drowzes.
I turn to watch his face,
but his face is not your face,
after the heated calisthenics of these olympics,
this oldest shell game on earth.
He falls back into his private self
(What was his name again?)
unlike you and I when we were us
falling together afterwards
into a glow of each other.

In the red light on his placid face,
delighted we shared
(as much as he dared)
I in the red blush of my satisfied shell
rueful for what you and I once enjoyed,
nearly always good in bed,
but for your losing-day to losing-day attitude,
that ruled then ruined us,
incompatible over breakfast
for letting the flame go out.
I can hardly forgive you.
You blew it. You blew it out.
I can hardly say it:
I loved you so much I hate you.

Sensual Mutuality...

SLEEP IN
HEAVENLY PEACE

Tonight was our first time together: Christmas Eve.

"Let's go home," you said. "Let's go to my place." You didn't say, "Hey, let's go fuck!" So I smiled and followed you silently into the night. All year long I've seen you standing around The Ramrod looking tough. I wanted you. I wanted to touch you through your leathers.

Once last summer I caught a glimpse of your sweaty pecs and shoulders and arms. I wanted to hold on to you. Even more, I wanted you to hold me. But summer left. Fall came. You disappeared for awhile. Now this winter you've come back.

You looked at me. For once, I pinned on my balls; I returned your stare. You looked hard, experienced, disciplined, gentle. My cock hardened. I wanted you more.

"Come home with me," you said. "We'll build a fire. You can see my tree."

I wanted sex. I needed a little TLC. You seemed to suggest something sex sometimes lacks during the holidays. Genuine human affection.

You broke out your best wine. We shared a smoke.

Your masculine arms embraced me. Held me. You, a leatherman, held me. Your face filled me with trust. I opened to you, silently, while the FM played stereo carols.

You gave me tenderness: tenderly you slipped your dick wet from my mouth into my willing ass; tenderly you greased your strong, pliable hand and filled me full of your strength; more tenderly you slipped your dick into your hand inside my ass and jerked yourself off inside of me. The throes of your cuming triggered my load out and up my belly, onto my chest, all the way to my face where you kissed and licked my seed through your thick moustache into your warm mouth.

Now you're laid back asleep. Your tree glows. Your fireplace warms me. My face feels good against your drowsy belly. You're an experienced leather guy. I'm new to it all. I like it. I like you. I guess even a leatherman is allowed to get a little sentimental during the holidays.

I'll lie here awhile, dozing with you, keeping watch with you by night, and in the morning it will be Christmas.

You'll make strong black coffee. Your big cock will swing easy between your thighs. We'll shower.

I'll offer to drop you by the friends you promised to visit as I go on my way to visit the friends I promised to visit.

You'll say you will call me in the afternoon to see how I'm doing.

"Fine," I'll say.

I never lie.

I loved hundreds of men this last year and I'll love hundreds more in the year to come; but right now with you, on your belly, because I am with you, because of what, tonight, has passed between us man-to-man, because I nearly always love the man I'm with, I love you now.

And that's, omigod, enough.

AFTERWORD

GAY AMERICAN LITERATURE

by Claude Thomas

"Jack Fritscher invented the South of Market prose style, and its magazines," wrote critic John F. Karr establishing a timeline for gay literature in *The Bay Area Reporter*, June 27, 1985. Fritscher's particular SOMA style, invented young, remains classic, current, inventive, hip, and hot, with a range from traditional fiction to cyber-punk.

Fritscher is epicentric to gay male literature. He was the right writer in the right place at the right time. In 1972, he wrote his hardcore novel, *Leather Blues,* which critic Michael Bronski praised as high male romance. By 1977, he was the founding San Francisco editor of *Drummer*, the first masculine-identified magazine of gay liberation. The Fritscher-driven *Drummer* issues remain legendary and collectible.

He created an original, actual vocabulary for the main themes of the Golden Age of Liberation. He developed and, in some cases brought to print for the first time, the themes that have since become evergreen staples of gay publishing: the concept of "gay pop culture" itself, leather, cigars, rubber, cowboys, daddies, bears, bodybuilders, gay sports, water sports, bondage, fisting and nipple play. In 1978, he pointedly added to the masthead of *Drummer* "The Magazine of American Gay Popular Culture." By 1984, Fritscher's cult-status leather writing was being referenced for its original psychological insight by scholars such as Martin S. Weinberg, Colin J. Williams, and Charles Moser in *The Official Journal of the Society for the Study of Social Problems*, McGill University, Montreal, Quebec.

Fritscher brings into the gaystream of men's erotic writing an alert sense of mainstream American literature. He spent his sophomore year in high school pouring over *Leaves of Grass* and *Ulysses* trying to find the dirty parts he'd been warned about, and finished quite happy to find the esthetic. He was raised on John Dos Passos' *USA Trilogy*, Thomas Wolfe's *Look Homeward, Angel*, Scott Fitzgerald's *The Great Gatsby*, Ernest Hemingway's short stories, Norman Mailer's *The Naked and the Dead*, J. D. Salinger's *The Catcher in the Rye*, John Updike's *Rabbit Run* and *Pigeon Feathers*, Flannery O'Connor's *A Good Man Is Hard to Find*, Arthur Miller's *The Crucible* and *Death of a Salesman,* Edward Albee's *The American Dream* and *Who's Afraid of Virginia Woolf,* and virtually every word written by Tennessee Williams. In 1967, he came out in Chuck Renslow's Gold Coast Bar in Chicago, and wrote, at Loyola University of Chicago, his doctoral dissertation, *Love and Death in Tennessee Williams.*

In 1968, as a founding member of the American Popular Culture Association, he took particular notice—and notes—of the gay liberation movement exploding exponentially with the Vietnam War protests. In San Francisco in 1971, he actually wrote in his journals the first words of his signature novel, *Some Dance to Remember,* in a room at the legendary Barracks Baths, above the Red Star Saloon, on Folsom Street at Hallam Mews. *Some Dance to Remember* defines the twelve years: 1970-1982. "If one can learn American history from the novels of Gore Vidal, one can learn gay American history from *Some Dance to Remember,*" David Perry wrote in *The Advocate*. Michael Bronski in *Firsthand* critiqued: "*Some Dance to Remember*, a mammoth saga of San Francisco gay life which spans the Sixties to the Eighties, is so bursting with plots, characters, energy, and ideas that it is...a great epic....an ambitious work and a rarity in modern fiction: a novel of ideas...telling the truth of gay men's lives." Critic Jack Garman wrote in the literary magazine, *Lambda Book Report:* "As a document of our times and our lives, *Some Dance to Remember* has no peer."

Besides creating this "Proustian...*recherche*" novel dubbed "mythic" by *The Advocate*, Fritscher's eye, ear, and pen have filled the dreamscape of gay magazines with a gift for language that Ian Young compares to the poet Dennis Cooper whose limit-pushing novel became the controversial 1995 film, *Frisk*, directed by Todd Verow. Editor-in-Chief Anthony DeBlase printed in *Drummer* #139, May 1990, an actual photograph of *Remembrance of Things Past* to illustrate a feature article, surveying gay history, authored by Fritscher, who once was photographed in Paris at Père-Lachaise, laughing—quite iconoclastically—sitting next to the black marble tomb of Proust himself.

As a premier magazine writer of fiction and features, as journalist, and as photographer, Fritscher, with more than 5,000 pages in print, is a most prolific artist diversely dedicated to the literary culture of gay magazines which he injects with fresh words and photographs that stimulate the intelligent imagination and broaden the conceptual vocabulary of sex. (See the formative Fritscher versions of *Drummer* issues 19-30, and *Son of Drummer*—all of which he edited and mostly wrote.) He is adamantly not part of the United States' current *fin de siecle* fad of political correctness which he deems no more than a tantrum of leftover, failed Marxism: "The fundamentalist p. c. stone wall will fall exactly as did the Berlin Wall." Fritscher's writing, wrote Carrie Barnett, Jeff Zurlinden, and Allen Smalling in *Au Courant*, "is about as far as you can get from politically-correct, stylistically-orthodox, writer's-workshop fiction, and we like it all the better for it!"

Literary erotica is the most interactive art because of its double dedication to orgasm of the body and the mind. About anthologies of Fritscher's short stories, Q wrote in *The Philadelphia Gay News*: "Jack Fritscher is a master of gay prose pornography....He plays with the brain, man's most accessible and effectively reached sexual organ....The manner in which he manipulates language, sensuality, feeling, nuance, style, atmosphere, and even one's visual sense...is...sensational." Couple the five basic plot-lines in all of world literature with the maybe twelve actually available sex acts, 26 letters of the alphabet, seven kinds of punctuation, eight parts of speech, and a bag full of transitive Anglo-Saxon verbs and it becomes evident that refreshment of these plots and acts and literary devices is totally dependent on the writer's inventive gift. Fritscher, who spends much time in Ireland, is ethnically mixed Irish, and in the Celtic tradition of the *seanachie* [the Irish story teller], he brings genuine plot, motivation, character, and a lyric and rhythmic voice to the *mise en scene* of the landscape of lust about which *Gay Times*, London, wrote "he creates as an *evocation poetique*."

Taking his cue from the poetic evocations of Tennessee Williams who wrote great, defining, mainstream roles for women, Fritscher has written many stories, two plays, and two screenplays about women. He defines himself as a humanist: "Neither a feminist nor a masculinist be." His 1976 "gender" play, *Coming Attractions*, produced in San Francisco by the Yonkers Production Company on a double-bill with Lanford Wilson's *The Madness of Lady Bright*, was the first play written in San Francisco about women in San Francisco coping with the new breed of gay men in San Francisco. The three women's roles in *Some Dance to Remember* (1990) are crowned by the star-turn of the lesbian protagonist of his 1997 novella, *The Geography of Women,* and by his 1997 screenplay written for Beijing Films about the historical Chinese woman, Golden Orchid, titled *Water from the Moon*. Born under the sign of Gemini, on the summer solstice, during the bright noon hour of the longest daylight of the year, the same day as Lillian Hellman, Fritscher balances his yin and yang fairly with his animus and anima, but buoyed by the nature of his physiology, he prefers yang and animus: the actual, true-north preference of masculine-identified homosexuality.

So it is no betrayal of his Whitmanesque philosophy of humanism to sing the songs of men. Actually, his homomasculine preserve of stories about men is inclusive in a very specific way for a specific demographic: the endangered species of masculine-identified gay men surviving in an age of virus and over-the-top male-bashing. (One sworn Streisand-identified critic, crippled by his own fundamentalist cant, went self-satirizingly ballistic censuring and censoring *Some Dance to Remember* because he misperceived the novel as a triumph of butch men over feministic gay men, and, so, not at all politically correct, as if all gay novels are duty-bound to be about queens. Fritscher responded: "Matriarchy need not replace patriarchy, because both have been replaced by democracy."

Actually, Fritscher has never said or anywhere written that masculine gay men are superior in any way to effeminate gay men, drag queens, straight women, or straight men.) In *Drummer*, Fritscher early on in the 70's coined the Jungian-like term "homomasculinity" to give broader reach to the male ethos than the crotch-focused term "homosexuality." The gay press reveals the actual raw desires of its readers in gay magazine "Classified Ads." In these populist columns real people articulate their sincere primal ISO desires. The gay lonely-hearts-club band seems always in constant search for straight-acting, straight-appearing men. Fritscher, sniffing the irony, is sensitive to this quintessential gay yearning. (Actually, the main character in *Some Dance to Remember* is a gay-friendly straight, but no one ever mentions that little quirk.) He gives voice for that subclass of gay men who actually are masculine-identified and discriminated against for being naturally butch. In his stories, everyone is sexually experienced. These are not the tales of sensitive souls coming out. They are not tales of drag and queens. They are not tales of homosexual despair and suicide. These tales are bawdy Chaucerian tales of humor, lust, and pleasure. Outside the literary fantasy, Fritscher, in reality, advocates absolute abstinence or monogamy.

Fritscher in his gift for language has a long list of words and concepts he coined or introduced to American gay literature back when the rocks in Stonewall were still hot: *mutualist, homomasculinity, homomuscularity, gaystream, manstream, leatherstream, sadomachismo, perversatility, mountainman,* and in 1981, *bear,* in *The California Action Guide.* In his 1972 novel, *Leather Blues,* he redefined S&M as "sensuality and mutuality," and coined in *Drummer* the phrase "the Second Coming Out" for a vanilla gay man's emergence into leather. In 1979 he founded with Mark Hemry the first leather 'zine *Man2Man,* which was Richard Bulger's acknowledged model for *Bear* magazine in 1987. The actual 1990's magazine *International Leatherman* took its title from *Some Dance to Remember*; Fritscher also created and titled the *Drummer*-affiliated magazine, *Tough Customers.*

Fritscher's only political theme concerns the anxiety of war. In "Goodbye, Saigon," a memory tale, the past comes insouciantly "prousting" back, and the reader is reminded that the Vietnam war was only a twenty-four-hour plane flight away from Castro Street and Christopher Street and that the protested war—not ended until May, 1975 (more than half of the 70's)—proactively transformed the character of the 1970's gay liberation movement. The *realpolitik* of the fear of death in war drove young draft-age men to libidinous heights of public sex: the more extravagantly gay a man was the less likely the Selective Service was to draft him. Gay sex meant survival.

Even so, comradeship in war, as a reason for genuine man-to-man bonding, affection, love, and sex, is celebrated in the long story, "The Shadow Soldiers," which dramatizes the payback for the American invasion of Vietnam. Reading such rough-sex texts caused critic Michael Bronski in *Gay Community News* magazine, to place Jack Fritscher's writing in a new stream of romantic gay writers including the veteran Sam Steward (Phil Andros) whose erotic publication career Fritscher revived in *Drummer*, and the neophyte John Preston whose *Mister Benson* draft-manuscript Fritscher mentored, edited, polished, and serialized in *Drummer*. As a particular emotional influence, Fritscher's brother, a career military man, served two tours in Vietnam and was caught in the horror of the Tet Offensive; the character of the Vietnam vet in *Some Dance to Remember* is not, however, based on his brother, except, Fritscher states, "to the extent that all writing begins in autobiography and ends in allegory." Certainly, Fritscher's war-torn "Wild Blue Yonder" is an absolutely beautiful story, a romantic notion built not only out of the poet William Blake, but of Fritscher's own childhood of missing men and dead soldiers during the stateside horror of World War II blackouts and shortages.

His "The Assistant Freshman Football Coach" is a Socratic-Platonic romance extolling the mystical sexual union of teacher and student, intellect and athlete in a bittersweet campus relationship in a time of war. Characteristically, this story of a college English professor alludes to American poet Robert Frost's "Stopping by Woods on a Snowy Evening." The actual verbability of the author shines through in the highly alliterative line so casually woven: "...a student and teacher breaking taboo in a war-torn time of broken totems." Fritscher played team contact sports in high school and college before his years of experience in bodybuilding circles and leather playrooms. In many of his stories, these athletic experiences borne out of the boxing ring and the gridiron become a measure of sexual psyche. "He took [my dick up his ass] like a man. I don't mean like the cliche. I mean like a man." In "Football Coach" and elsewhere, Fritscher means not like the stereotype in a gay story, and not "like a man" in a politically-correct story, but like the Jungian archetype of perfect animus.

This is important, because storytelling, especially erotic storytelling, is a shorthand mix of archetypes and stereotypes. "Usually," Fritscher wrote, "the archetypes are the good guys we identify with and the stereotypes are the bad guys we hate." Erotica thrives on, and thrills to, familiar archetypes of slang, like calling a blond man a "Swede" or a "Polack" because the archetype, like the stereotype, connotes a whole character so thoroughly.

"The Shadow Soldiers" is, like the survivalist "The Old Man and the Sea," a symbolic story of courage. Written shortly after the last helicopters lifted off the roof of the American embassy at the fall of Saigon, this rather unique story is actually about straight men allowing themselves to regard each other tenderly, sexually, without guilt. What torturous sex there is is not gay sex; it is not even sex, because it is simply rape. Few gay writers ever address either the tragedy of Vietnam or the happy side of the golden age of sexual liberation of the 70's. Fewer would equate them. In fact, Fritscher has never shied away from the twin realities of war and sex. Both fascinate him. He is the writer who named the 70's "The Golden Age of Sexual Liberation." His survival stories from the 70's equipped him for the survival stories that became standard in the HIV 80's as in his high-sex, high-comedy novella, *Titanic*, published in *Uncut* (September 1988) and in *Mach* #35 (March 1997). In fact, he peels back history, folds time, and reveals the 70's in many stories, as in *Some Dance to Remember* with its heavy-duty Vietnam subplot that has eluded some reviewers who comment only on the novel's reflection of gay history as if their horizon is the rim of the gay ghetto, as if they are not citizens of the wider society.

Fritscher, like his bicoastal lover, Robert Mapplethorpe,
finds it inappropriate to live in any ghetto. He daringly disas-
sembles the Art Reich ghetto of New York City in his 1994
autobiographical memoir *Mapplethorpe: Assault with a Deadly
Camera*. In *Mapplethorpe*, like "The Shadow Soldiers" with
its martyrdom and triple "crucifixion," he demonstrates the
long continuing tradition in western culture of the imagery of
religious suffering ending in Mapplethorpe's own suicide-
martyrdom by virus. Mapplethorpe's photographs, Fritscher,
the art critic, points out are virtual violence worthy of theologi-
cal consideration. Consider Mapplethorpe's crucifix, gun, and
knife photographs, and his portraits of gay "saints," and himself as Satan, Jesus, and, finally, as Death itself. In the home-
front war story, "Goodbye, Saigon," which is the same erotic
genre as Tennessee Williams' classic, "Desire and the Black
Masseur," the staccato beat of language is powerful poetry.
Actually, this parable of a hawk and a pacifist seems a retell-
ing of belief and faith and honor in the upper room where the
glorified Christ, dead and risen, invites the Doubting Thomas, the apostle, to place his fingers in the bloody wound in
Christ's side. *Eros* and *thanatos*, *love* and *death*, are the two
major themes in his work.

Fritscher loves American popular culture as much as he
loves American literature. The war story, "From Nada to Mañana," has its genesis somewhere in Michael Cimino's *The Deer
Hunter* as his "Foreskin Prison Blues" in *Stand by Your Man
and Other Stories* is spun out of Jon Voight's iconic masculinity in *Runaway Train*. Even Prince Sodom is described from
movie iconography in the wonderful coinage, "Conneryian,"
after the look of Sean Connery in *Zardoz*. These stories, as
much as the pop-culture novel *Some Dance to Remember*, exist in the world of American movies.

The melodic capture of language in "Nada/Mañana" is
typical of Fritscher's Irish-American tongue, and the moon-
lit images are typical of his filmic eye. As auteur, he has
composed and directed more than 125 feature-length videos; two of his documentaries of the photographer-painter,
George Dureau, are in the permanent collection of the Mai-
son Europeenne de la Photographie, Paris. His rebellious
coffee-table book of erotic photographs, *Jack Fritscher's*

American Men was published in London, 1995, and in it there is none of the usual coffee-table fare of faceless, svelte gymbo-modelles leaning in artsy shadows holding hoola-hoops. The use in "Nada/Mañana" of the present tense makes fiction, usually written in the past tense, come as alive as a news report. Actually, "Nada/Mañana" can be read as a performance piece for an actor after the manner of Joseph Conrad's *The Heart of Darkness* in Francis Ford Coppola's *Apocalypse Now*. If one reads the reincarnation story, "Wild Blue Yonder," outloud, the writer's rhythms are melodic. He is a philosopher of the yearning heart who has the ability to write: "Can you imagine being dead...and jealous?" His description of being inside the orgasm that conceives the writer himself has to be one of the most innovative plot twists ever ginned up to reunite two lovers. In the same vein, "Big Doofer at the Jockstrap Gym" is a droll, comic parody of and paean to muscular masculinity where, at orgasm, trees bend, dogs howl, crops fail, trailer parks twist into wreckage. This is erotic literature of desire, because the voice speaking is wise, funny, and living in a butch-camp that works erotically and frankly, causing in the reader the shock of recognition: he's been reading my dreams!

In the tradition of romantic literature, Fritscher's content of the classic ideal embraces beauty and terror. The advice-column format makes "Wait Till Your Father Gets Home" a horror story of child abuse or a nostalgic memoir of a Daddy-Son relationship that gay magazines ritually glorify each issue. Each of Fritscher's stories is actually based on a principle of homomasculinity, and each piece features sexual climax and intellectual payoff. "S&M Ranch," debating city-versus-nature values, raises the price of an existential poker chip to a bet where normal folks might not understand the coded feelings in the story which is not about brutality, but about transcendence. Fritscher so actually believes in the doctrine of Transubstantiation that when the word becomes flesh in this story, and flesh transcends words, he offers a peek into a psychology fit for a monastic retreat where fasting and mortification of the flesh lead to crystalline mystical clarity of spirit. There is religious poetry in "S&M Ranch": "The sound of the whip...the sting and the pain and the welt and the wait for the next crisscross blow."

The characters assume high-sex nicknames: MacTag, El Cap, Firbolgs [ancient Irish forbearers], Peter Eton-Cox, Dogg Katz, Rip, and Strip. Throughout his writing Fritscher is very careful about naming his characters. *Some Dance to Remember* would be a quite different novel if the dropdead blond musclegod were not named "Kick," the sister were not named "Kweenie," and the video pornographer were not called "Solly Blue." Certainly, in the sci-fi fantasy cyber-punk story "RoughNight@Sodom.cum," a huge metaphysics opens up precisely because of the name of "Prince Sodom."

If ever a "cult" story reveled in and revealed the devotion of true believers, "Sodom.cum" is the HIV equivalent of the *Holy Roman Martyrology* of Christian martyrs replayed masterfully in an age of sex devotees embracing a killer virus that comes as part of the sex act. When sex is unsafe, nothing is safe, and the only joy left for many is to die a martyr. Fritscher wisely stops short of intoning the words of Transubstantiation: "This is my body. This is my blood." The outlaw "Sodom.cum" is *Quo Vadis* minus the bourgeois Hollywood Code. Most moralists would write this story a different way, or have a hero come to everyone's rescue. In Fritscher's fantasy world the point is that no one even wants to be rescued, the way gay people don't want to be "rescued" from being gay.

"Sodom.cum" is an Antonin Artaud comic book of sensuality about the erotics of death. This is an over-the-top romp from the Theatre of Cruelty that runs smack into the taboo of death where most people won't admit they fantasize, unless they are devotees of the gay *Katharsis* magazine or the gladiator novels of Aaron Travis/Steven Saylor. In his memoir, *Mapplethorpe*, Fritscher wrote that people freaked out over Robert's photographs not because they were about sex, but because they were about death in the manner of Baudelaire and Rimbaud. To keep an even keel that elevates ecstasy over freakout, Fritscher expects his erotica to be read the way he writes: dick in hand. It's no wonder that at the 1997 Key West Writers' Conference, yet another Mapplethorpe friend, Genet biographer Edmund White, fanning his flushed face in the tropical heat, came grinning up to meet Jack Fritscher for the first time and said the career-summing statement: "Is it just me, or have you all used up all the oxygen?"

While written sound effects often lack lustre, Fritscher uses sound effects judiciously well to keep the pop-art of "Sodom.cum" skipping along like a cartoon on some adult MTV channel. Perhaps a proper Irish *seanachie* would recommend reading "RoughNight@Sodom.cum" on a night of the full moon to understand the reverse-mirror and reverse-morality and reverse-pleasure of its story. "In the gay world," of course, as Fritscher writes, "everything is always reversed through the looking glass and over the rainbow." What makes Fritscher's writing important is that he writes great magazine fiction that transcends the genre and must be regarded simply as sparkling gay fiction that will be read a hundred years from now.

In the imploding title story, "Rainbow County," written in 1997, a particular group of people is observed historically at a particular place in a particular time: the first lift-off of gay culture at 18th and Castro in San Francisco. The barber shop fictionalized in this story actually had a base in fact, existing as it did on the southwest corner of 18th and Castro over the drugstore-pharmacy that became the Elephant Walk Bar where the San Francisco police beat up the patrons during the fiery White Night Riot, May 21, 1979. (At the following night's peaceful counter-demonstration, which was also a street-party celebrating Harvey Milk's birthday, May 22, 1979, Jack Fritscher first met Mark Hemry 100 feet away from 18th and Castro under the marquee of the Castro Theatre.) "Rainbow County" is actually a two-person performance piece. It reads like a treatment for a black-and-white movie at Robert Redford's Sundance Film Festival, or an indie production at the Irish Film Centre. In this collection, "Rainbow County" is an unexpected surprise with its quiet, daylight sadism and brutality. It is a love *pas de deux* reminiscent of J. D. Salinger's "Franny and Zooey" spun out of a Holden Caulfield with a serial killer's (and a serial promiscuist's) mindset.

In the existential geography of "Rainbow County," the barber and the immigrant are both archetypes, as is the female painter, who is a sorceress and shape-shifter. The emblematic theme of leather jackets and fathers is repeated

Rashomon-like from other stories in other books told in other ways by Fritscher. The story is constructed almost purely in dialog by brilliant little tricks and ticks of small talk that make the characters' psychology stream on. Fritscher is a master ventriloquist with dialog. As a dramatist, he has a keen ear expressed in a diversity of voices. His two-character play, the actual title piece in Fritscher's First Fiction Collection, *Corporal in Charge of Taking Care of Captain O'Malley and Other Stories*, is a minimalist classic performance script built solely on dialog. Historian Winston Leyland included Fritscher's complete one-act play, *Corporal in Charge of Taking Care of Captain O'Malley*, in the literary canon of his critically-acclaimed master work, *Gay Roots: An Anthology of Gay History, Sex, Politics, and Culture*, 1991. Of the Second Collection of twenty-two short stories written by Jack Fritscher, critic Richard Labonté wrote in *The Advocate,* and said in review in *In Touch*: "In *Stand by Your Man*, Fritscher writes with a blessed combination of erotic ingenuity and poetic intelligence, depicting the most wonderfully suggestive sex scenes in a delightfully wry, ironic, sweaty, urgent and dirty voice...There's more range in this one book of 22 stories than in many anthologies with 22 different authors."

—Claude Thomas,
Temple Bar, Dublin

"Afterword" ©1997 Claude Thomas

Claude Thomas' cover-feature regarding the publication of *Some Dance to Remember*, titled "Sex, Lies, and Gay Fiction: A Candid Interview with Jack Fritscher" appeared in *Torso* magazine, December 1990: Publisher, The Mavety Group; Editor-in-Chief, Stan Levanthal. *Torso* photograph of Jack Fritscher by Dan O'Neill. Research for "Gay American Literature" was conceptualized and composed from reading the actual fiction texts, author interviews, and research at www.JackFritscher.com.

Also by Jack Fritscher

Fiction Books
Leather Blues, novel, 1972 and 1984
Corporal in Charge of Taking Care of Captain O'Malley and Other Stories, 1984, 1999/U.K. (The First Collection)
Stand By Your Man and Other Stories, 1987, 1999 (The Second Collection)
Some Dance to Remember, novel, 1990
The Geography of Women, 1998
Titanic: Forbidden Stories Hollywood Forgot, 1999 (The Fourth Collection)

Non-Fiction Books
Love and Death in Tennessee Williams, Doctoral Dissertation, 1967
Popular Witchcraft: Straight from the Witch's Mouth, 1971
Television Today, 1972
Mapplethorpe: Assault with a Deadly Camera, 1994
Mapplethorpe: El fotographo del escandalo, 1995

Photography Book
Jack Fritscher's American Men, London, England, 1995

Writing in Other's Books
Vamps and Tramps: New Essays, Camille Paglia, essays
Censorship: An International Encyclopedia, Derek Jones, England, essays
Gay Roots: Twenty Years of Gay Sunshine: An Anthology of Gay History, Sex, Politics, and Culture, Winston Leyland, one-act play
Best Gay Erotica 1997, Douglas Sadownick and Richard Labonté, fiction anthology
Leatherfolk: Radical Sex, People, Politics, and Practice, Mark Thompson, essay anthology
Mystery, Magic, and Miracle: Religion in a Post-Aquarian Age, Edward F. Heenan, essay anthology
Challenges in American Culture, Ray B. Browne, essay anthology

The Leatherman's Handbook, "Gay History Introduction,"
25th Anniversary Edition, Larry Townsend, nonfiction

Writing in Scholarly Journals
"William Bradford's *History of Plymouth Plantation,*"
The Bucknell Review
"Religious Ritual in the Plays of Tennessee Williams,"
Modern Drama
"2001: A Space Odyssey,"
The Journal of American Popular Culture
"The Boys in the Band in *The Boys in the Band,*"
The Journal of American Popular Culture
"*Hair*: The Dawning of the Age of Aquarius,"
The Journal of American Popular Culture

Photographs Appearing in Other's Books
*The Arena of Masculinity: Sports, Homosexuality, and the
Meaning of Sex*, Brian Pronger, London, 1990
Narrow Rooms, James Purdy [cover], London, 1997
Ars Erotica: An Encyclopedic Guide, Edward Lucie-Smith,
London, 1998

Writing and Photography in Magazine Culture
Jack Fritscher's fiction, essays, and photography appear
regularly or variously in the following magazines: *Drum-
mer, International Leatherman, Honcho, Thrust, The James
White Review, Skin, Skinflicks, Dungeonmaster, Inches, In
Touch, Checkmate, Powerplay, Bear, Classic Bear Annual,
Son of Drummer, Bunkhouse, Mach, Man2Man Quarterly, Un-
cut, Foreskin Quarterly, Hombres Latinos, Just Men, Stroke,
Rubber Rebel, Eagle* from *The Leather Journal, Hippie Dick,
Gruf, William Higgins' California, Men in Boots Journal,
GMSMA Newsletter, Hot Ash Hot Tips, The California Ac-
tion Guide, Adam Gay Video Guide, Dan Lurie's Muscle
Training Illustrated, Hooker, Expose, California Pleasure
Guide*, and others.

**For further bibliography and gay history, visit
www.JackFritscher.com**

ACKNOWLEDGEMENT

Acknowledgement and gratitude to the many magazine publishers and editors who have framed these stories into print over the years, and to the artists who illustrated the stories. Their roles in periodical publishing are often overlooked, underestimated, or lost to history.

"The Shadow Soldiers" appeared in *Man2Man Quarterly* #4, June 1981, and *Man2Man Quarterly* #5, September 1981: Publisher, Mark Hemry; Editor-in-Chief, Jack Fritscher. Also appeared as cover-featured lead fiction in *Drummer* #127, April 1989: Publisher, Anthony F. DeBlase; Editor-in-Chief, Fledermaus; four pen, ink, and marker-pen illustrations by "Skipper" through courtesy of Palm Drive Video Publishing. Appearance also in *Powerplay* #15, August 1997: Publisher, Bear-Dog Hoffman; Managing Editor, Joseph W. Bean; Editor, Bob Fifield; drawing by Ricky Ellsworth.

"Goodbye, Saigon" appeared as "Wound-Sucking Cocksucker" in *Man2Man Quarterly* #3, March 1981: Publisher, Mark Hemry; Editor-in-Chief, Jack Fritscher. Appearance also in *Powerplay* #17, Spring 1998. Publisher, Bear-Dog Hoffman; Managing Editor, Peter Millar; Editor, Bob Fifield. Drawing by Ray Schulze (RAS).

"Rough Trade" appeared as "Chico Is the Man" in *Son of Drummer,* June 1978: Publisher, John Embry; Editor-in-Chief, Jack Fritscher. Photograph illustration by Bob Heffron. Art Direction by A. Jay/Al Shapiro. Appeared as "The Poem of Summer" in *Thrust,* Volume 11, Number 2, August 1997: Arts Editor, Armando Aguilar/Jimmy Jizz.

"From Nada to Mañana" appeared as "El Capitan" in *Uncut,* Volume 1, Number 6, July 1987: Editors, John Rowberry and Aaron Travis/Steven Saylor. Rapidograph ink-drawing illustration by REX. Also appeared as "El Capitan: The Hard of Darkness" in Brush Creek Media's *Hombres Latinos,* Fall 1996: Publisher, Bear-Dog Hoffman; Managing Editor, Joseph W. Bean; Editor, Bob Fifield.

"RoughNight@Sodom.cum," appeared in *Mach* #37, October 1997: Publisher, Bear-Dog Hoffman; Managing Editor, Peter Millar, Editor, Bob Fifield.

"Foot Loose" appeared in *Drummer* #29, May 1979: Publisher, John Embry; Editor-in-Chief, Jack Fritscher. Photograph illustration by John Trojanski. Art Direction by A. Jay/Al Shapiro.

"Wild Blue Yonder" appeared in *Uncut*, Volume 2, Number 1, September 1987: Editors, John Rowberry and Aaron Travis/ Steven Saylor. Pencil drawing illustration by PEN. Also appeared in Brush Creek Media's *Classic Bear Annual #2*, February 1997: Publisher, Bear-Dog Hoffman; Managing editor, Joseph W. Bean; Assistant Managing Editor, Peter Millar; Editor, Rich Iremonger. Pencil-drawing illustration by Walt Henry.

"Wait Till Your Father Gets Home" appeared in premiere edition, *Man2Man Quarterly* #1, January 1980: Publisher, Mark Hemry; Editor-in-Chief, Jack Fritscher. Also appeared in *The California Action Guide*, October 1982: Publisher, Michael Redman; Editor-in-Chief, Jack Fritscher. Photograph illustration by Mark Hemry.

"Big Doofer at the Jockstrap Gym" appeared as "Doofer" in *Inches,* Volume 3, Number 12, February 1988: Editors, John Rowberry and Aaron Travis/Steven Saylor.

"Photo Op at Walt Whitman Junior College" appeared as "Wet Stough" in *Drummer* #28, March 1978 with ten photographs by Jack Fritscher and David Sparrow: Publisher, John Embry; Editor-in-Chief, Jack Fritscher. Art Direction by A. Jay/Al Shapiro. Also appeared in *The James White Review*, Fall-Winter 1997.

"Assistant Freshman Football Coach" appeared as "4th Down! 12 Inches to Go!" in *Inches,* Volume 4, Number 1, March 1988: Editors, John Rowberry and Aaron Travis/Steven Saylor. Painting illustration by Dan Marx. Appearance also in *Mach* #39, May 1998: Publisher, Bear-Dog Hoffman; Managing Editor, Peter Millar; Editor, Scott McGillivray. Three photographs provided by Le Salon.

"Father and Son Tag Team" appeared in *Inches*, Volume 3, Number 7, September 1987: Editors, John Rowberry and Aaron Travis/Steven Saylor. Line-drawing illustration by the Hun. Appearance also in *Mach* #41: Publisher, Bear-Dog Hoffman; Managing Editor, Peter Millar; Editor, Bob Fifield.

Illustrations included a drawing by Mike Thorn and a photograph by Brush Creek featuring Palm Drive Video model, Tom Howard.

"Rainbow County," *Mach* #43: Publisher, Bear-Dog Hoffman; Managing Editor, Peter Millar; Editor, Bob Fifield.

"The Real Cowboy" appeared in *Man2Man Quarterly* #5, Fall 1981: Publisher, Mark Hemry; Editor-in-Chief, Jack Fritscher, and in *The California Action Guide*, Volume 1, Number 3, September 1982: Publisher, Michael Redman; Editor-in-Chief, Jack Fritscher.

"S&M Ranch" appeared in *Man2Man Quarterly* #2, December 1980: Publisher, Mark Hemry; Editor-in-Chief, Jack Fritscher. Appearance also in *Powerplay* #19, September 1998: Publisher, Bear-Dog Hoffman; Managing Editor, Peter Millar; Editor, Ray Massie. Two pointilist drawings specific to the story created by Ricky Ellsworth.

"Sleep in Heavenly Peace" appeared in *Drummer* #25, December 1978: Publisher, John Embry; Editor-in-Chief, Jack Fritscher. Photograph illustration by John Trojanski. Art Direction by A. Jay/Al Shapiro. Also appeared as "2 All a Goodnight" in the last issue of *Man2Man Quarterly* #8, December 1981: Publisher, Mark Hemry; Editor-in-Chief, Jack Fritscher. Pencil-drawing illustration by Sable.

All of the characters and narrative in this collection of short fiction, including historic names, persons, places, events, products, and businesses as dramatized, are fictitious, or are used fictitiously. Events and characters are not intended to portray actual events or actual persons, living or dead, and any similarity or inference is unintentional and entirely coincidental.

SOME CRITICS PROFILE
JACK FRITSCHER'S WRITING

"Veteran author, Jack Fritscher, is an anarchist of Gay sexual prose, the man who invented the South of Market prose style...as well as its magazines..."
—**John F. Karr,** *Bay Area Reporter*

"Gore Vidal...James Baldwin...Andrew Holleran...Jack Fritscher...classic!" —**David Van Leer,** *The New Republic*

"Jack Fritscher's prose is...stark, subtle, smooth and suggestive, richly erotic." —**Richard Labonté,** *In Touch.* "Jack Fritscher's short-story anthology *Stand by Your Man* [is] the most literate of the lot of erotic fiction in a strong year of gay literature." —**Richard Labonté,** *The Advocate.* "Fritscher's *Corporal in Charge of Taking Care of Captain O'Malley* is a collection of twenty-one assertively sexual and imaginatively arousing pieces...elegant fantasies...rough-and-tumble orgies of the mind...the title tale is actually a twenty-page torrent of S&M wordplay"
—**Richard Labonté,** *In Touch*, Los Angeles

"Fritscher's cool quiet sadomasochistic material in *Leather Blues* is sometimes heavy-duty S&M...surreal mix of dreams and memories...almost Proustian in his associations...a power and beauty that is breath-taking...Fritscher shows us just how good the choice of words can be."
—**T. R. Witomski,** *Connection*, New York

"...from the pen of *Drummer*'s original daddy, its founding San Francisco editor-in-chief, Jack Fritscher. Devotees...will find a lot to like...literate, funky, honest...even funny by intent...a good read." —*NBN* **Newspaper**

"Jack Fritscher is a master of gay prose pornography, a rarity in our...video-oriented culture....He plays with the brain, man's most accessible and effectively reached sexual organ....The manner in which he manipulates language, sensuality, feeling, nuance, style, atmosphere, and even one's visual sense...is enough to guarantee...sensational status for many, many years." —**Q,** *Philadelphia Gay News*

"Jack Fritscher has roamed the furthest corners of sexuality, and can lead you on head trips unequaled by any other Gay writer I know of. You may resist, as I did, some of the aggression, machismo, and sexual practices only to be won over by Fritscher's prose....[He] writes with sweat and wit, dirt and desire. Fritscher is a knee to the groin....His sex...is aggressive, abusive, extreme, and at times (I have to say it), politically incorrect. But his free-wheeling prose creates a believable world of hedonistic sensuality. Forms of sex some readers might find unpalatable in life become arousing within the realm of fantasy, and Fritscher's work is clearly such. Within Fritscher's forbidden world we are safe, and that is what fiction is for....Fritscher, as a key creator of *Drummer* magazine, is godfather to the contemporary South of Market man..."
—**John F. Karr**, *Bay Area Reporter*

"Jack Fritscher writes...wonderful books, full of careful writing and a fine sense of words. Full of compassion and humor...full of hot horny fantasies that make good one-handed reading...his writing surges with lyricism and insight....Fritscher creates his text from images, memories, and fantasies...His writing becomes a frieze, a fine carving, lovingly crafted....He shows man as tester and prover, as erotic dreamer, as self-lover, and as shaman crossing old barriers and old prejudices...There is a world of insight packed into his metaphors."   —**Geoff Mains, author**
of *Urban Aboriginals*, **in** *The Advocate*

"Jack Fritscher's writing is a potent aphrodisiac. The reader will pant for his own chance at manhandling (or being manhandled) during a stimulating read....Fritscher knows the rhythms of writing fuckprose. Like Rechy, he joins words in powerful couplings...remarkably hot sex scenes....Fritscher is a poet of porn [who through fantasy will] chase away periods of safe-sex melancholy."
        —**Joseph D. Butkie**, *Bay Area Reporter*

"S/M Fiction [has become] unabashedly romantic...the endless quest for love...Phil Andros...John Preston...Jack Fritscher ....*Corporal-in-Charge* by Fritscher is perhaps the best book of the lot. It is a collection of short pieces, all of which deal with S/M and individual consciousness. Like Genet's work, Fritscher's are essentially masturbatory fantasies which deal in a closed world of the imagination. They are as violent, cruel,

and explicit as any of the other writing [by Andros and Preston whose *Mr. Benson* Fritscher edited]—and as romantic ....Fritscher is actually talking about the fantasy of romance. His work is not romantic *per se*, but rather, is how we think and talk about sex and romance....Fritscher's *Leather Blues*...is explicit sexuality with the theme of the young man learning from the older. It is also a masculine version of true love...between equals, both of whom have learned to love themselves and one another. [Such transcendentally "cruel" romance] explores and expands our sexualities—and our lives and minds...a way to keep anchored to tradition so that we can go out of ourselves without ever losing ourselves...Readers want their sexuality reaffirmed, and graphically drawn...by presenting an S/M sexuality in the confines of romantic tradition...The S/M makes the emotional content more varied and vital. It is the romance which makes the more frightening aspects...palatable and easier to deal with."
—Michael Bronski, *Gay Community News*, Boston

"Fritscher...is at his best in his erotic, inventive use of language...Fritscher is truly our Pynchon of Porn."
—Thor Stockman, *GMSMA News*, New York

"Jack Fritscher and his high-brow, gutter-level ruminations [offer] privileged glimpses of that unique cock-stiffening domain of which Fritscher is the sole demiurge....As a writer, Fritscher is hard to categorize....He's a jittery stylist with a kinetic verbal sense....[His style] works spectacularly....There's enough ghettoized angst to keep the Manhattan gay literati wired for months."   **—Aaron Travis/Steven Saylor,**
Drummer **Magazine**, San Francisco

"...a very particular style and rhythm....The subject matter is as varied as Fritscher's imagination, which seems endless and without remorse. What may really surprise you is that amid the graphic descriptions of every act known to man, there are actually ideas here." **—***Drummer* **Magazine**, San Francisco

"Jack Fritscher's gift for language makes me think of the poet Dennis Cooper...a strong element of romanticism....unlike most writers of dirty stories, Fritscher loves words as well as what they describe...one of the hottest books...."
—Ian Young, author, *The Stonewall Experiment,*
in *The Body Politic*, Toronto

"Jack Fritscher does for gay writing what his bicoastal lover Robert Mapplethorpe did for photography."
—**Tom Phillips,** *We the People*

"As a document of our times and our lives, Jack Fritscher's novel *Some Dance to Remember* has no peer."
—**Jack Garman,** *Lambda Book Report*

Research www.JackFritscher.com

RAINBOW COUNTY
AND OTHER STORIES

This 3rd collection of fiction, *Rainbow County and 11 Other Stories,* won the National Small Press Book Award as "Best Erotic Book 1998." This is author Fritscher's 12th book. In total, his books have sold to date more than 100,000 copies, and his name recognition is high from many years of publication in more than 25 gay magazines. He is best known for his biographical memoir of his life with his lover Robert Mapplethorpe, *Mapplethorpe: Assault with a Deadly Camera,* and for his epic novel, *Some Dance to Remember,* which *The New Republic* called a classic comparable to Gore Vidal and James Baldwin.

Photograph of Jack Fritscher, San Francisco 1998, ©Mark Hemry